NIGHTS OF
RAIN AND STARS

NIGHTS OF RAIN AND STARS

Maeve Binchy

McArthur & Company
Toronto

First published in Canada in 2004 by
McArthur & Company
322 King Street West, Suite 402
Toronto, Ontario
M5V 1J2
www.mcarthur-co.com

Library and Archives of Canada Cataloguing in Publication

Binchy, Maeve
Nights of rain and stars / Maeve Binchy.

ISBN 1-55278-431-2

I. Title.

PR6052.I46N53 2004 823'.914   C2004-903320-4

Printed in Canada by Webcom

10 9 8 7 6 5 4 3 2 1

For dear good Gordon
who has been such a supportive and kind person
that nobody would believe it if I were to write him into a book!
Thank you with all of my heart.

Chapter One

Andreas thought he saw the fire down in the bay before anyone else did. He peered and shook his head in disbelief. This sort of thing didn't happen. Not here in Aghia Anna, not to the *Olga*, the little red and white boat that took visitors out to the bay. Not to Manos, foolish headstrong Manos whom he had known since he was a boy. This was some kind of dream, some trick of the light. That could not be smoke and flames coming from the *Olga*.

Perhaps he was not feeling well.

Some of the older people in the village said that they imagined things. If the day was hot, if there had been too much *raki* the night before. But he had gone to bed early. There had been no *raki* or dancing or singing in his hillside restaurant.

Andreas put his hand up to shade his eyes and, at the same time, a cloud passed overhead. It wasn't as clear as it had been before. He must indeed have been mistaken. But now he must pull himself together. He had a restaurant to run. If people came all the way up the hilly path, they would not want to find a madman, someone crazed by the sun fancying disasters in a peaceful Greek village.

He continued fixing the red and green plastic-covered cloths with little clips to the long wooden tables on the terrace outside his taverna. This would be a hot day, with plenty of visitors at lunchtime. He had laboriously written the menu on the blackboard. He often wondered why he did it . . . it was the same food every day. But the visitors liked it; and he would put 'Welcome' in six languages. They liked that too.

The food was not special. Nothing they could not have got in two dozen other little tavernas. There was *souvlaki*, the lamb kebabs. Well, goat kebabs really, but the visitors liked to think they were lamb. And there was *moussakas*, warm and glutinous in its big pie dish. There were the big bowls of salad, white squares of salty feta cheese and lush red tomatoes. There were the racks of *barbouni*, red mullet, waiting to be grilled, the swordfish steaks. There were the big steel trays of desserts in the fridge, *kataïfi* and *baklava*, made from nuts, honey and pastry. The chilled cabinets of retsina and local wines. Why else did people come to Greece? People came from all over the world and loved what Andreas, and dozens like him, could provide.

He always recognised the nationality of any visitor to Aghia Anna and could greet them in a few words of their own language. It was like a game to him now, after years of studying the way people walked and reading their body language.

The English didn't like it if you offered them a *Speisekarte* instead of the menu, the Canadians did not want you to assume they were from the United States. Italians did not like to be greeted with a *Bonjour* and his own fellow countrymen wanted to be thought of as important people from Athens rather than tourists from abroad. Andreas had learned to look carefully before he spoke.

And as he looked down the path he saw the first customers of the day arriving.

His mind went on to automatic pilot.

A quiet man, wearing those shorts that only Americans wore, shorts that did nothing for the bottom or the legs, but only pointed out the ridiculous nature of the human figure. He was on his own and stopped to look at the fire through binoculars.

A beautiful German girl, tall, tanned, with hair streaked by the sun or a very expensive hairdresser. She stood in silence, staring in disbelief at the scarlet and orange flames licking over the boat in Aghia Anna bay.

A boy, also in his twenties, small and anxious-looking with glasses that he kept taking off and wiping. He stood open-mouthed in horror, looking at the boat in the bay down below.

A couple also in their twenties, exhausted after the walk up the hill; they were Scottish or Irish, he thought – Andreas couldn't quite make out the accents. The boy had a sort of swagger about him, as if he were trying to tell some imaginary audience that the walk had not been difficult at all.

In their turn, they saw a tall man, slightly stooped, with grey-white hair and bushy eyebrows.

'That's the boat we were on yesterday.' The girl had her hand over her mouth in shock. 'Oh, my God, it could have been us.'

'Well, it isn't, so what's the point in saying that?' her

boyfriend said firmly. He was gazing in disdain at Andreas's laced-up boots.

And then, there was the sound of an explosion from down in the bay and, for the first time, Andreas realised that it was true. There *was* a fire. Not just a trick of the light. The others had seen it too. He could not put it down to an old man's failing eyesight. He began to tremble and hold on to the back of a chair to support himself.

'I must telephone my brother Yorghis, he is in the police station ... maybe they don't know about it, maybe they cannot see the fire from down there.'

The tall American man spoke gently. 'They see it, look, there are lifeboats already on the way.'

But Andreas went to make the phone call anyway.

Of course there was no reply from the tiny police station up the hill from the harbour.

The young girl was peering down at the innocent-looking blue sea where the ragged scarlet flames and the black smoke seemed like a grotesque blot in the middle of a painting.

'I can't believe it,' she said over and over. 'Yesterday he was teaching us to dance on that very boat, *Olga*, he called it, after his grandmother.'

'Manos – that's his boat, isn't it?' asked the boy with the glasses. 'I was on his boat, too.'

'Yes, that is Manos,' said Andreas gravely. *That fool Manos with too many people on the vessel as usual, with no proper catering facilities but insisting on pouring drink into them and trying to make kebabs with some out-dated gas cylinder.* But none of the people of the village would ever say any of this. Manos had a family here.

They would all be gathered now, down by the harbour, waiting for news.

'Do you know him?' asked the tall American with the binoculars.

'Yes, indeed, we all know everyone here.' Andreas wiped his eyes with a table napkin.

They stood as if transfixed, watching the distant boats arriving and trying to douse the flames, the bodies struggling in the water hoping to be picked up by the smaller craft.

The American lent his binoculars to anyone who wanted to see. They were all at a loss for words; too far away to go and help, there was nothing they could do, but still they couldn't stop looking at the tragedy unfolding below on that innocent, beautiful, blue sea.

Andreas knew he should make some move to serve them but somehow it seemed crass. He didn't want to leave what was left of Manos and his boat and the unsuspecting tourists who had gone out for such a happy holiday cruise. It would be too insensitive to start telling these customers about stuffed vine leaves and seating them at the tables he had been preparing.

He felt a hand on his arm. It was the blonde German girl. 'It's worse for you – this is your place,' she said.

He felt tears come to his eyes again. She was right. It *was* his place. He had been born here, he knew everyone in Aghia Anna, he had known Olga, the grandmother of Manos, he knew the young men putting their boats out into the tide to rescue the victims. He knew the families who would be standing waiting at the harbour. Yes, it was worse for him. He looked at her piteously.

Her face was kind but she was practical too. 'Why

don't you sit down? Please do,' she said kindly. 'There's nothing we can do to help them.'

It was the spur he needed. 'I'm Andreas,' he said. 'You're right, this is my place, and something terrible has happened here. I will offer you all a Metaxa brandy for the shock and we will say a prayer for the people in the bay.'

'Is there nothing, *nothing* that we can do?' asked the English boy with the glasses.

'It took us about three hours to get up this far. By the time we got back I guess we'd only be in the way,' said the tall American. 'I'm Thomas, by the way, and I think we'd better not crowd the harbour. See – there are dozens of people there already.' He offered his binoculars so they could see for themselves.

'I'm Elsa,' said the German girl, 'and I'll get the glasses.'

They stood with tiny glasses of the fiery liquid in their hands and raised a strange toast in the sunshine.

Fiona, the Irish girl with the red hair and a freckled nose, said, 'May their souls and all the souls of the faithful departed rest in peace.'

Her boyfriend seemed to wince slightly at the expression.

'Well, why not, Shane?' she asked him defensively. 'It's a blessing.'

'Go in peace,' said Thomas to the wreckage. Now the flames had died down and they were in the business of counting the living and the dead.

'*L'chaim*,' said David, the English boy with the glasses. 'It means "To life",' he explained.

'*Ruhet in Frieden*,' said Elsa with tears in her eyes.

'*O Theos n'anapafsi tin psyhi tou*,' said Andreas,

bowing his head in grief as he looked down on what looked like the worst tragedy that Aghia Anna had ever known.

They didn't order lunch, Andreas just served them. He brought them a salad with goat's cheese, a plate of lamb and stuffed tomatoes, and afterwards a bowl of fruit. They spoke about themselves and where they had been. None of them was a two-week package tour visitor. They were all in it for the long haul – several months, at least.

Thomas, the American, was travelling and writing articles for a magazine. He had a year off, a proper sabbatical from his university. He said that they were much sought after . . . a whole year with their blessing to see the world and broaden his mind. Teachers of every kind needed a chance to go out and talk to people of other countries, otherwise they could get caught up in the internal politics of their own university. He looked somehow a little far away as he spoke, Andreas thought, as if he were missing something back in California.

It was different with Elsa, the German girl. She seemed to miss nothing she had left behind. She said she had grown tired of her job, she realised that what she had once thought of as important was in fact shallow and trite. She had enough money saved to finance a year's travel. She had been on the road for three weeks and never wanted to leave Greece.

Fiona, the little Irish girl, was more uncertain. She looked at her moody boyfriend for confirmation as she spoke of how they wanted to see the world and find somewhere to settle where people wouldn't judge them, want to improve them, or try to change them. Her boyfriend said nothing either to agree or disagree, just shrugged as if it were all very boring.

David spoke of his wish to see the world while he was still young enough to know what he liked and maybe join in. There was nothing sadder than an old man who found what he was looking for decades too late. Someone who had not shown the courage to change because he had not known what opportunities for change there were. David had only been a month on his road of discovery. His mind was filled with all he had seen.

But even as they talked and told each other a little of their lives in Düsseldorf, Dublin, California, and Manchester, Andreas noted, they said nothing of the families they had left behind.

He told them of life here in Aghia Anna and how the place was rich today, compared to his childhood when no tourists ever came by and a living was earned in the olive groves or minding goats on the hills. He spoke of brothers long gone to America, and his own son who had left this restaurant after an argument nine years ago and who had never come back.

'And what did you argue about?' asked little Fiona, with the big green eyes.

'Oh, he wanted a nightclub here and I didn't – the usual thing about age and youth, about change and not changing,' Andreas shrugged sadly.

'And would you have had a nightclub if it meant he would have stayed at home?' Elsa asked him.

'Yes, now I would. If I had known how lonely it would be to have my only son in Chicago, far across the world and never writing to me ... then, yes, I would have had the nightclub. But I didn't know, you see.'

'And what about your wife?' Fiona asked. 'Did she not beg you to get him back and open the club?'

'She had died. Nobody left to make peace between us.'

There was a silence. It was as if the men were nodding and understanding completely and as if the women didn't know what he was talking about.

The afternoon shadows grew longer. Andreas served them little coffees and none of them seemed to want to leave. From high on the hill here at the taverna they could see down below at the harbour a hellish scene was unfolding. A sunny day had turned into death and disaster. Through the binoculars, they saw bodies on stretchers, and crowds gathering and people pushing to see if their loved ones were alive or dead. They felt safer here, up the hill, and even though they knew nothing of each other, brought together like this they talked as if they were old friends.

They were still talking as the first stars came into the sky. Now, down in the harbour they could see the lights of flashing cameras and of television teams recording the tragedy to tell to the world. It hadn't taken long for news of the disaster to get to the media.

'I suppose they have to do it,' said David with resignation. 'But it seems so ghoulish, monstrous, preying on people's lives in a tragedy.'

'It is monstrous, believe me, I work in it. Or worked, anyway,' Elsa said, unexpectedly.

'A journalist?' David asked with interest.

'I worked on a television current affairs show. There's somebody like me now, at my desk in the studio, asking questions at long distance of someone down there in the harbour: how many bodies have been recovered, how did it happen, are there any Germans among the dead? What you say is true – it *is* monstrous. I'm glad to be no part of it now.'

'And yet people do have to know about famines and wars – otherwise how can we stop them?' Thomas asked.

'We'll never stop them,' Shane said. 'It's a matter of money. There's big money in this kind of thing, that's why it's done, that's why anything's done in the world.'

Shane was different from the others, Andreas thought. Dismissive, restless, anxious to be somewhere else. But then he was a young man, it was natural that he would want to be with his attractive little girlfriend, Fiona, just the two of them, rather than having a conversation with a lot of strangers high on a hill on a hot day.

'Not everyone is interested in money,' David said mildly.

'I didn't say you had to be, I'm just saying it's what gets things going, that's all.'

Fiona looked up sharply as if she had been down this road before, defending Shane for his views. 'What Shane means is that that's the system – it's not the God in his life nor in mine. I certainly wouldn't be a nurse if it was money I was looking for.' She smiled around at them all.

'A nurse?' Elsa said.

'Yes, I was wondering, would I be any use down there, but I don't suppose . . .?'

'Fiona, you're not a surgeon, you're not going to amputate a leg down there in a harbour café,' Shane protested. There was a sneer on his face.

'But, you know, at least I could do *something*,' she said.

'For God's sake, Fiona, get real. What could you do, tell them in Greek to keep calm? Foreign nurses aren't in high demand at a time of crisis.'

Fiona flushed darkly.

Elsa came to her rescue. 'If we were down there I'd say you'd be invaluable but it would take us so long I think we're better off to be up here, out of people's way.'

Thomas agreed. He was looking through his binoculars again. 'I don't think you'd even be able to get near to the wounded if you were there,' he said reassuringly. 'See, there's such confusion.' He passed her the glasses and with trembling hands she looked down at the distant harbour and the people jostling each other.

'Yes, you're right, I see,' Fiona said in a small voice.

'It must be wonderful being a nurse, I guess it means that you're never afraid,' Thomas said, trying to make Fiona feel better. 'What a great career. My mother is a nurse, but she works long hours and doesn't get paid enough.'

'Did she work while you were a kid?'

'Still does. She put my brother and me through college and we got careers out of all that. We try to thank her and give her a rest, a place to live, but she says she's programmed to keep going.'

'What career did you get out of college?' David asked. 'I have a degree in business studies but it never got me anything I wanted to do.'

Thomas spoke slowly. 'I teach nineteenth-century literature at a university.' He shrugged as if it weren't a big deal.

'What do you do, Shane?' Elsa asked.

'Why?' He looked back at her directly.

'Don't know, probably it's because I can't stop asking questions. It's just that the rest of us said. I suppose I didn't want you to be left out.' Elsa had a beautiful smile.

He relaxed. 'Sure, well, I do a bit of this and a bit of that.'

'I know.' Elsa nodded as if this were a reasonable answer.

The others nodded too. They also knew.

Just then, Andreas spoke very slowly. 'I think you should all call and tell them back at home that you are alive.'

They looked at him, startled.

He explained what he was thinking. 'As Elsa says, this will be on the television news tonight. They will all see, they may know you are here in Aghia Anna, they will think that you might be on the boat of Manos.' He looked around him. Five young people from different families, different homes, different countries.

'Well, my mobile phone doesn't work here,' Elsa said cheerfully. 'I did try a couple of days ago and I thought, so much the better, now it's a real escape.'

'It's the wrong time of day in California,' Thomas said.

'I'd get the answering machine, they'll be out again at some business function,' David said.

'It would only be another earful of "Dear, dear, look what happens when you leave your nice, safe job and go gallivanting round the world,"' said Fiona.

Shane said nothing at all. The notion of phoning home had just never occurred to him.

Andreas stood up at the table and addressed them. 'Believe me, when I hear there has been a shooting in

Chicago or a flood or any disaster, I wonder to myself, could my Adoni be caught up in it? It would be so good if he were to ring . . . just a short message to say that he is safe. That's all.'

'His name was Adoni?' Fiona said in wonder. 'Like Adonis, the god of beauty.'

'His name *is* Adoni,' Elsa corrected.

'And *is* he an Adonis, with the women, I mean?' Shane asked with a grin.

'I don't know, he doesn't tell me.' Andreas had a sad face.

'You see, Andreas, you're the kind of father who *does* care. Some fathers don't,' David explained.

'Every parent cares, they just have different ways of showing it.'

'And, of course, some of us have no parents,' Elsa said in a light voice. 'Like me, a father long disappeared, a mother who died young.'

'But there must be someone in Germany who loves you, Elsa,' Andreas said, and then thought perhaps he had gone too far. 'I tell you, my telephone is there in the bar. Now I will open a bottle of wine to celebrate that we were here tonight, with all our hopes and dreams still left to us as we sit in another night of stars.'

He went inside and could hear them talking out on the terrace.

'I think he really *does* want us to use his phone,' Fiona said.

'Well, you just said what you'd be letting yourself in for,' Shane objected.

'Perhaps it's making too much of it all,' Elsa wondered.

They looked down again at the scene below. And there was no argument, this time.

'I'll call first,' said Thomas.

Andreas stood polishing glasses and listening to their calls. They were a strange little group gathered today in his taverna. None of them seemed at ease with the people they called. It was as if they were all running away from something. Each of them sounded like someone escaping from a bad situation.

Thomas's voice was clipped. 'I *know* he's at day camp. I just thought . . . no, it doesn't matter . . . believe me, I had no agenda. Shirley, please, I'm not trying to make trouble, I was just . . . All right, Shirley, think what you like. No, I haven't made any plans yet.'

David sounded apprehensive. 'Oh, Dad, you're at home, yes, well, of course you should be. It's just that I wanted to tell you about this accident . . . no, I wasn't hurt . . . no, I wasn't on the boat.' A long silence. 'Right, Dad, give my love to Mum, won't you. No, tell her there's nothing definite about when I'm coming back.'

Fiona's conversation was hardly about the boat tragedy at all. No one seemed to let her talk about it. It was, as Shane had predicted, some kind of plea for her to come home. 'I can't give you a date yet, Mam, we've been through this a million times. Where he goes I go, Mam, and you must make your own plans for that – it would be much better that way.'

Elsa's conversation was a mystery. Andreas spoke German, and he understood perfectly. She left two messages on answering machines.

The first was warm: 'Hannah, it's Elsa. I am in this glorious place in Greece called Aghia Anna and there was a terrible accident today. People died in a boat tragedy. In front of our eyes. I can't tell you how sad it was. But in case you wondered was I involved in it, I wanted to tell you I'm one of the lucky ones ... Oh, Hannah, I do miss you and your kind shoulder to weep on. But I weep a lot less now, so possibly I did the right thing to come away. As usual I'd prefer you not to say that you heard from me. You're such a friend – I don't deserve you. I'll get in touch soon, I promise.'

Then she made a second call and this time her voice was ice cold. 'I wasn't killed on that boat. But you know that there are times I would not mind if I had been. I don't pick up e-mails so save your energy. There is nothing you can say, nothing you can do. You've done and said it all. I only called you because I imagine the studio is hoping that I was either burned in that pleasure-boat fire or that I am standing on the harbour waiting to give an eye-witness account. But I am miles away from it, and even more miles away from you, and that's all I care about, believe me.'

And Andreas saw the tears on Elsa's face as she replaced the receiver.

Chapter Two

Andreas knew that none of them wanted to leave his place. They felt safe here on his terrace, far from the tragedy unfolding below. And far from their own unhappy lives back home.

He wondered, as he had wondered so many nights before, about families. Was it just the argument about the nightclub that had driven Adoni away? Was it a need to be free, away from the old ways? If he had to do it all over again, would he have been more open and giving, supported his son to go and see the world before he settled down?

But then these young people were all doing that and yet they were still having problems at home. He had heard that in all their conversations. He left their wine on the table and sat in the shadows with his worry beads moving from hand to hand while they talked. As the evening came and more wine was poured they grew relaxed and seemed to want to talk. They were no longer secretive about their home lives.

Poor little Fiona was the most eager of all.

'You were right, Shane ... I shouldn't have called, it just gave them another chance to tell me what a mess I was making of my life, and how they can't get their silver wedding plans organised until they know where I am going to be. Five months left, and my mother, who thinks that a take-away Chinese meal is entertaining, is now worrying about a party! I told her straight out that I hadn't a notion of where we'd be then, and she starts to cry. She's actually *crying* about a party, and here we are with all those people down at the harbour who really *do* have something to cry about. It would make you sick.'

'Told you.' Shane inhaled. He and Fiona were smoking a joint; the others didn't join in. Andreas didn't approve, but now wasn't the time to make heavy rules.

Thomas spoke up. 'I had no luck either. Bill, my little boy, who might actually care about me, was out at day camp. My ex-wife, who would love to think that I had perished on Manos's boat, was less than pleased by the call. Still, at least the boy won't look at the news and worry about me.' He was philosophical about it.

'How would he know that you were even in this area?' Shane obviously thought the phone calls home were a waste of time for everyone.

'I sent a fax with my telephone numbers. Shirley is meant to put it up on the bulletin board in the kitchen.'

'Does she?' Shane asked.

'She *says* she does.'

'But has your son called?'

'No.'

'Then she doesn't, does she?' Shane had it all figured out.

'I guess not, and I don't imagine she'll call my mother either.' Thomas's face was set in hard lines. 'I wish I had thought of calling Mom instead. But I wanted to hear Bill's voice, and then Shirley got me so upset ...'

Finally David spoke quietly. 'When I called, I was getting ready to leave a nice calm message on the answering machine – but they were at home and it was my father . . . And he said . . . he said that if nothing had happened to me, what was I ringing about?'

'He didn't really mean that, you know,' Thomas said, soothingly.

'You know the way people always say the wrong thing, just because they're relieved,' Elsa added.

David shook his head. 'But he *did* mean it, he really didn't see the point, and I could hear my mother calling out from the sitting room, "Ask him about the award, Harold, is he coming home for that?"'

'Award?' the others asked.

'It's a pat on the back for having made so much money, like the Queen's Award for Industry. That sort of thing. There's going to be a big reception and a ceremony. Nothing else on earth matters to them except this.'

'Is there anyone else at home who could go to the ceremony in your place?' Elsa asked.

'Well, there's everyone in Father's office and his friends from Rotary and the golf club, and Mother's cousins . . .'

'You're an only child then?' Elsa said.

'That's the problem. That's the whole problem,' David replied sadly.

'It's *your* life, do what you want to,' Shane shrugged. He couldn't see what the problem was.

'I suppose they just wanted to share the honour with you,' Thomas said.

'Yes, but I wanted to tell them about the tragedy and people dying, and all they could do was to start talking about this function and wanting to know if I would be home in time for it. It's monstrous.'

'It might be a way of saying, "Come home", mightn't it?' Elsa suggested.

'Everything's a way of saying, "Come home", but "Come home and get a good job and help your father in his business", and that is not what I am going to do, not now, not ever.' David took off his glasses and wiped them.

Elsa had said nothing about herself. She sat looking far out to sea over the olive groves at the coastline of the little islands where all those people thought they would be spending a sunny holiday afternoon. She felt everyone looking at her, waiting for her to talk about the phone call *she* had made.

'Oh, what response did I get? Well, I think that there's nobody at home in Germany! I called two friends, got two answering machines, and they'll both think I'm mad, but what the hell?' Elsa gave a little laugh. There was no hint that she had left a vague, cheery message on one machine and tense, almost hate-filled words on the other.

From the shadows Andreas looked at her. The beautiful Elsa, who had left her job in television to find peace in the Greek Islands, had certainly not found it yet, he told himself.

They were quiet again on the terrace now, thinking about their phone calls and wondering how they would have played the scene if they had to do it all over again.

Fiona *might* have said to her mother that there were so many anguished mothers and daughters looking for each other down at the harbour it had made her need to talk to home, and that she was sorry for all the anxiety she was causing, but just because she was a grown-up woman and had to lead her own life it didn't mean that she couldn't love her mam and dad as well. They couldn't have got so upset if she had said that, if she had talked about her mother's plans and just said over and over that she *did* care about them and that she would try to be home for the silver wedding. They would have to wait and see.

David thought he *might* have said that he was visiting many places and learning a lot about the world. He could have told them that today there had been this sad tragedy on a beautiful Greek island, and it had certainly made him stop and think about how life was so short and how it could end so unexpectedly.

His father enjoyed proverbs and sayings. David might have told him that there was a proverb that said, 'If you love your child, send him on a journey,' and he could have said that his plans weren't firm yet but he felt every day was a learning experience which would make him a better person. It might have worked: it couldn't have been worse than the empty chasm he had created.

Thomas realised that he should have called his mother, not Shirley. It was just that he had been so hoping to talk to Bill and hadn't been able to resist the possibility that the boy might be there. Mom was the one he should have phoned. He would have told her that he had not been involved in the tragedy and asked her to tell Bill. He could have told his mother that, as he sat with people he had never met, he had told them what a great woman she was and how grateful he was that she had paid for his education by taking on extra night work. Mom would have loved that.

Elsa alone thought that she had handled her calls well.

They both knew she was in Greece, but they did not know exactly where and she had left them no way of getting in touch with her. She had said exactly what she wanted to say to each of them. She had been vague and gentle to one; she had been curt and cold to the other. She would not have changed a word.

The phone rang and Andreas started. It might be his brother Yorghis, calling from the police station. Maybe he was calling to let him know about the dead and the casualties.

But it wasn't Yorghis, it was a man speaking German. He said his name was Dieter and he was looking for Elsa.

'She is not here,' Andreas said. 'They all went back to the harbour a while ago. Why do you think she is here?'

'She can't have left,' the man said, 'she only called me ten minutes ago. I have traced the number she called from ... where is she staying, please? Forgive me for sounding so urgent, but I really do need the information.'

'I have no idea, Herr Dieter, no idea at all.'

'And who was she with?'

'A group of people – I think they leave this village tomorrow.'

'But I must find her.'

'Sincerest regrets at not being able to help you, Herr Dieter.' He hung up, and turned to find Elsa standing looking at him. She had come in from the terrace when she heard him speaking German on the telephone.

'Why did you do that, Andreas?' Her voice was steady.

'I thought it was what you would want me to do, but

if I was wrong the telephone is still here – please telephone him again.'

'You were not wrong. You were absolutely right. Thank you very much, very much. You were very right to turn Dieter away. Usually I am strong but tonight I could not have had that conversation.'

'I know,' he said gently. 'There are times when you will say too little or too much. It's best then not to have to say anything at all.'

The phone rang again.

'You still don't know where I am,' she warned.

'Of course,' he said with a bow.

This time it was his brother Yorghis.

Twenty-four people dead.

Twenty from abroad and four from Aghia Anna: not only Manos but also his little nephew who had proudly gone out for the day to help his uncle. A boy of eight. And the two local boys who had worked on the boat, young men with their lives ahead of them.

'It's a very dark time for you, Andreas,' Elsa said, her voice full of concern.

'These are not bright days for you either,' he answered.

They sat there, each thinking their own thoughts. It was as if they had always known each other. They would talk when there was something to say. Elsa spoke eventually.

'Andreas?' She looked outside; the others were talking together, they couldn't hear.

'Yes?'

'Will you do one more thing for me?'

'If I can, yes, of course.'

'Write to Adoni. Ask him to come home to Aghia

Anna. To come back now. Tell him that your village has lost three young men and a boy, that you all need to see the face of someone who left, someone who *can* come back.'

He shook his head. 'No, my friend Elsa, it would not work.'

'You mean you won't try to make it work. What's the worst that can happen? He can write and say no, thank you. That's not the end of the world, compared to all that has happened here tonight.'

'Why do you want to change the lives of people you don't know?'

She threw back her head and laughed. 'Oh, Andreas, if you knew me in my real life, that's what I do all the time, I'm a crusading journalist – that's what the television station calls me, my friends say I'm just interfering, meddling. I'm always trying to keep families together, get children off drugs, get litter off the streets, get integrity into sports . . . It's my nature to change the lives of people I don't know.'

'And does it ever work?' he asked.

'Sometimes it works. It works enough times for me to want to keep at it.'

'But you've left?'

'Not because of the work.'

He looked at the telephone.

She nodded. 'Yes, you're right, it's because of Dieter. It's a long story. Some day I will come back here and tell it all to you.'

'You don't need to.'

'I do, oddly, but I'd also love to know you had written to Adoni in Chicago. Tell me that you will.'

'I was never a great letter-writer.'

'I'd help to write it for you,' she offered.

'Would you?' he asked.

'I could try to speak with your voice, though I might not get it right.'

'Well, neither might I.' Andreas looked sad. 'Sometimes I think I know the words and I imagine myself putting my arms around him and he says, "Papa" – other times I imagine him being very stiff and hard and saying that what has been said cannot be unsaid.'

'If we were to write a letter then it has to be one that will make him say "Papa",' she said.

'But he would know it was not from me, he knows his old father does not have the power of words.'

'It's often the timing that's most important. He will read in the newspapers, even in Chicago, of this tragedy, this disaster back home in Aghia Anna. He will want to hear from you. Sometimes things are bigger than we are, more important than our little fights.'

'And could that be the same for you and Herr Dieter?' he asked.

'No.' She shook her head. 'No, that's different. Some day I'll tell you, I promise you I will.'

'No need to tell me your business, Elsa,' he said.

'You are my friend, I want to tell you.'

But they heard the others approaching.

Thomas was the spokesman. 'We must let you sleep, Andreas, tomorrow will be a long day,' he said.

'We think we should go back down the hill, back to where we are staying,' David began.

'My brother Yorghis is sending a truck up this way for you soon. I told him I had friends who would need a lift; it's a long way.'

'And can we pay you now for our meal – our long day and night with you?' Thomas asked.

'As I told Yorghis, you are friends, and friends do not pay for their food,' he said with dignity.

They looked at him: old, slightly bent, poor, working hard in a place where they had been the only customers today. They *had* to pay him yet they couldn't insult him.

'You know, Andreas, it would make us feel bad to go away from here without sharing in the cost of our meal together, as if we were all friends in a way,' Fiona began.

Shane saw it differently. 'You heard the man say he doesn't want the money.' He looked around at them all, people who couldn't see a free day's eating and drinking when it was staring them in the face.

Elsa spoke slowly. She had a way of capturing their attention. The others all stopped to listen. She seemed to have tears in her eyes.

'What do you say that we make a collection for the family of Manos and his little nephew and the other people who died in front of our eyes today? There will undoubtedly be a fund for them. We can gather what we think our food and drink here would have cost in another taverna, and then get an envelope and put on it, "From the friends of Andreas".'

Fiona had an envelope in her shoulder bag. She took it out and without a word they poured their euros on to a plate. The sound of the police truck was heard coming up the hill.

'You write the message for the people, Elsa,' Fiona suggested.

And Elsa did with a steady hand.

'I wish I could write in the Greek language,' she said to Andreas, and looked at him as if they shared a secret.

'It's fine – your generosity, all of you, is very fine in any language,' he said, sounding very choked. 'I was never good at writing any sort of letter.'

'It's just the first words that are always the hardest, Andreas,' she persisted.

'I would begin *"Adoni mou,"*' he said haltingly.

'Now you're halfway there,' Elsa said, and held him to her for a quick moment before they climbed into the truck to go back down the hill to the little town which had changed so much since the night before, even though the stars looked exactly the same.

Chapter Three

They travelled in silence as the little van bumped its way down the hill. They all knew that they would never forget tonight. It had been a deep and emotional long day. In a way they had learned too much about one another to feel any sense of ease and comfort with each other. But they all hoped that they would indeed see the old man Andreas again. He had told them that he had a putt-putt bike with a trailer attached to it and that he came down the bumpy road to what he called The Town every day to buy supplies.

None of them slept well that night. The only thing that united them was that they could not lie under warm, dark Mediterranean skies and find sleep. They tossed and turned, the starlight too bright somehow and seeping into their bedrooms. A million little pinpoints up there preventing them from getting the sleep they needed.

Elsa stood on the tiny balcony of her apartment hotel and looked out at the dark sea. She was staying at the Studio Apartments, run by a young Greek man who learned the property business in Florida and had returned with the idea of having six little self-contained units here:

simply furnished, Greek rugs on the wooden floors, colourful Greek pottery on the shelves. No one balcony overlooked the others. He charged a lot by Aghia Anna standards but his apartments were always full.

Elsa had seen an advertisement for them in a travel magazine and had not been disappointed.

From her balcony the dark sea looked so safe and comforting, even though twenty-four people had perished outside that very harbour earlier and that same water had not been able to rise and douse the flames.

She understood for the first time why someone very sad and lonely might want to end their life in the arms of the sea. It would be foolish, of course, there was nothing romantic about drowning. Elsa knew that it wasn't just a matter of closing your eyes and being swept gently away from the problems of life. You would thrash about and struggle for breath and panic. She wondered had she meant what she said in the message to Dieter . . . that she wished she too had died today?

No, she hadn't really meant it. She didn't want to fight with all her strength against overpowering torrents of water.

But yet in a way, in one way, it would have solved everything. It would have sorted out the terrible situation she was running fast away from but which was following her everywhere. She knew she wouldn't sleep for hours. There was no point in lying down. She pulled out her chair and sat with her elbows on the little wrought-iron balcony, looking at the patterns the moonlight was making on the water.

David's little room was too hot and stuffy. It had been fine up to now but tonight was different. The people in the house were wailing too loudly for anyone to sleep. Their son had died on Manos's boat today.

When David had walked into the house and discovered the family and friends comforting each other he had been stricken. He had shaken hands awkwardly and fumbled for the words to express what could not be said. They spoke little English, and they looked at him wild-eyed as if they had never seen him before. They hardly noticed when he came downstairs again to walk in the night air. Their grief was too great.

David wondered what would have happened if he had died on the boat. It could so easily have been. He had just chosen one day for a tour rather than another. People's lives are changed or destroyed by casual choices like that.

Would there have been wailing like this in his home? Would his father have rocked forward and back in misery? Or would he have said grimly that the boy had chosen his life and he had to live with that choice and die by it.

Suddenly David felt very anxious as he walked around the sorrowing town. He wondered if he might meet some of the people he had spent all that time with. Not Fiona's awful boyfriend Shane, of course, but any of the others.

He thought he would go to a small taverna where people were still sitting talking about the terrible events of the day. He might even meet and speak to Fiona about Ireland, a place he had always wanted to go.

He could have asked her about nursing, and if it really was as rewarding as people said. Did you get a glow of pleasure as patients got better? Did they remember you and write and thank you? Were English people welcome in Ireland as tourists or as workers, had all that hostility died down? Were there any crafts courses in the west of Ireland? David had often thought he would like to be a potter. Do something with his hands, anything far from the world of making money.

Or he could have asked Thomas about his writing: what kind of thing he wrote, why he was going to be so long away from his university, how often he got to see his little boy.

David loved to listen to people's stories. It was why he was so useless in his father's investment broking business.

Clients needed him to tell them what to spend and how. David was much more interested in asking about their houses as homes rather than investments. He unsettled them by wanting to know would they have dogs or an orchard when what they really wanted to talk about was a quick turnover.

As he walked he saw Elsa on her balcony but didn't call out to her. She was so calm and in control, the last thing she needed was a bumbling fool like him in the middle of the night.

Thomas had booked himself for two weeks into a little apartment over a craft shop. It was owned by an eccentric woman called Vonni – in her late forties or so, always dressed in a different floral skirt and a black shirt. She looked like someone you would have to give money to for her next meal, Thomas had thought – but in fact she owned this splendid luxury apartment which she let out to visitors. It was expensively furnished and had some valuable little figurines and pictures.

Vonni was Irish originally, he gathered, though she

didn't want to talk about herself. She was a perfect landlady in that she left him alone. She offered to take his clothes to a local laundry and she left an occasional basket of grapes or a bowl of olives on his doorstep.

'Where do you live while I stay here?' he had asked at the start.

'I sleep in an outhouse,' she had replied.

Thomas was unsure if she was joking or was in fact somewhat simple in the head. And he asked her no more – he was happy in Vonni's place.

He would have been happy in somewhere one-tenth of the price, but he needed a phone in case Bill wanted to call him.

Thomas had always resisted the cellphone back in the States. Too many people were slaves to it. He felt it would be intrusive on his travels, and anyway people were always complaining that they couldn't get a signal in remote places. And what did it matter how many euros he spent on an apartment with a telephone? He had nothing else to spend his professor's salary on, and even his poetry was beginning to earn him money.

A prestigious magazine had paid for him to go abroad and write travel articles, in his own style from wherever he wanted. It had been the perfect assignment when he'd realised that he needed to get away. And he had badly needed to get away. He had wanted to write about Aghia Anna, but the world's press would be arriving tomorrow and Aghia Anna would already be notorious.

Once he had thought it would be easy to go on living in the same town as his ex-wife, seeing his son Bill as often as possible, keeping a civilised and non-combative relationship with Shirley. After all, he didn't love her any more so it was easy to be polite.

People had even admired them for being so non-judgemental, so unlike the other bitter couples who had separated and who revisited the scenes of their resentment over and over.

But now things were different.

Shirley's new boyfriend was Andy, a car salesman she had met at the gym. When Shirley announced that she was getting married to Andy it changed everything.

It meant that things would be easier if Thomas were not around.

She explained that she had found a real and permanent love. She hoped that Thomas would remarry also.

Thomas remembered how he had filled up with bile at the patronising way she spoke. As if she were rearranging the furniture.

Thomas had been surprised to find how much he had resented it. Andy wasn't a *bad* guy, it was just that he'd moved too easily into the house which Thomas had bought for himself, Shirley and Bill.

'Because it's all so much *easier*,' Shirley had explained.

Bill had said that Andy was okay, and that's just what he was: *okay*. But he was a bit of a jock and not into reading, not into holding a book with Bill at night and saying, 'Come on, you choose what to read and we'll read it together.'

And, to be fair, Andy had sensed the awkwardness of it all. He had suggested that Thomas visit Bill between five and seven when he, Andy, was in the gym.

It had been reasonable, sensible, sensitive even, but that had annoyed Thomas even more. As if he were being tidied away to a place that didn't impinge on their lives. Every time he visited he had come to hate the house more: the jars of vitamins and health supplements all over the kitchen and bathrooms, the rowing machines in the garage, the magazines about health and fitness on the coffee tables.

When the chance to get away came Thomas was sure he was right in taking it. He could keep in touch with his boy by phone, by letter, by e-mail. There would be less chance of getting annoyed or resentful.

He had convinced himself it was better for everyone.

And for the first few weeks it had worked well. He didn't wake up angry any more, nor drive himself crazy thinking about his son's new household. The break had been a good thing.

But the events of today had changed everything. All those people dead, a village plunged into mourning. He could hear the sounds of their crying floating up to him over the harbour.

There was no way he could sleep, and his thoughts kept buzzing round like angry insects.

Thomas paced Vonni's apartment all night. Sometimes he looked down at the hen-house at the end of the tangled, vine-filled garden. Once or twice he thought he saw her tousled head at the old window – but then again, it might have been an elderly hen.

Fiona too was awake in their room in a cramped little house outside town.

It belonged to a thin anxious woman called Eleni, who had three little boys. There didn't seem to be any sign of a husband. She didn't normally take guests. Fiona and Shane had found the place by knocking at various doors and offering a small handful of euros in return for overnight accommodation. Shane had been adamant. They had no serious money to throw away on luxuries like a bed for the night. They must get the cheapest on offer.

Eleni's simple house proved to be the cheapest around.

Now Shane lay sprawled in the chair asleep, the only one of them who had managed to get a night's rest. Fiona couldn't sleep because Shane had said out of the blue that they should move on next day.

She had been startled.

They had both thought Aghia Anna the kind of place where they might stay a while. But now Shane had changed his mind.

'No, we can't stay. It's going to be a creepy place after all this,' Shane had said. 'Let's get out, we'll get a boat to Athens tomorrow.'

'But Athens is a big city . . . it will be so hot,' she had protested.

But Shane said that he had a fellow to see, someone there he just had to meet.

Nothing at all had been mentioned about this fellow they were to meet when Fiona and Shane had set off a month ago. But Fiona knew from experience that it was not wise to upset Shane over something so trivial.

And in a way it was trivial whether they were here or in Athens after all.

It was just that she had wanted to go to the funeral for Manos, the handsome, sexy Greek who had pinched her bottom and said she was *orea*, which meant wonderful, *beautiful*.

He was a silly guy, but good-tempered and cheerful, he thought all ladies were *orea*, he drank wine from the bottle and he danced Zorba-like dances for them, revelling in the pictures that were taken of him for albums all over the world.

But there had been no harm in him, he didn't deserve to die with his little nephew and his work-mates and all those tourists who had been having such a great time.

And Fiona would have liked to see the people from today again. The old man, Andreas, had been so gentle, so generous. Thomas, the college professor, was a wise, good person, and she might even have encouraged David a little to be more outgoing.

And as for Elsa . . .

Fiona had never admired anyone so much, for knowing exactly what to say and when to say it. No wedding ring, and yet she must be about twenty-eight. Fiona wondered who she had telephoned in Germany.

Shane was still asleep in the chair.

Fiona wished that he had not brought out the pot in front of Andreas and the others today, and that he had been a bit nicer to them all. He could be so prickly and difficult at times. But then he had lived a confused life with no love in it.

Not until he had met Fiona, that was. And she alone knew how to reach the real Shane.

The room was very hot and poky.

She wished they could have stayed somewhere a little better. Then Shane might not want them to move on so quickly tomorrow.

During the night, as the stars shone down on the bay, Andreas wrote a letter. He wrote several versions and decided that the last one was the best. By morning he was ready to post the first and only letter he had written in nine years to his son in Chicago.

When the sun came up he got on his putt-putt bike and made the journey to the town.

When the sun came up on Aghia Anna, the phone rang in the tasteful apartment over the craft shop.

It was Thomas's son Bill calling him.

'Dad, you okay?'

'I'm great, son, just fine. Thank you for calling. Your momma gave you my number?'

'It's on the board, Dad. It's just Mom says it's always the middle of the night out there. Andy said I should try anyhow.'

'Say thanks to Andy.'

'I will, Dad. He got out a map of the world to show me roughly where you are, when we saw the fire on television. It must have been scary.'

'Well, it was sad,' he said.

'It's a long way away, where you are, Dad.'

Thomas yearned to be beside his boy. It was a real ache. But he had to remain cheerful otherwise what was the point of all this?

'Nowhere's a long way away these days, Bill, the phone is always there. Listen to you! You could be in the next room.'

'Yeah, I know and you always liked to travel,' the boy agreed.

'I do, and so will you one day.'

'Sure. And I called Gran to tell her you were okay and she said you are to take care.'

'I will, Bill, believe me, I'll take care.'

'I've got to go now. Bye, Dad.'

He was gone but the sun had come up and the day was beautiful. His son had called. Thomas felt alive and for the first time in a long time he felt how good everything was.

When the sun came up on Aghia Anna, Fiona went to the bathroom and suddenly realised that her period was six days late.

When the sun came up on Aghia Anna, Elsa walked down towards the harbour. She passed by the church, which had become a temporary morgue; then, as she rounded the corner, she saw with horror that among the crowds of people arriving from Athens was a German television crew from her own network setting up shots of the still-smouldering wreck which had been towed into the harbour.

She knew the cameraman and the sound man. And they would have known her had they seen her. And then Dieter would know where she was and would be here in a matter of hours.

She backed carefully into a little café and looked around wildly.

Inside were old men playing a form of backgammon – no help there. Then at a table she saw David, worried David from yesterday, the kind English boy who had said there was no pleasing his father.

'David,' she hissed.

He was overjoyed to see her.

'David, can you go and get a taxi and bring it here for me? I can't go outside. There are people out there I just don't want to see, can you do that for me, *please* . . .'

He seemed alarmed that she was so different from yesterday, so out of control by comparison. But, mercifully, he seemed to understand.

'Where will I tell it you're going?' he asked.

'Where were *you* going today?' she asked, wildly.

'There's a place about fifty kilometres away, a little temple and an artists' colony. It's called Tri ... Tri ... something. It's on a little gulf. I was going to get a bus there.'

'We'll take the taxi there,' she said firmly.

'No, Elsa, we'll go out and get on a bus, a taxi would cost a fortune, believe me,' David argued.

'And I *have* a fortune, believe me,' she said, handing him a wad of notes. 'Please, David, just be full of guts and act now, this minute, and take a chance this once ...' She looked at him and saw his face fall. Why had she spoken so cruelly and harshly, as good as telling him she thought him a weakling?

'I mean that it's a crazy thing for someone you hardly know to ask, but I need your help, I'm begging you. I'll tell you all about it when we get to this place. I haven't committed a crime or anything, but I am in trouble and if you don't help me now then honestly I don't know what I'll do.' She spoke from the heart, not acting, but with the same intensity she summoned up so well for the camera.

'There's a line of taxis in the square. I'll be back in five minutes,' said David.

And Elsa sat down in the dark café, unconcerned that every eye in the room was directed towards the tall blonde goddess who had marched into such an unlikely place, offered a nervous young man with spectacles what looked like a year's wages, and was now sitting, waiting, with her head in her hands.

Chapter Four

Fiona had quite a long time to wait until Shane woke up. He lay there in the chair with his mouth open, his hair damp and stuck to his forehead.

He looked so vulnerable when he was asleep. She longed to stroke his face but she didn't want to wake him until he was ready.

The room was hot and stuffy, the people of the house had left their clothes in it and it smelled like a second-hand shop.

Downstairs she could hear the tired Eleni, whose eyes were red with weeping over the tragedy, calling to her three little sons. Neighbours kept calling in, obviously telling the story over and over to each other, all of them shocked by the tragedy.

She wouldn't disturb these people by going down, not until Shane woke, until he was ready to go.

When he did wake he was not in good humour.

'Why did you let me sleep in the chair?' he asked, rubbing his neck. 'I'm as stiff as a bloody board.'

'Let's go and have a swim – that will make you feel better,' she tried to encourage him.

'Easy for you – you've been sleeping in the bed all night,' he grumbled.

This was not the time to tell him that she had been awake most of the night, thinking about poor Manos, whose body lay in the local church beside that of his little nephew and so many others who had died on his boat. And it was certainly not the time to tell him that she could very possibly be pregnant. That must certainly wait until he was awake, alert and not complaining of pains in his shoulders.

Anyway they were going to Athens today, so he had said. He had a man to meet, something to do.

'Will we pack before breakfast?' she asked.

'Pack?' he said, puzzled.

Perhaps he had forgotten the whole idea.

'Don't mind me, I don't know where I am half the time,' Fiona said with a laugh.

'You can say that again . . . Here, I'm going to bed for a bit and you could go and get us a couple of coffees. Okay?'

'It's a long way to the café – it would be cold by the time I got back.'

'Oh, Fiona, ask them for it downstairs. It's only coffee, after all, and you know all those *please* and *thank you* words that they like.'

Words that most people like, Fiona thought to herself, but didn't say so.

'Sleep for a couple of hours, then,' she said to him, but he didn't hear her as he was asleep already.

She walked along the beach back towards the town, her bare feet kicking the warm sand at the edge of the water, and letting the Mediterranean tickle her toes. She could not believe that this was happening. Fiona Ryan, the most sensible of her whole family, the most reliable nurse on the whole ward, had thrown up her job to go off with Shane, the man they had all warned her against.

And she might now very possibly be pregnant.

It wasn't just her mother who had rejected Shane as the other half of her life, it was all her friends, including Barbara, her best pal since they had been six years of age. And her sisters, and her fellow nurses.

But what did they know?

And anyway love was never meant to be uncomplicated, think of any of the great love stories and you realised that. Love had nothing to do with meeting a nice *suitable* person, someone who lived nearby, who had a good job, who wanted a long engagement and to save a deposit on a house.

That wasn't love, that was compromise.

She thought about the possible pregnancy and her heart lurched. There had been a couple of times, fairly recently, when they had not been careful. But there had been times like that in the past too and nothing had happened.

She felt her flat stomach. Was it possible that a speck which could become a child was growing there, someone who would be half Shane and half her? It was too exciting to imagine.

In front of her on the beach she saw the strange baggy shorts and over-long T-shirt of Thomas, the nice American man that they had spent the day with yesterday.

He recognised her and called out, 'You look happy!'

'I am.' She didn't tell him all the reasons, and the way her mind was filling up with wild wonderful plans, for living here in Aghia Anna, bringing up a child with these people, Shane working on the fishing boats or in the restaurants, she helping the local doctor, maybe even as midwife. These were all dreams for the future, dreams that would be discussed later when Shane had his coffee, she would tell him then.

'My son called me from the States. We had a great conversation.' Thomas couldn't help sharing his own good news.

'I'm so very glad.'

This man seemed to care about only one thing: the little boy called Bill whose picture he had shown them during their long time together. A little boy like any other with blond hair and a toothy grin but the most special child in the world to Thomas, as to any parent.

She dragged herself back from that train of thought. 'You know I *thought* he might call you back last night – I felt it when you were telling us about him.'

'Let me buy you a coffee to celebrate,' he said, and they walked together along to a small taverna near the beach. They talked easily as they had yesterday, about the tragedy, about how hard it was to sleep, and to believe that all those people had begun yesterday with coffee in a taverna like this and now were lying dead in the church.

Fiona explained that she had walked into town to buy bread and honey for their breakfast, and she would give some to the people in the house where they were renting a room so that in return she could make a cup of coffee for Shane when he eventually woke up.

'We were meant to be going to Athens today, but I think he's too tired,' she said. 'In some ways I'm actually rather glad he's too tired. I like this place. I want to stay on.'

'So do I. I'm going to walk up in those hills, and I want to stay for the funeral for some reason.'

She looked at him with interest. 'So do I, and it's not just ghoulish wanting to see it all first hand, I wanted to be part of it.'

'Wanted? Does that mean you'll not stay?'

'Well, we don't know what day it will be and, as I said, Shane says that he wants to go to Athens.'

'But surely if *you* want to . . .' His voice trailed away.

Fiona saw the look on his face. The same look that eventually came over everyone's face when they met Shane. She stood up.

'Thanks for the coffee. I'll go now.'

He seemed disappointed, as if he had wanted her to stay. She too would like to have stayed talking to this nice, easy man, but she couldn't risk Shane waking up and not finding her there.

'Thomas, do you think I could give you some money for flowers in case . . . well, in case people do have flowers for them all.'

He put up his hand. He knew she didn't have much money. 'Please – I'd love to get the flowers and I'll put "Rest in peace" from Irish Fiona.'

'Thank you, Thomas, and if you see the others, David and Elsa . . .'

'I'll say that you and Shane had to go to Athens and you said goodbye,' he said very gently.

'They were very nice, you were all great people to be with . . . I wonder where they are now?'

'I saw them both heading out of town in a taxi together this morning,' Thomas said. 'But it's a tiny place. I'll see them again.'

He watched her go and buy the great warm bread and

the little pot of local honey to take back to that selfish young man and he sighed. A professor, a poet, a writer – and he didn't understand the smallest thing about life and love.

Like why Shirley found him cold and distant and found the empty-headed Andy a delightful companion. Thomas remembered their conversations as the sun had set yesterday; he hadn't understood the lives that were being described there, either. Like why David's father, who should be so proud and happy to have such a son, kept the boy at arm's length and managed only to say the wrong thing, the hurtful thing.

Thomas had no idea what could have happened to that gorgeous German girl Elsa that had her running away from her homeland with haunted eyes.

He would never begin to understand such things, he told himself with resignation. Better not to attempt it.

He looked up and saw Vonni crossing the street.

'*Yassu*, Thomas,' she said.

'*Yassu* – isn't it such a tragedy? I expect you knew him, Manos?'

'Yes, I knew him as a toddler, a schoolboy, he was wild then, wild always. He would steal things from my garden so I gave him a job working in it. That sorted him out.' She seemed pleased with the memory.

Thomas felt an urge to talk to her, ask her why she had come to this island – but there was something about Vonni that discouraged any intimacy. She was always too quick with a jokey remark that headed you off.

'Anyway he has to deal with God tonight and, knowing Manos, he'll get by on charm.' She shrugged and moved away.

Thomas knew that was the end of the conversation.

He watched Vonni continue down the street towards her craft shop. There would be little business today. He wondered if she would even open her little shop.

He saw her shake hands with passers-by, easy and at home in this place.

Elsa bent down in the taxi and hid her head under a scarf until they had left the town. Only then did she straighten up. Her face looked strained and anxious.

'Why don't I tell you what I know about this place we are going to?' David offered.

'Thank you. That would be perfect.' She lay back and closed her eyes while his words rolled over her. Apparently it was the site of a minor temple that had had some excavation work but the money had dried up so it had been left in a semi-exposed state. Nobody knew all that much about the temple, the excavations had yielded little in the early stages. But there were those who said it was well worth a tour.

And an artists' colony had started there years ago, which was still going strong. Even today, silversmiths and potters came there from all over the world. It wasn't at all over-commercialised, and the artists brought their wares to town to sell.

David looked at her from time to time as he spoke.

Her face was relaxing. Obviously, she didn't want to tell him what she was frightened of so he wouldn't ask. Better to go on burbling away about this place they were visiting.

'Am I boring you?' he asked her suddenly.

'No, why on earth do you think that? You are restful and soothing,' Elsa said with a wan smile.

David was pleased. 'I often bore people,' he said

frankly. He wasn't self-pitying or asking to be contra-dicted. He was stating a matter of fact.

'I doubt it,' Elsa said, quickly. 'I think you are a very peaceable person to be with. Is that the right word or should it be "peaceful"?'

'I like peaceable,' David said.

She patted his hand and they sat back companionably in the taxi, looking up to one side of them where goats clambered on the rugged hillside, and down at the sparkling blue sea on the other. The sea that looked so friendly and inviting now but had taken the lives of so many yesterday.

'When will the funeral be?' Elsa suddenly asked the taxi driver.

He understood the question but didn't know the words to reply.

'*Avrio?*' he said.

'*Avrio?*' she repeated.

'Tomorrow,' David said. 'I just learned fifty words,' he added apologetically.

'That's forty-five more than I learned,' Elsa said, with a trace of the old smile coming back to her face. '*Efharisto*, David my friend, *efharisto poli*.'

They drove on along the dusty road. Friends indeed.

Shane felt a lot better after the coffee, bread and honey. He said that they would have one last day in this crazy place and leave for Athens on the following day. Boats to Athens left the harbour every couple of hours, it was no big deal.

He wondered where they would find a place with some action.

'I don't think there'll be much action today or tonight

– the whole town is full of press and investigators and officials. You know the funeral is tomorrow, the people downstairs told me.' Fiona longed to ask if they could leave after the funeral. But she had so much to tell him during the day she could let that question wait a while. 'There's a lovely little place I saw out on a point – they catch fish and grill them straight from the sea, will we go there, do you think?'

He shrugged. Why not? The wine was probably cheaper there than in the fancy places by the harbour anyway. 'Come on, let's go there then, Fiona, and don't spend hours and hours struggling to say "Me going – you staying" to all these people downstairs.'

She laughed at herself good-naturedly. 'I don't think I'm quite as bad as that, I just try to say thank you to Eleni for being so nice to us and that I'm sorry about what happened to their friends.'

'It's not *your* fault. For *Christ's* sake.' Shane was in one of those moods where he would fight about anything.

'No, of course it isn't, but it doesn't hurt to be polite.'

'They're being well paid for our staying here,' he grumbled.

Fiona knew they were paying practically nothing – if the family had not been so poor they wouldn't have moved out of their bedroom. But this was not the time to argue the point with Shane.

'You're right, we should go now before it gets too hot,' she said, and they walked down the shabby stairs and through the crowded kitchen past the family who sat bewildered by the scope of the tragedy. She longed to stop and sit there with them, to murmur consoling phrases to them, little Greek sentences she had heard everywhere: *Tipota, Dhen pirazi.*

But she knew that Shane was anxious for his first cold beer of the day. She had so much to tell him today, this was no time for delay. It would soon be noon and it was very hot. They should go to the taverna on the sea straight away.

The day was indeed becoming very hot.

Thomas decided against going up into the hills, he should have left much earlier in the morning for that kind of trip. He looked into the craft shop. He had been right. Vonni had not opened for business. She had put a notice in the window in Greek. Black-edged and short, he had seen similar ones in other places. He had been told that it said: 'Closed out of respect'.

Vonni was asleep in her chair. She looked tired and old. Suppose she really slept in the hen-house? When there was an empty bedroom in the apartment? She could easily sleep in there – but he knew better than to ask her.

The shops were closed but there was plenty to see. And if the truth be told he didn't want to move far from the little town that was shrouded in grief. He would walk along the coast to a simple place on a point which he had seen last week. There had been a wonderful smell of grilling fish when he had passed it a few days back, and it would be just the spot to sit and look out to sea and think. He was glad that he had remembered it.

There had been some raggedy umbrellas there that would protect him from the sun, and a cool breeze coming in from the sea. Just the place to go.

*

Elsa and David's taxi arrived in the old square that was the centre of Kalatriada.

The driver wondered where to leave them.

'Here is just fine,' Elsa had said, paying him handsomely. David had wanted to share the cost but she insisted it was her treat. They stood and looked around the village where they had arrived up twisty, perilous roads. It was not a popular tourist spot. A place that most certainly had not been discovered by developers.

The sea was far below, down another narrow track. Half the buildings around the square seemed to be tiny restaurants or cafés, and there was a selection of pottery shops.

'I'm sure you want to go and find your temple,' she said to him. 'This is a good safe place you brought me, I can hide here.'

'I'm in no great rush to see the temple,' David said. 'I can sit with you for a while.'

'Well, after all those turns and corners, I must say I would love a coffee,' Elsa smiled. 'But truly this is a fine place to come to, I can breathe properly here. You really are my hero, you know.'

'Oh, hero, you say!' David laughed at the idea. 'Not my usual role, I'm afraid.'

'Now don't try to tell me that you're normally cast as a villain.' Elsa was cheerful again.

'No, nothing as dashing. The buffoon more often,' he admitted.

'I don't believe it for a moment,' Elsa said.

'That's because you don't know me, you haven't seen me in my real life where I just mess everyone up.'

'That's not so. You told us that you don't see eye to

eye with your father. That's not a hanging offence, half the men in the world feel the same way.'

'I've let him down in everything, every single thing, Elsa. Honestly, if he had been given any other kind of son it would have worked. A ready-made business, a position of honour in the community. A lovely home – but it all choked me and made me feel trapped. No wonder he despises me.'

'Shall we sit here, do you think?' Elsa indicated the nearest place and sat down on a broken-looking chair in a very basic café.

The waiter came and spread a piece of waxed paper on another chair.

'Better chair for the lady,' he said.

'They're all so nice here,' she marvelled.

'Everyone's nice to you everywhere, Elsa, you are so full of sunshine.'

David ordered two *metrios*, the medium-sweet coffees. They sipped them companionably.

'I didn't *know* my father, David, he left us early but I had many, many arguments with my mother.'

'You see, that's probably more healthy. In my case there aren't any real arguments at all, it's all sighs and shrugs,' David said.

'Believe me, I said far too many things to my mother, far, far too much criticism, if I had my time over I would have said less. But that's women and their mothers, they always say!'

'What kind of things did you argue about?'

'I don't know, David. Everything. I used to say that my way was right and hers was wrong. Her clothes were awful, her friends, you know, the usual destructive things.'

'I don't know, you see. Because we don't talk at all.'

'If you had it all over again what would you do?' Elsa asked.

'The same, mess it up I imagine.'

'That's so defeatist. You're young. Much younger than me, your parents are alive, for you there is time.'

'Don't make me feel worse, Elsa, please.'

'Of course not, I just think it's fair to tell you we share something but I don't have a chance to put it right. My mother's dead.'

'How did she die?'

'In a car crash with one of her unsuitable friends.'

David leaned over and patted Elsa's hand. 'It was quick and I am sure it was painless for her,' he said.

'You are such a kind boy, David,' she said in a shaky voice. 'Finish your coffee and we'll go and investigate Kalatriada. And then at lunch I'll tell you my problems and you can give *me* advice.'

'You don't have to, you know,' he said.

'Peaceable David,' she said with a smile.

'Where's this place you said was so good?' Shane grumbled. His attention was drawn by a noisy bar they passed. 'Maybe this place would be fine,' he suggested.

It wasn't at all the kind of place where she could have told him the news so Fiona refused to consider it. 'Much too expensive – tourist prices,' she said. And that settled it. They moved towards the fish restaurant on the point.

Andreas sat with his brother in the police station. Yorghis's desk was piled high with reports about the accident. His phone had been ringing constantly. Now there was a lull.

'I wrote to Adoni today,' Andreas said slowly.

'Good, good,' Yorghis said after a little time.

'I didn't say sorry or anything.'

'No, of course not,' Yorghis agreed.

'Because I'm *not* sorry. You know that.'

'I know, I know.' Yorghis did not need to enquire why his brother had written to the long-estranged son in Chicago. He knew why.

It was because the death of Manos and all the people on the boat had shown them how very short life was. That was all.

Thomas passed the television crews and photographers in the square beside the harbour. It was a job like any other, he supposed, but they did seem somehow like a swarm of insects. They didn't gather where people were having a good time and getting on with life, only where there had been a disaster.

He thought about Elsa, that golden handsome German girl. She had been fairly dismissive of her own role in it all. He wondered where she had been going today in the taxi. Perhaps she even knew these German television crews who were gathered around the harbour. Greece was a popular destination for Germans, there were even two German visitors said to have lost their lives on Manos's boat. But even though he looked, she was nowhere to be seen. She must not have come back from her taxi ride. He walked on to the restaurant on the point.

David and Elsa walked around the ruins of the temple. They were the only visitors.

An elderly guide asked them for half a euro and gave

them a cloakroom ticket in return, also an ill-written and near incomprehensible account of what the temple had once been.

'There could be a fortune made from writing a proper leaflet in German,' Elsa said.

'Or even in English,' David laughed. They wandered back to the square.

'Let's see about this great lunch I'm going to take you to,' she said.

'I'm easy, Elsa … look, the waiter where we were before is waving at us, I'm happy to go back there if you are.'

'Of course I am – I'd prefer to, as it happens. But then I wanted something more grand because I have to ask another favour of you.'

'You don't have to pay me with an expensive lunch, and I don't think Kalatriada has a posh restaurant anyway.'

Their waiter ran out, delighted to see them. 'I knew you come back, lady,' he said, beaming all over his face. He brought a dish of olives and little bits of cheese, he indicated the kitchens where they could see dishes kept warm in the big heated cabinets. Proudly he opened up each dish so that they could choose what they would eat.

They sat companionably and talked as if they were old friends.

They wondered what it would be like to have grown up in a small hill village like this instead of in big cities as they had.

They marvelled at the tall blond Scandinavians who had come from the northern cold to work here as jewellers and potters. It was only when they were sipping the dark sweet coffee that Elsa said, 'I'll tell you what this is about.'

'You don't have to, we're having a lovely day.'

'No, I have to tell you, because, you see, I want us not to go back to Aghia Anna tonight. I want us to stay here, stay until tomorrow when the funeral is over.'

David's mouth opened. *'Stay here?'*

'I can't go back to the town, David, my television crew is there, people will recognise me, they'll tell Dieter, our boss back home, and he'll come and find me. I couldn't bear that.'

'Why?'

'Because I love him so much.'

'So that's bad – if the man you love comes to find you?'

'If it were only as simple as that,' she said, and she took his two hands and held them to her face. He felt the tears splash down over his fingers and on to the table.

'I understand that of course we have to stay here in Kalatriada tonight,' said David, who felt that he was indeed becoming more like a hero every hour of this day.

It was early. Fiona and Shane were the only people in the restaurant. The waiter left them alone with the fish and the wine by the dark blue sea and white sand. Shane had drunk two beers and a glass of retsina very quickly. Fiona watched him, waiting for the right time to tell him her news. Finally, when she could wait no longer, she put her hand on his arm and told him that she was six days overdue. She said that since she had been twelve years old she had never been one day late. And with whatever medical knowledge she had as a nurse she felt sure that this was not a false alarm and that it really did mean they were pregnant. And she looked hopefully into his face.

She saw disbelief written all over it.

He drank another glass of wine before he spoke. 'I can't take this in,' he said. 'We took precautions.'

'Well, we didn't . . . all of the time. If you remember . . .' She was about to remind him about one particular weekend.

'How could you be so stupid?' he asked.

'Well, it wasn't only me.' She was hurt.

'God, Fiona, you really have a way of spoiling everything and wrecking everyone's life,' he said.

'But we *did* want children, we said, you said . . .' Fiona began to cry.

'One day, I said, not now, you're such a fool, not now that we're only a month out on the trip.'

'I thought . . . I thought . . .' She struggled to speak through her tears.

'What did you think?'

'I thought we might stay here, you know, in this place and we could bring up the baby here.'

'It's not a baby, it's a six-day-overdue period.'

'But it could be a baby, *our* baby, and you could get a job in a restaurant maybe, and I could work too . . .'

He stood up and leaned across the table to shout at her. She could hardly hear the things he was saying, so hurtful and cruel were they all. She was a whore, like all women. Scheming and plotting to get him tied down with a brood of children and make him work as a *waiter*. A waiter in a god-forsaken place like this.

She must get rid of the baby and never think of

coming up with this kind of fairy story again. Never. She was a stupid, brainless fool.

She must have argued with him, none of it was clear, but then she felt the stinging blow on her face with such a shock that she had begun to reel back as he was coming at her again with his fist clenched.

The ground was coming up at her, she felt sick, she was shaking all over. Then she heard the running and shouting behind her and two waiters held Shane back and Thomas, who had arrived from nowhere, was pulling her away, guiding her to a chair.

She closed her eyes as he dabbed her face with cold water.

'You're all right, Fiona,' he said as he stroked her hair. 'Believe me, you're all right now.'

Chapter Five

The restaurant gave Thomas the number of the police station. Fiona heard Shane laugh when he heard that the call was going to be made.

'Waste of time, Thomas, she's not going to press charges, and even if she does, it's only a domestic. That's what they'll say. Even worse, a *foreign* domestic, no chance of anything holding up.' He reached for another glass of wine.

The two waiters looked at Thomas as if for advice. Should they let Shane drink or should they restrain him?

But Thomas just nodded slightly. The drunker Shane got, the worse the impression he would make when Yorghis, the brother of Andreas, turned up to deal with things.

He went into a back room to make the call privately and introduced himself to the policeman on the phone, who immediately knew who he was.

'You were one of the generous people who gave such a donation to the family of Manos.'

'It was really your brother who did that, he didn't charge us for the meal.'

'He said you were friends.' It seemed clear to Andreas's brother.

'And we are proud to be his friends, but, sir, we have a problem ...' Thomas explained it all to Yorghis who understood the situation instantly. There was remarkably little red tape. Then Thomas quietly asked the waiters to take Shane into a back room and lock him in. Shane didn't even put up a struggle.

'It's a waste of time, a waste of police time, believe me, you'll be sorry when they've been and gone. Know-it-all Thomas bleating on yesterday about not being able to communicate with your son. You couldn't communicate with a cat, Thomas, you don't have the style.'

'And you do, of course, and with the fists,' Thomas said.

'Very droll, very droll indeed.'

'They don't take kindly to hitting women here, you'll discover that shortly.'

'I'll walk out of here with that girl on my arm, it's happened before, it will happen again.' He looked cocky and confident.

Thomas felt the bile of anger rise in his throat and he realised that his hand had turned into a fist without his intending to do it.

Shane saw and laughed. 'Don't tell me you're going to behave like a man at last,' the boy sneered at him.

But the anger had left Thomas almost as soon as it arrived. He was calm again. 'Leave him some wine, I'll pay,' he said to the waiters, and went to sit down beside Fiona, whose tear-stained face showed someone still in shock.

'It will be fine,' he said, stroking her hand.

'It will never be fine,' she said with a terrible finality.

'We survive, you know, that's why we're all here roaming the earth instead of being extinct.'

And then he didn't say any more while they waited for the police van to arrive. They sat there listening to the waves crashing against the rocks under the restaurant. Her face looked sad and empty, but Thomas knew that he was some kind of strength and company for her just by being there.

When Yorghis arrived he told Shane that an assault had been seen by three independent witnesses, that he would be locked up in the police station for twenty-four hours.

'But she didn't mind.' Shane's voice was slurred now and nervous. 'Ask her. I love her, we're together, we might even be going to have a baby – right, Fiona? Tell them.'

She still had her eyes closed.

'That's not important,' Yorghis explained. 'The complaint has not been made by this lady, what she says is irrelevant.' Then he handcuffed Shane and helped him into the police van.

The van had driven off in the sun when people started to arrive for their lunch. The waiters were relieved. They were young and inexperienced, it had all been disturbing, a fracas, the arrival of the police van, an arrest, but order had been restored and trade had not been interrupted. It had been a busy morning so far.

Fiona had said nothing during the whole time but now she started to cry. 'I wish I had a friend, Thomas,' she said.

'I'm your friend.'

'Yes, I know, but I meant a woman friend like

Barbara back home, she'd tell me what to do, she'd advise me.'

'Do you want to call her? I have a telephone in my apartment,' he suggested.

'It's not the same now. Too much water under the bridge, too many times when she offered to help and I didn't listen, she couldn't understand how much has changed. How much has happened.'

'I know, you'd have to start too far back.' He was sympathetic.

'I *could* talk to Elsa, but we don't know where she is, and anyway, she might not want to listen to all my complaints,' Fiona said sadly, wiping her eyes with a napkin.

'We could find out where she is, I saw her getting into a taxi this morning with David. I don't know where they were going. But why don't we have something to eat to build you up a little?'

'You sound like my mother.' She gave a weak little smile.

'I'm good at mothering skills,' he said. 'When you are strong enough to walk we'll go and ask the taxi drivers. They won't have forgotten someone like Elsa.'

'It's a bit feeble of me really.'

'She's very warm and sympathetic ... she's just the person to talk to,' he reassured her.

'Do you think so?'

'Yes, I do. Oh, Fiona, another thing?'

'What?'

'Is it true what he said that you might be pregnant?'

'He said that? I didn't realise.' There was a pathetic hope in her face again.

'He only said it hoping to get out of trouble.'

'I thought he might have been pleased.'

'No. I don't want to be cruel but he didn't sound pleased. Might it be true?'

'It might.' She sounded glum.

'We'll have an omelette and then we'll go interrogate the taxi drivers. If they can't remember Elsa then they're certainly not worthy to be called men.'

He was right. They all remembered the German blonde and the small man with glasses. The man who had taken them to Kalatriada said it was a wonderful fare.

'Let's go there,' Thomas said, and offered the startled taxi driver his second great fare of the day.

It was certainly a twisty road up through the hills. Once they got to the small town of Kalatriada it was easy to find Elsa and David. The place was not very much more than a big square ringed with cafés and craft shops. Elsa's blonde hair was hard to miss as she bent over some pottery plates in a little shop. There was hardly any need for explanations. It was obviously not a coincidence. And Elsa panicked.

'Anyone looking for me?' she asked urgently. Her eyes looked wild and frightened.

Thomas went straight to the point. 'In a way, Elsa. We were hoping that you and Fiona could have a talk. She's been a bit upset, you see.'

'I can see that,' David said, looking at the livid red mark on Fiona's cheek.

'Next one would have broken her nose,' Thomas said grimly.

'Well, certainly we'll have a talk.' Elsa had her hand on Fiona's arm. 'Sorry for immediately thinking it was about me but I have a few problems, which is why David and I are staying here tonight.'

'Staying?'

'Staying here?' Fiona and Thomas spoke together, amazed.

'Sure, it's a nice place, isn't it, and there's a lovely little hotel over there on the other side of the square. We have two rooms. Fiona can share with me and you men can share a room. Is that suitable, do you think?' Elsa's confident smile was back, and it seemed the most natural thing for four people who had never met until yesterday to be having a mini holiday that none of them had expected in a tiny village called Kalatriada. A place that only David had ever heard of. They all agreed that it was very suitable indeed.

This time yesterday they had barely met. Today they were involved in each other's lives.

They talked easily about everything. It was as if they were old friends who had grown up in the same neighbourhood instead of four strangers from four different lands.

It would not be like last night when they were all so emotional about the accident and the effect of their phone calls home. Last night when they had begun to talk intimately as soon as the stars came into the night sky. Tonight was different. A storm was coming.

The family who ran the little hotel seemed to show no surprise at the ill-assorted group of people with no luggage who had turned up so unexpectedly. They all seemed pleasant easy-going people, a little strained, but then they had been in Aghia Anna where that terrible tragedy had happened. Maybe they knew people on the boat that had been lost.

Irini was the woman who ran the hotel. She looked tired and bent as she got them towels and a little cake of soap. Her smiles warm but weary, she appeared to do all the cleaning and cooking while three men sat playing a board game in the corner; not one of them helped her.

'A lot of work to be done by the women's movement here in this house, I think,' Elsa whispered to Fiona as they went upstairs to claim their room.

'You could probably start with me, Elsa,' Fiona said humbly. 'You don't need to look much further than at me to see a victim.'

Elsa's face was full of sympathy. 'Sleep for a little,' she urged. 'Everything is better after a couple of hours' sleep.'

'I want to tell you about him, and why he does what he does,' Fiona began.

'No, you don't. You want to hear me say you're perfectly right to go back to him, and that he didn't mean it.'

Fiona's eyes opened wide.

'Maybe I *will* say that but not now, Fiona, you are too tired and upset to hear anything at all. Rest now. We'll talk later, there's all the time in the world.'

'And you?'

'I'll sit here and look at the mountains,' Elsa said.

To her amazement Fiona felt her eyelids become heavy and soon she was breathing deeply.

Elsa sat in the little cane chair and watched the shadows come down over the valley.

There was rain tonight, covering the blanket of stars.

'Do you play chess, Thomas?' David asked.

'Badly,' Thomas admitted.

'Me too, but I have a little chess set, would you care for a game ... no expectations of high standards.' The boy looked drained but he didn't look as if he wanted to confide or talk. Chess could be a substitute.

They set up a little table by the window, and as the night shadows fell and the downpour began they played chess together happily.

Irini knocked on both bedroom doors.

They could not eat out of doors, too much rain, but they could sit inside and see the square in Kalatriada, she said. She made no comment on the great bruise starting to emerge on Fiona's face.

They all came down to the table with its blue and yellow check cover. And with the background of old men clicking dice and counters from the backgammon game in the corner, they all began to eat the kebabs and salad that Irini proudly produced for them.

'*Orea*,' David said. '*Poli poli kala!*'

Irini's tired face smiled a big toothless smile. She might only be forty, Elsa thought, less even. It was no life here for her, but she was surrounded by the people she knew and liked, and now four guests were praising the simple food and saying it was beautiful.

Once Elsa had been so sure and confident about everything. She would have *known* what was wrong with Irini's life. Now she was not so sure. Possibly it was better for Irini to live here in this beautiful village between the mountains and the sea, one of those men at the backgammon tables might be her husband, another her father. There were children's clothes flapping on the line. She probably had a family, little children who knew everyone in the village.

There was a case to be made that she might be much better off here than if she had gone, like Andreas's son, looking for brighter lights in Chicago.

Elsa sighed. It had been much easier when things had been certain. Once Elsa would have urged Fiona to look hard at Shane and realise that he would never love her, and was probably incapable of loving anyone. She would have said that although no woman should advise another to have a termination, Fiona should consider all aspects of carrying Shane's child to term. But nowadays Elsa was not at all certain about what was the right thing for anyone to do.

She realised that she had been daydreaming and dragged herself back to the conversation at the table. She had come away to clear her mind, not to sit confused and brooding as she had a few weeks ago in her apartment until she bought her ticket to Athens.

She must pay attention and not allow herself to drift off like this again. Thomas was talking about his landlady.

'She's a real character, Vonni, been here for years apparently, she never talks about herself, but she speaks Greek like a native. She knows this place Kalatriada well, she said, she comes every few weeks or so to buy pottery to sell in her craft shop.'

'She's from Ireland, Andreas told me yesterday,' Fiona said. 'I was thinking about her only today . . . you know if she could stay here, maybe I could.' Her small pale face looked very sad.

'Did she come here with anyone, do you think?' Elsa wanted to inject some reality back into the discussion before Fiona started living in some fantasy world where she and Shane might raise a family here in the purple Greek mountains.

Thomas didn't know. He told them that although Vonni was so open and friendly you didn't ask her questions.

David had been in Vonni's craft shop and talked to her, she had chosen a good range of items, he thought ... she had to walk that difficult line between stocking touristy things for visitors and good taste.

'I really like the fact that she doesn't seem obsessed by money and I wouldn't say she has much,' David said.

'No, I think she's fairly pushed for a living,' Thomas agreed. 'She teaches English, and she sleeps in a sort of shed out back so that she can let me rent her place.'

'How old is she?' Elsa asked.

'Fifty to sixty,' David said.

'Forty to fifty,' Thomas said at the same time. They all laughed.

'Well, so much for dressing ourselves up to please men,' Elsa said with a wry smile.

'No, Vonni doesn't dress up, she wears a T-shirt and a coloured skirt, and open sandals. I don't expect she ever wore makeup.' Thomas was thoughtful. 'It's oddly restful, somehow.' He seemed miles away, as if thinking of some other woman who did dress up and applied a lot of makeup regularly.

'Do you fancy her then, this restful woman of uncertain age?' Elsa teased him.

'No, not remotely, but she does interest me. I called her before dinner tonight in case she saw no lights in her place and wondered whether I'd disappeared on her.'

'That was thoughtful of you,' Fiona said in wonder. It wasn't the kind of thing Shane would have thought of.

'She told us not to dream of getting a taxi again, that we should take the bus from the square, one leaves every two hours. I told her that I thought we would all probably go back tomorrow for the funeral, I checked that we wouldn't be in the way. She told me that it would be appreciated. Is that okay with everyone?'

'It's fine with me,' David said.

'Yes, and I can go to the police station and talk to Shane,' Fiona said eagerly. 'He will be so sorry and upset by now, now that he's had time to think it all through.'

The others didn't catch her eye. Elsa was the only one who hadn't spoken.

'Elsa?' Thomas spoke gently.

'I might just stay on here for a couple of days, you know, I could join you all later.' It seemed to need an explanation. She hesitated and then decided to speak. 'It's a little bit awkward, you see, I'm trying to avoid someone, and I would prefer to hide out a little until he has gone away.' She looked at three blank faces. 'I know it sounds stupid but it's just the way things are. I ran away from Germany, from my friends, from a good job that I loved . . . just to get away from him. It would be stupid to meet up with him again in a tiny place like Aghia Anna.'

'And you are certain he's there?' Thomas asked gently.

'Yes, this is just his sort of story. No one does human interest better than he does. That's why I ran away here with David.' She looked at David gratefully.

'We could all keep him away from you.' David was busy living up to his heroic role in all this.

'We could tell Yorghis, you know, Andreas's brother

... he would warn him off if he tried to stalk you or harass you.' Thomas was reassuring.

Elsa looked from one to the other. 'No, it's not that, I'm not afraid of him, I'm afraid of myself, that I might go back to him and then all this – all the business of coming here – would have been such a waste of time.' Her lip was trembling. Elsa the cool, confident Elsa.

They were perplexed.

'I'd stay with you, Elsa,' Fiona began. 'Only I have to go to the police station and check about Shane.'

'You don't *have* to, Fiona, you just want to,' Elsa said.

'Well, I love him, *you* must understand that.' Fiona was stung by this remark. 'Seriously, Elsa. You have to be in love with this fellow otherwise you wouldn't be so afraid of meeting him.'

Thomas intervened. It was getting too serious between the women.

'We've all had a long day ... suppose we meet here for breakfast at eight. We could get the nine o'clock bus ... those of us who want to go. Is that okay?' He had a gentle voice, but from years of teaching students he had an air of authority.

They realised he was right, and started to move off.

'Just a moment,' Elsa said. 'I'm very sorry, Fiona, I was rude to you, you have every right to go and see the man you love. And I apologise for putting my own selfish affairs before other people's tragedy. Of course I'll come to the funeral with you and I would be delighted to have the protection of kind friends like you.' She looked from one to the other, her eyes over-bright, as if the smile was hiding a lot of tears.

Chapter Six

In the holding cell at the back of the police station, Shane sat with his head in his hands. He needed a cold beer very badly but he was highly unlikely to get one from that ignorant Greek policeman, the brother of the tiresome Andreas up in the taverna.

Where *was* Fiona? He would have thought that she would be here by now. He could send her down to the fish bar at the harbour to get him three cold cans. Of course he would have to do the *sorry, sorry* bit, explaining that he had been so upset by the way she had sprung things on him, he couldn't help his reaction.

He banged the plate which had held hard bread against the door.

Yorghis pulled back the shutter and peered in. 'Yes?'

'My girlfriend, I'm sure she's been to see me, have you kept her away from me? You can't get away with this, you know, people in custody have a *right* to see family and next of kin.'

Yorghis shrugged. 'Nobody came.'

'I don't believe you.'

'Nobody came.' Yorghis began to move away.

'Look – I'm sorry, I didn't mean I didn't believe you

exactly, it's just that, you see, we are very close and I expected . . .' His voice trailed away.

'It didn't look as if you were very close yesterday,' Yorghis said.

'No, you don't understand, we have a very passionate relationship, naturally it explodes from time to time.'

'*Endaxi*,' Yorghis said.

'What does that mean?'

'It means right, or okay, or whatever you say.' Yorghis moved off.

'Where is she?' Shane cried.

'I heard she left Aghia Anna yesterday,' Yorghis called over his shoulder.

'I don't believe you!' Shane shouted.

'Believe what you like, I was told she took a taxi and left the place.'

Shane sat there in disbelief. It couldn't be true. Fiona would never leave without him.

'*Kalimera sas*, Yorghis, you look worried.' Vonni stopped to lean on the wall of the police station.

'Well, we have all these crowds of cameramen trampling on everyone for the funeral, the station is full of accident investigators and insurance officials, I have eleven different reports still to compile and I have this young pup in a cell. I don't know what to do with him.'

'The boy who hit the Irish girl?' Vonni asked. Nothing happened that she didn't know about.

'Yes. I wish he were hundreds of miles from here.'

'Well, export him so.'

'What?'

'That's what we used to do in Ireland years ago: if some tearaway was causing trouble the judge or the guards would say that if he was on the mail-boat to England that night no further action would be taken.'

Yorghis smiled in disbelief.

'No, it's true, terrible thing to do to England, send our dregs over there, but we thought, well, England is bigger, it can cope.'

'I see.'

'Suppose you put him on the eleven o'clock boat to Athens. Seriously, Yorghis, he'd be out of here before the funeral starts, it would be an ease to everyone.'

'And indeed Athens is big enough to cope with him.' Yorghis stroked his face thoughtfully.

Vonni's lined, tanned face broke into its wide smile. 'True, Yorghis, Athens is well big enough,' she agreed.

'You can't order me off the island,' Shane said.

'Take it or leave it. We have no time to deal with you now. Locked up here until next week then a prosecution – maybe jail. That's on the one hand. On the other, you get a free trip to Athens. You choose. You have ten minutes.'

'What about my things?' Shane asked.

'One of my boys will drive you past Eleni's house. You can pack your rucksack and be on the boat at ten-thirty.'

'I'm not ready to go yet.'

'Suit yourself,' said Yorghis, turning to leave the cell.

'No – wait a minute, come back. I think I'll go.'

Yorghis ushered him out to the police van. Shane got in sulkily.

'Bloody strange way of running a country,' he said.

Back in Eleni's house he noticed that Fiona's things were still there in the room.

'I thought you said she had gone away.'

Eleni explained in Greek that the girl would be back that day. The young policeman knew better than to translate. His boss wanted this violent boy aboard the 11 a.m. ferry and out of his jurisdiction. No point in delaying things because that foolish girl was coming back and it wasn't as if he had been asking much about her anyway.

He watched while Shane stuffed his clothes into his bag. He made no attempt to pay Eleni for the room. He didn't even say goodbye as he left in the police van.

The bus from Kalatriada wound its way through the little hill villages as it headed slowly towards Aghia Anna.

Old women in black got on and off, saluting everyone: some of them carried vegetables which they might be going to sell at a market, one woman had two hens. A young man played the bouzouki.

At one stage they stopped at a wayside shrine with a statue of Mary the Mother of God. Bunches of flowers had been laid around it.

'This is amazing,' Thomas said. 'It looks as if it was all set up by central casting somehow.'

'Yes, or the Greek Tourist Board,' Elsa agreed.

But apart from that they said little. They were all lost in their own thoughts and concerns about the day that lay ahead of them.

Elsa wondered what were the odds against Dieter and his television team turning up in this tiny village where she had run to flee from him.

Fiona hoped that Shane would feel much calmer now. Perhaps she could persuade that nice old man Andreas to put in a word for Shane, maybe they would let him out for the funeral.

Thomas worked out how he could ask Vonni to sleep in the spare bedroom of her own apartment rather than in that terrible shed. He did not want to patronise her, just to make her see sense.

David looked out at the families of children who waved at the passing bus. He wished he could have had brothers and sisters who would have shared the load. If he had a brother who had trained as an accountant, a sister who had read law and another brother who had not been academic but who had gone into Dad's business when he was sixteen and learned it from the ground up – then he, David, would have been properly free to go and learn about pottery somewhere like Kalatriada.

He sighed as he looked out at the hills covered in olive groves. Instead of that, here he was, tortured with guilt. Last night Fiona had mentioned Catholic guilt. She didn't even begin to know what Jewish guilt was like!

Vonni gave English lessons to the children in the big room behind her craft shop. She suggested that she would teach them a verse of an English hymn which they could sing at the funeral. It might be a small consolation to the English-speaking relatives who had been arriving on every boat for the past thirty-six hours, coming to the scene of the tragedy. She might even find something in German too. She would enquire.

Everyone thought it was a good idea.

And it would distract the children too, take them away from weeping households for a while. The families were grateful to Vonni as they had been for years and years since first she had come to Aghia Anna as a young girl. She had grown older with them all, spoke their language, taught their children, shared the good times and bad. A lot of them could not even remember why she had come here in the first place.

As Thomas went up the whitewashed steps to the apartment above and let himself in, he paused, unbelieving.

He heard the voices of little children singing: 'The Lord's my shepherd, I'll not want . . .'

It had been a long time since he had been in church. Possibly at his father's funeral. That was the last time he had heard it sung. He paused, stricken, in the sunshine. This funeral was going to be even sadder than he had thought.

Andreas and his brother Yorghis stood beside the ferry.

Shane avoided their eyes.

'Is there anything you would like to do before you leave?' Andreas asked.

'Like what? Like congratulate you on your legendary Greek hospitality for example?' Shane sneered.

'Like write a letter to your girlfriend.' Andreas was curt.

'I don't have any paper or pen,' Shane said.

'I do.' Andreas offered both.

'What am I to say? That you and your Gestapo brother threw me out? That's not going to cheer her much, is it?' Shane looked very belligerent.

'She might like to know that you are safe and well, and free . . . and that you'll contact her when you are settled.'

'She knows that.'

The pen and paper were still in Andreas's hand. 'A few short words perhaps?' the old man urged.

'Oh, for God's sake.' Shane turned away.

They blew the whistle to show the boat was about to leave. The young policeman escorted Shane on deck and came back to Andreas and Yorghis.

'It's better he doesn't write to her,' he said to the older men.

'Possibly,' Andreas agreed. 'In the long term certainly, but in the short term it will break her poor little heart.'

David and Fiona walked with Elsa back to her apartment.

'Look, nobody around,' David said. It was true. The streets which had thronged with press and bureaucrats were quiet now.

'I wish I could stay longer, I just have to check Shane is all right,' Fiona apologised, as she went up the hill towards the police station. From down in the harbour they all heard the hooting of the 11 a.m. ferry as it left for Athens. At midday another boat would arrive carrying even more people coming to attend the funeral.

'Would you like me to stay with you here, Elsa?' David asked.

'Just for five minutes so that I don't run away again,' she laughed.

'You won't do that.' He patted her hand.

'I hope not, David. Tell me, did you ever in your life love anyone obsessively, foolishly?'

'No. I never loved anyone at all,' he said.

'I'm sure that's not so.'

'I'm afraid it is, it's not something to be proud of at twenty-eight.' He was apologetic.

'You're exactly the same age as I am!' she exclaimed in surprise.

'You put your years to better use than I did,' he said.

'No, you wouldn't say that if you knew. I'd prefer never to have loved. Maybe I can get back to where I was before all this. That's what I'd choose more than anything.' Her eyes were far away.

David wished he knew what to say. It would be wonderful to be able to say the right thing, to make this sad girl smile. If only he knew a joke or a funny story to lift the mood. He racked his brains. He could only think of the golf jokes his father told.

'Do you play golf, Elsa?' he asked her suddenly.

She was startled. 'A little,' she said. 'Were you thinking of a game?'

'No, no, I don't play, I was actually thinking of a golf joke to try to cheer you up a little.'

She seemed touched. 'Tell it to me then.'

David sought the joke and sort of retrieved it. It was about a man whose wife had died out on the golf course. His friends had sympathised and the man had said no, it wasn't too bad, the worst thing was picking her body up and carrying her on to the next hole as he played each shot.

Elsa looked at him expectantly.

'That's it, I'm afraid.' David was miserable. 'You see, golfers are meant to be so obsessed ... that he sort of carried the corpse rather than give up on the game ...' he stopped, appalled at himself. 'Look, I'm so sorry, Elsa, on the day of a funeral to tell such a stupid story ... I'm such a fool.'

She reached out and stroked his cheek. 'No, you're not, you are a dear gentle person, and I'm so happy to have you here. Let's make ourselves a little lunch together?'

'Or I could take you out for an *omeleta tria-avga* ... they love you to ask for that ... you know, stressing you want three eggs.' He looked enthusiastic at the thought of it all.

'I'd prefer not to be out there if you don't mind, David. I feel safer in here. We could eat on the terrace and see without being seen. Would you hate that?'

'Of course not, I'd love it,' said David.

And he went to Elsa's fridge happily to take out feta cheese and tomatoes and make them lunch.

'Hallo, I wonder if I could speak to the police chief, please.'

Yorghis stood up wearily.

Fiona stood there in a little blue cotton dress with a white wool shoulder bag. Her hair falling over her face didn't hide the bruise. She looked frail and unable to cope with the hand that life had dealt her.

'Come in, *Kyria*, sit down,' he said, offering her a chair.

'You see, my friend stayed here with you last night,' she began, as if Yorghis ran some up-market bed and breakfast instead of Aghia Anna's jail.

Yorghis spread out his hands in front of him. She looked so anxious to see this boy, so forgiving of what he had done. How did young pigs like that get good women to love them? And now he had to tell this girl that he had gone an hour ago on the ferry without a backward glance. He found it hard to select the right words.

'Shane is very sorry, he may not sound it to you but he *is*,' she began. 'And in a way a lot of it was my fault, I told him something all the wrong way instead of explaining it properly . . .'

'He has gone to Athens,' Yorghis said baldly.

'No, he can't have, not without me, not without telling me. No, no. It's not possible.' She looked at him with a distraught face.

'On the eleven o'clock ferry.'

'Did he not leave me a note? Tell me where he's going? Where I should meet him? He *can't* have gone just like that.'

'He will get in touch when he's settled, I'm sure he will.'

'But where? Where will he write to me?'

'He could write a letter here, I suppose,' Yorghis said, doubtfully.

'No, you know he wouldn't do that!'

'Or maybe to the place where you and he were staying.'

'No, he wouldn't be able to remember Eleni's house, or where it was. No, I must go on the next boat, I'll find him,' she said.

'No, my dear girl, no, Athens is a huge place. Stay here. You have good friends here, stay until you are stronger.'

She was weeping now. 'But I have to be with him . . .'

'There will be no more boats leaving today, because of the funeral. Please, please be calm. It's better that he left.'

'No, no, how could it be better?'

'Because otherwise he would be in jail, locked up. At least he is free.'

'Did he leave me any message?'

Yorghis said, 'It was all in a great hurry you see.'

'Anything at all?'

'He *did* ask about you, wondered where you were.'

'Oh, why did I go away? I'll never forgive myself for the rest of my life . . .'

Yorghis patted her shoulder awkwardly as she sobbed. Over her shoulder, down at the foot of the hill, he saw Vonni passing by with her little troupe of children and he had an idea.

'Andreas tells me you are a nurse?' he said.

'I was. Yes.'

'No, you are always a nurse . . . could you do something to help? Do you see Vonni down there, she's looking after the children during the funeral, I know she'd love you to give her a hand.'

'I'm not sure I could help anyone just now . . .' Fiona began.

'That's often when we help best,' Yorghis said. He called out something in Greek. Vonni called something back. Fiona looked wistful.

'You know, if we could live here and have our child, we would learn Greek and be part of the place like she is.' She spoke almost to herself but Yorghis heard her and felt a lump in his throat.

Thomas felt restless; he wished that the funeral would begin soon and end soon. There was a heavy air of expectancy hanging over the little town. He couldn't settle until these people had been laid to rest. And indeed he was anxious that the television teams and journalists should leave. And things could go on like they had before.

Well, not exactly as before.

Not for the family of Manos and the other boys who had died. Some of the visitors were going to be buried here, some would be put into coffins and taken back to England and Germany.

But it would be better for everyone when this day was over.

He had promised to collect Elsa at her apartment and walk with her to the little church. He hoped that she would not meet this man she was avoiding and seemed so afraid of. There was too much pain in her face when she talked about him.

It would be very crowded there. Whoever he was, he might not see Elsa.

'I'm Fiona,' she said to the lined, tanned woman.

'A Dub?' the woman asked.

'Yes, and you? They told me you were Irish too?'

'I'm from the west,' Vonni said. 'But a long, long time ago.'

'And what are you doing with the children?'

'Their families are all at the house of Manos.' Vonni spoke English with an Irish accent but in a slightly foreign way, as if it were her second language. It probably was by this stage. 'I thought we would go a little outside the town and pick some flowers on the hill, will you help me?'

'Yes, of course, but I'm useless – what will I say?'

'They're meant to be learning English. Keep saying *very good* and *thank you*. I think they've mastered that much.' Vonni's lined face cracked into a huge smile that lit up everything.

'Sure,' said Fiona, brightening up for a moment and stretching out her hands to two five-year-olds. They all walked together in a straggling line down the dusty road out of town to pick flowers for the church.

Thomas saw the priests walk together in twos. Tall men with long robes with their grey hair tied back in little buns under their black headgear. They looked pale and solemn, and Thomas wondered what would make a young Greek man from this sunny island choose a life in religion. But then, back in sunny California he knew people, even in the faculty, men who were in Holy Orders – that young priest who taught mystic poetry, the Methodist preacher who also lectured in Elizabethan literature. These men were strengthened by their faith. It could be exactly the same for these Greek Orthodox dignitaries.

Thomas knew it was now time to go to the church. He went to Elsa's apartment as he had promised and was surprised to hear voices inside. Perhaps she had met her friend after all.

He was disappointed, but cheered up when he realised that of course this guy wouldn't be with Elsa, he would be out filming the funeral.

He knocked on the door and was surprised when David opened it.

'It's only Thomas,' David called out. It wasn't much of a welcome.

'Well, I *did* tell Elsa that I'd walk with her to the church,' Thomas said huffily.

'Lord, I'm sorry, Thomas, I don't know what's wrong

with me today, I can't say the right thing to save my life. It's just that we thought ... we were afraid that ...'

Elsa came out to join them. She was wearing a smart cream linen dress with a navy jacket. She had dressed formally for the ceremony.

Thomas had a tie in his pocket in case it would be appropriate. Now he realised that it would.

'Thomas, I asked David to answer the door for me because I am so paranoid – I still think that Dieter will come calling. Forgive me.'

'What's to forgive?' Thomas was putting on his tie at the little mirror in the hall.

'I should have gone home for a tie too.' David was worried.

'No, you look fine, David,' Thomas said, and they set out together following the crowds to the little church. The people stood on both sides of the street winding up from the harbour. Their heads were bowed, the conversation low.

'I wonder where Fiona is?' David whispered.

'Up there at the precinct feeding lover boy biscuits through the bars,' Thomas said.

'She *does* love him,' Elsa said, as if offering some sort of excuse.

'You should have seen him hit her,' Thomas said.

'If she's up at the station, she's there on her own, all the police are here,' David observed.

Then a great hush came over the crowd and they stood in silence at the approach of the funeral party. Lines of men and women walked behind the coffins in a little procession. Their tear-stained faces and black clothes seemed totally wrong for the bright sunshine, the blue sea and the whitewashed buildings.

Behind them walked the English and German families who had come so unexpectedly to this Greek village to bury their loved ones. They looked around them bewildered and confused, as if they were taking part in a play where they hadn't learned their parts.

Every shop, taverna and business in Aghia Anna had closed. The fishing boats stood idle, all of them flying a flag at half mast. Bells tolled from the monastery in the valley beyond. The television cameras of half a dozen countries filmed the scene. There was room in the little church for only a tenth of the people gathered to sympathise. Crackling speakers relayed the service to the people outside. And unexpectedly, in the middle of the Greek prayers and music, came the sound of children singing 'The Lord's My Shepherd'. The sound of the English people sobbing in the church could be heard. Thomas wiped a tear from his face.

Then there was a verse from the German hymn '*Tannenbaum*', and Elsa too cried openly.

'It was my friend Vonni who taught them that,' Thomas whispered.

'Well, you must tell her that she's done a fine job in breaking our hearts,' David whispered back.

When the congregation came out of the church and prepared to walk the short journey up to the graveyard, Elsa spotted Fiona. She was with Vonni and the children, all of whom had armfuls of wild flowers. Fiona was holding tight the hands of two little boys.

'Another day, another surprise,' Thomas said. 'Who would have thought she would have got her act together.'

'It's probably to take her mind off him,' Elsa decided.

Yorghis made an announcement. The families would

like to go alone to the burial service in the graveyard. They thanked people for coming to the church to sympathise, but now they wanted to be alone. They had asked the café owners and restaurants to open again and for life to carry on. They were sure everyone would understand.

Reluctantly the television teams agreed. This was not a situation where arguing would do any good. The children marched with Vonni and Fiona towards the small graveyard. Open graves waited among the old stones and the crumbling walls.

'This is an unreal day and we haven't even lost anyone,' Thomas said.

'I don't really want to be alone just now,' Elsa appealed.

'I could treat you to a glass of retsina and a little plate of *kalamari* and olives down at the harbour. Look, they're all putting out chairs,' Thomas said.

'I think Elsa would feel happier out of the public eye,' David countered.

'Sure, I forgot. Listen, I have some nice cold retsina in my place, you know, over the craft shop.' They were reluctant to leave each other and so they thought it would be a good plan.

'Is there a way we can tell Fiona where we are?' Elsa wondered.

'It might mean involving what Thomas calls "lover boy".' David was doubtful.

'No, I'd say he's still well locked up,' Thomas said. 'So is that an okay plan then?'

'Very okay,' Elsa smiled. 'I'll just go back home and get a scarf for the evening breeze then I'll go get some olives in Yanni's on the way back and see you at your place.' She seemed happy with what had been arranged.

Thomas was soon tidying up his sitting room, and getting out glasses. David walked around looking at the books.

'Did you bring all these from California?' he asked, astonished.

'No, a lot of them are Vonni's. I do really wish that she'd sleep here, you know.'

'What?'

'She sleeps down there at the end of the yard, it's a shed and there are hens and the Lord knows what else in it.'

'I don't believe you.' David looked in surprise at the dilapidated building. They chatted easily for a while as they set out paper napkins and little plates.

Eventually David said what they were both thinking. 'Elsa is a very long time getting the olives, isn't she?'

There was a long pause.

'I suppose she met him,' Thomas said.

'And went off with him,' David said.

Elsa saw Dieter as soon as she came out of Yanni's delicatessen. He was talking to Claus, the chief camera-man, and looking at his watch. Elsa knew they would have hired a helicopter if they had felt they could not wait for slow ferries to take them back to Athens.

The pictures and commentary would be in Germany already, sent by modem.

She moved back into the doorway of Yanni's shop but not quickly enough.

Dieter had seen her.

She could see him running towards her.

'Elsa! Elsa!' he called, pushing past the people in the narrow street. His face was flushed and his eyes were bright. She had forgotten how handsome he was, like Robert Redford in his early years.

There was no escape: he was beside her.

'Dieter?' she said uncertainly.

'Darling Elsa, what are you *doing* here, what did you mean by running away?' He stood with his hands on her shoulders, admiring her and drinking her in.

Any attempt at discretion had been abandoned. But then Claus had probably known anyway. Like half the television company had probably known.

She said nothing, just looked into his very blue eyes.

'Claus heard you were here, someone from the other networks saw you yesterday, but I didn't believe them. Oh, my dearest lovely Elsa – how very, very good to have found you.'

She shook her head. 'You haven't found me, you've just met me by chance. Now I must go.'

She saw Claus move back discreetly: he wanted no part of this lovers' quarrel.

'Elsa, don't be ridiculous – you leave your job, you leave me, no explanation for either . . . you think there is nothing to discuss?'

His face was working with emotion; she had never seen him so upset. He called out to the cameraman, 'Claus, I'm going to stay the night here, you go back with the others and I'll call you tomorrow.'

'Don't stay for me, Dieter, I beg you. And if you try to force me or threaten me, I swear I'll get the police. They've locked up one man yesterday for threatening a woman here, they'll have room in his cell for another.'

'Threaten you, Elsa?' He was astounded at the idea.

'As if I would! I *love* you, Elsa, is it so demanding and mad that I ask you to tell me why you left me? With no explanation?'

'I wrote to you,' she said.

'Twelve lines,' he said, reaching into his jacket. 'I carry it everywhere, I know it by heart, I am always hoping one day I will read it and it will make sense.' He looked so confused she felt herself softening.

'It's all there,' she said.

'Nothing is there, Elsa. I'll go away, leave you alone, I swear, if you tell me. Just tell me why you threw away two years like that. You know why . . . I don't. We have always been fair with each other. Be fair now. You owe me that much.'

She was silent. Perhaps she did owe him more than a twelve-line letter.

'Where are you staying? Let me come to your place,' he asked quickly, seeing her hesitation.

'Not my place, no – where are you staying? The Anna Beach?'

It was the one vaguely touristy, comfortable place. She would have expected him to stay there.

'Yes, exactly,' he agreed.

'Right, I'll go there with you, we can talk in a corner of the café, the sort of veranda looking over the sea.'

He seemed to expel a sigh of relief.

'Thank you,' he said.

'First I have to leave a message.'

He produced his mobile phone.

'No, I don't know the number.' She went to the counter and gave the olives back to Yanni. There was some discussion and it was agreed. Yanni's little brother would take the bag of olives and a note to the apartment over Vonni's craft shop. She scribbled something on a piece of card.

'You didn't even write this guy twelve lines – I suppose I should be flattered,' Dieter said.

She smiled at him. 'No, it's not a guy, well, it's two guys actually, but you know what I mean.'

'I love you, Elsa,' he said with great intensity.

'You were so helpful today, Fiona, the parents said to thank you very much.'

'It was nothing, I love children.' Her voice was sad.

'You will have your own one day.'

'I don't know, Vonni, I really don't. Did you have children?'

'One,' Vonni said. 'A son, but it wasn't what you'd call straightforward.' Her tone meant that the subject was now closed. But she was not shutting Fiona out. She was prepared to talk, but not about her son.

'I meant it, you *are* good with children, it doesn't matter that you don't speak their language.' Vonni was praising.

'Vonni, I could be pregnant now,' Fiona said in a rush. 'In fact I'm certain I am and . . . well, it's not what you'd call straightforward either.'

'And the young man who has gone to Athens – does he know?'

'Sort of, I told him badly, you see.'

'You shouldn't be on your own now,' Vonni said. 'I'd ask you home but I'm living in what Thomas calls the hen-house.'

'I'll go to Elsa's place,' Fiona said. But there was no reply there.

The people in David's house said he had not come home, either.

Vonni escorted her to the craft shop.

'I'll wait here until I see you have someone to be with,' she said, and stood in the street as Fiona went up the steps to the apartment.

Vonni saw Thomas open the door and welcome her in, then she went back to the harbour. She was going to go to help in the kitchen of Manos's family, where there was plenty of food but nobody to serve it or wash up afterwards. Vonni would stay there as long as she was needed.

'They sent him away to Athens, before I could see him,' Fiona wept.

'Maybe it was all for the best,' David said. Then he saw the expression on Fiona's face. 'What I mean is, it gives a cooling-off period for everyone, then he'll be back or something,' he finished lamely.

'Or he'll write,' Thomas added doubtfully.

'Where's Elsa?' Fiona asked suddenly. Elsa might say something helpful, unlike these well-meaning men.

There was a silence.

Then Thomas said, 'She was coming back here but she met someone . . .' he began.

'The German guy,' David said.

'And she went off with him?' There was naked envy in Fiona's voice.

'Apparently,' Thomas and David said at exactly the same time.

Chapter Seven

At the Anna Beach most of the journalists were at the checkout desk. Another job was over, another disaster recorded, and now they were heading off to the next one. They'd pick up the story again when the investigators had reached their official conclusions and produced their report.

Dieter and Elsa went over to the big rattan chairs and low tables of the conservatory. Below them the dark blue sea lapped innocently against the rocks. It was impossible to believe that this very sea had taken the lives of so many people in the bay this week.

Dieter ordered coffee for two.

'Sorry,' Elsa called the waiter back. 'He is having coffee, I'm not, he ordered for me by mistake ... I would like an *ouzo* and water, please.'

'Please don't be difficult,' Dieter begged her.

'Difficult? Choosing what I want to drink?' she asked, perplexed.

'No, you know, scoring points,' he said.

'Oh, I'm way beyond that now. Anyway, Dieter, you wanted to talk, so here I am. Talk to me.'

'No, I wanted *you* to talk, I wanted you to tell me

why you disappeared, ran out on everything . . . to hide secretly in a backwater like this.'

'I'm not hiding,' Elsa said indignantly. 'I resigned from my work formally, I am here under my own name, when you asked me to come and meet you I came, so where's the secrecy bit? And why do you call it a backwater? Look over at that desk – half the world's media is here . . . plenty of action I'd say.'

'I hate it when you're flippant, Elsa, it's an act, and it doesn't suit you.'

The waiter arrived. Elsa poured some water into the aniseed drink and watched it go cloudy. Then she drained it in one gulp.

'That was fast!' He was startled and amused as he began to sip his coffee.

'Well, why don't you finish yours too – then we can go to your room?'

'*What?*' he looked at her in astonishment.

'Your room,' she repeated as if he were a little deaf.

He stared at her, uncomprehending.

'Dieter, isn't this what it's about? You said talk, but you don't mean talk, do you? You mean screw.'

He looked at her, open-mouthed.

'Well . . . I . . . oh, come on, Elsa, there's no need to be crude about it all. That's not what we had.'

'Sorry, I thought that's just what we had every night you came to my apartment, and lunchtime too, when it could be managed.'

'Elsa, I love you, you love me, why on earth are you reducing it all to such coarse words?'

'So you don't want me to go to bed with you?' She looked at him innocently.

'You know I do.'

'Well, finish your coffee and get your key,' she said.

'Thank you, Vonni, nobody but you would think of coming here to wash dishes on a night like this.' Maria, the widow of Manos, stood in her kitchen looking at all the clean dishes and the polished glasses.

'How are you managing in there? Are the relations being a help?'

'Most of them, yes, but some say he was irresponsible and that's no help.'

'Oh, there are always people who say the very wrong thing, they sort of specialise in it,' Vonni assured her.

'You sound as if you have had experience of it.'

'I could write a book about it. Who has upset you most?'

'My sister, I think. She told me I should look for a new husband soon, before I lose my looks. Manos is not cold in his grave and she tells me this.'

'This is the sister married to the miser on the other side of the island?'

'Yes.'

'Well, she's hardly a world authority on love, ignore her. Who else?'

'My father-in-law, he says I'll never manage to raise his grandchildren here, that we should all go to Athens to live with him. I'd hate it, Vonni, really I would. I couldn't go.'

'Of course you couldn't. Tell him you'll think about it for a year. Say you heard that no one should make a decision for twelve months after a bereavement, say it's an old custom.'

'Is it?' Maria asked.

'It is back in Ireland, but you don't need to tell him where the tradition came from, just say it's well known.'

'He'll start making plans if he thinks I might.'

'No, be very firm, say no plans until a year from now. In a year you can say the children can't leave their school or whatever.'

'Did you really have things like this to worry about, funerals where they say the wrong thing? You always look so calm.'

'After my mother's funeral, my sister wrote and told me that I was a scourge and a lash for my mother's back, that she never slept easy in her bed because of me.'

'Oh no, Vonni, that can't have been true.'

'I was wild when I was young, much more irresponsible than your Manos ever was. I was very hurt, I thought for a long while that it might indeed be true, but then I remembered that I made my mother laugh too, something my boring, serious sister never did, so I cheered up then.'

'And do you stay in touch with your sister? I would like to go back into the other room and slap *my* sister's face,' Maria said.

'Yes, so did I for a long time, but life is much easier if you don't slap them. Believe me. I send her a birthday card and a Christmas card every year.'

'And does she reply?'

'She sends me cards when she goes to the opera in Italy, or a classical tour of Spain, just to show me how cultured she is. But she is lonely, she has no real friends. I am a million times better off in this warm, welcoming place. I can afford to send her polite greetings. You too, Maria, you are so lucky not to be married to that miser your sister chose, rejoice in it every day, and hang on in there. She'll be back with him counting coins in two days. Don't slap her this time.'

Maria laughed. 'You make me feel much better – I didn't think I would laugh again,' she said, putting her hand on the older woman's arm.

'Yes, you will,' Vonni promised her. 'Cry a lot, but laugh as well. It's how we survive.'

David didn't want to go back to the house where he was staying. The family were wiped out with grief over their dead son, he felt in the way. Fiona didn't want to walk all the way out to Eleni's house to sleep there alone in the knowledge that Shane had left her with no explanation, no letter, no message.

'Why don't you both stay here?' Thomas suggested suddenly. 'Fiona can have that room at the back, David can have the sofa bed.' He looked at their faces, both of them very grateful and relieved.

They nodded their acceptance, it was a great idea, they said.

It wasn't a night to be alone.

'Can I stay here in the station?' Andreas asked his brother Yorghis.

'I was just going to suggest it.'

'It's just that it seems a long way to go the whole way up that mountain road tonight, I'm not quite sure why.'

'Nobody wants to be alone on a night of such a sad funeral,' Yorghis said, reaching out and patting his brother's hand. 'I don't want to be alone either. I'm glad you want to stay.'

Neither of them mentioned the reason why they were alone.

They talked about the people who had come out today to mourn. They talked about their sister Christina and how she would have come to the funeral but she had to look after her family far away. No word was spoken about Andreas's son Adoni who lived in Chicago and was in contact with neither his home town nor his father. Adoni who would have gone to school along these roads with Manos.

No mention was made of Yorghis's wife who had left him over an incident many years ago. His wife always said that she was just being friendly to a tourist. Yorghis had seen it as being a great deal more than friendly. Words had been said that could never be taken back. She had long since gone back to her own people in Crete.

Yorghis went to one of the filing cabinets and brought out a bottle of Metaxa brandy and then he got some clean sheets and pillows.

'Are you giving me a cell?' Andreas asked.

'No, brother, you and I have spent enough years as boys sharing a room, it won't hurt us to do it again, two lonely old men, on a sad night.'

Vonni had served coffee and *baklava* to the family of Maria and Manos, and she was preparing to leave quietly when Maria came back into the kitchen.

'Vonni, can I ask you a favour?'

'Anything, Maria.'

'Could you stay here for the night, just one night? I don't think I can manage on my own tonight.'

'Of course I will.'

'You are such a good friend, the bed is too big, too empty for me.'

'I snore a bit, I'd better warn you,' Vonni apologised in advance.

'So did Manos, every night, even though he denied it loudly.'

'Dear Manos,' Vonni said fondly. 'I'm sure he would be pleased if I snored for a night or two in his place.'

The Hotel Anna Beach had little bungalows facing the sea. Dieter opened his bungalow door with his key and stood back to let Elsa go in first.

She didn't sit down but stood looking at the pictures on the walls, big blown-up photographs of the coast along Aghia Anna.

'Very cool,' she said admiringly.

'This is not what I had expected,' he said.

'But we have agreed that it's what you'd like,' she smiled.

'That's not a real smile, Elsa,' he began.

'You taught me to smile for television. Teeth and eyes, you said. Teeth and eyes. I remember it well.'

'Please, my love, you *are* my love. Please don't be brittle.'

'No, indeed, and let's not waste time either.' Elsa had already taken off her navy jacket. Now she drew the cream linen dress over her head and laid it neatly on the back of the chair.

He was still very unsure.

She removed her lace bra and pants and placed them on top of her dress, then finally she stepped out of her smart navy sandals.

'You are so beautiful, and to think I believed I'd never see you again.' He looked at her in open admiration.

'Not you, Dieter, you get everything you want.' She

put her arms around his neck and kissed him. And suddenly it was as if they had never been apart.

In the apartment over the craft shop, Fiona had gone to bed in the small white room that Vonni had furnished with a turquoise bedspread and a bright blue chair. The little white chest of drawers had a blue-framed mirror and some shells and pottery on top. It was cool and welcoming.

Fiona was weary and sad.

It had been a nightmare of a day, and further nightmares were ahead. She didn't think she would sleep. Too much had happened and the future was too frightening. How wonderful it would have been if Shane were still here and they might both have been able to stay with Thomas for a few days in this wonderful apartment. But even as she thought it Fiona knew she was fooling herself. Shane would have fought with Thomas about something. The way he always did with people. Out of insecurity.

She gave a little sob.

It was such a tragedy that people misunderstood Shane and brought out the worst in him.

She lay on the bed with its blue cover and cried herself to sleep.

In the room next door Thomas and David played chess. They heard the sounds of weeping through the wall.

'She's crying over that bastard!' David whispered in amazement.

'I know, it's beyond comprehension,' Thomas whispered back.

And they sat there and waited until the sobs had died down. Then they smiled at each other in relief.

'Do you know what we're like?' David said. 'We're like the parents of a toddler who won't go to sleep.'

Thomas sighed. 'Yes, there was always that moment of not wanting to leave the room until you were *sure* he was asleep, and then just when you crept to the door he'd call you back. They were great days really.' He looked sad, thinking about his son.

David thought hard about what to say. He so often got it wrong.

'It's hard to understand women, isn't it?' he said eventually.

Thomas looked at him thoughtfully. 'It sure is, David, the exact same thought was going through my mind. Fiona crying over that drunken brute who would have beaten her senseless, Elsa going off with the man she had run a thousand miles to escape, my wife who used to tell me she loved poetry and literature and art living with a bonehead who has some exercise machine in every room of my house.' He sounded very bitter.

David looked at him, stricken. It had not been a good thing to say after all.

Thomas shrugged. 'And you probably have your own women-are-unfathomable story, David,' he said.

'No, that's just the problem. I was telling Elsa before, I never really loved anyone. That makes me superficial, cold and shallow.'

Thomas smiled at him. 'No, you're a good guy, and I'm glad to have your company tonight. But you are *not* a skilled chess player. You didn't free up the squares around your king. He has no egress, poor fellow, it's checkmate, David, that's what it is.'

And for some reason they both found that very funny and laughed as loudly as they could while keeping the volume low enough so as not to wake the sleeping Fiona in the next room.

Dieter stroked Elsa's face.

'I must have been mad to think I had lost you,' he said.

She said nothing.

'It will all be fine again,' he said.

Still no reply.

'You could not love me like that and not mean it?' he said, just a little anxiously now.

Elsa lay there saying nothing.

'Speak to me, tell me this has all been nonsense, that you'll come back with me and it will all be fine again . . .'

She still said nothing at all.

'Please, Elsa . . . please?'

She got up slowly from the bed and put on the big white fluffy robe that was hanging on the bathroom door. She picked up Dieter's packet of cigarettes and lit one.

'You gave up!' he said accusingly.

She inhaled deeply and sat in the big bamboo chair looking at him.

'You'll come home with me, Elsa?'

'No, of course I won't. This is goodbye, you know this and I know this, so let's not be foolish, Dieter.'

'Goodbye?' he asked.

'Yes, goodbye. You are going home, I am going to go to . . . well, somewhere. I haven't decided exactly where yet.'

'This is insane, we were meant for each other, you know that, I know it. Everyone knows it.'

'No. Everyone does *not* know. A few people at work know and say nothing, because they take their lead from you. And because you do not want us to go public we have lived a secret life for two years. So less of the *everyone knows we are meant for each other* line.'

He looked at her, startled. 'We went into it, eyes open. Both of us,' he said.

'And I'm walking out of it, eyes open,' Elsa said calmly.

'You aren't the kind of woman to hold out for an engagement ring,' he said with scorn in his voice.

'Of course not. I didn't exactly hold out, did I? I slept with you the third time I met you. That's hardly playing games, withholding favours.'

'So what are we talking about then?' He was genuinely bewildered.

'I told you. I wrote it all down before I left.'

'You did like hell, you scribbled twelve jumbled lines that I still can't make head nor tail of. Life is not meant to be a guessing game, Elsa, we are both far too old for this sort of thing. What do you want? Tell me. If you're holding a gun to my head and saying we must be married, then all right. If that's what it takes, all right, that's what we'll do.'

'I've heard of better proposals,' she said with a smile.

'Stop playing the fool. If it's the only way I can have you with me, I'll marry you. Be *proud* to marry you,' he added as an afterthought.

'No, thank you, Dieter. I don't want to marry you.'

'So what *do* you want?' he cried, in near despair.

'I want to get over you, to forget you, to make you no longer any part of my life.'

'You took an odd way to show all that.' He looked down at the bed she had so recently left.

Elsa shrugged. 'I told you. I no longer trust you, I don't admire you or respect you any more. Sex has nothing to do with those things. Sex is just sex, a short amount of pleasure, excitement. You told me that yourself, if you remember.'

'I do remember, but it was in totally different circumstances. I wasn't talking about us, not about you and me.'

'Still, the principle is the same, isn't it?' She was ice calm now.

'No, it's not in my case, we were talking about a totally meaningless drunken encounter at a film festival with some very silly girl whose name I can't even remember.'

'Birgit. And she remembers you.'

'Only well enough to tell you and upset you over something that couldn't have mattered less.'

'I know, I realise that.'

'So tell me, Elsa, if you realise this, what in God's name is all this drama about? Why did you leave?'

'I wrote it in my letter.'

'You did *not* write it, you wrote some rubbish about responsibilities and lines having to be drawn. I swear I didn't know what you meant. I still don't know.'

His handsome face was working with emotion and his thick hair was tousled.

'Birgit told me about Monika,' Elsa said.

'Monika? Monika? But she was ages before I met you. We agreed that the past was past. Didn't we?'

'Yes.'

'So why bring her up? I swear I never saw her since I met you. Not even once.'

'I know.'

'So explain to me. I beg you. If you know I haven't seen or thought of Monika in years ... what is this about?'

'You haven't seen or thought of your daughter either.'

'Ah,' Dieter said. 'Birgit really went to work, didn't she?'

Elsa said nothing.

'It was never meant to happen. I told Monika I wasn't ready to be a parent, to settle down. She knew that from the very start. There were no grey areas.' He was beginning to bluster now.

'How old is she, Dieter?' Elsa's voice was level.

He was genuinely confused. 'Monika?'

'Gerda. Your daughter.'

'I don't know, I told you I have nothing to do with them.'

'You must know.'

'About eight or nine I suppose. But why do you keep probing it, Elsa? All that has nothing to do with us.'

'You fathered a child. That has something to do with you.'

'No, it has not. That was a long past incident in my life and not my fault. Monika was in charge of contraception. I have nothing to do with her child, never had and never will. We all began again.'

'But Gerda began with no father.'

'Stop calling her by her name, you don't know her, you're only repeating tittle-tattle from that bitch Birgit.'

'You should have told me.'

'No, if I had that would have been wrong too. You would have said I was always hanging around a child from a previous relationship. Be fair, Elsa, you would not have liked that either.'

'I'd have liked it a hell of a lot more than a father who opted out and left a child hoping and wondering.'

'That is fantasy talk, you don't know *anything* about that child.'

'It's my own story all over again. My father left home and I spent years waiting and hoping and wondering. Every birthday, every Christmas, every summer. I was so sure he would write or call or come to see me.'

'It was different in your case: your father *had* lived at home with you. You had a right to think he would always be around. In my case I had nothing to do with Monika's child. Not ever. There were no expectations.'

Elsa gave him a long look.

'What do you want me to do?' he asked eventually.

'Nothing, Dieter.'

'You'd come back to me if I made some kind of link to this totally strange child?'

'No, I will not come back to you ever.'

'But all this . . .' Again he looked at the bed where they had made love. 'Did it mean nothing to you?'

'You know it did. It meant goodbye,' she said, and put on her dress and her sandals. Slipping her underwear in her bag, she walked to the door.

'You *can't* do this!' he cried.

'Goodbye, Dieter,' she said and walked through the manicured little rock gardens of the Anna Beach towards the gate. Her navy jacket she had slung over her shoulder.

From his bungalow Dieter called after her. 'Don't go,

Elsa, please don't go. I love you so much. Don't leave me . . .'

But she walked on.

Vonni had realised there was no milk in Maria's house and that everyone would want it in the morning. As soon as Maria's breathing became regular Vonni slipped out of the big double bed and found a pottery jug. She would go to the Anna Beach where the kitchen would be open all night.

She was returning with the jug that they had willingly filled for her when she saw the beautiful German girl walking alone. There were tears on her face. Vonni pulled back behind a big bougainvillaea so as not to encounter her.

Then she heard a man calling and shouting. Vonni didn't speak much German but she could understand what he was saying. And if she was any judge at all, he meant it, whoever he was.

But Elsa did not look back.

Chapter Eight

Thomas had gone out for hot fresh bread and figs for their breakfast. He made a large pot of coffee and rattled the cups.

Fiona emerged pale and tired-looking but with a grateful smile. David had folded the light rug Thomas had given him, and plumped up the cushions.

He came eagerly to the breakfast table.

'He spoils us, Fiona, weren't we lucky to find a benefactor?'

'Oh, I know.' Fiona too was fervent. 'I feel much, much stronger today, I'm full of plans now, so I am.'

Thomas smiled at her. 'Tell us your plans,' he said.

'I'm going up to the station to see the chief of police, now that I'm calm and not hysterical. I'll ask him to help me find Shane, he might know where he would head for. We were only in Athens for twenty-four hours on the way here, but he loved Syntagma Square, perhaps Yorghis might know some policemen there who could get him a message. Then I'll go back to Eleni's and change my clothes. I've been wearing this dress for days, then I'm going to find Vonni and ask her does she need any help with the children.' Her eyes were bright and enthusiastic and the dead, defeated look had gone.

David too seemed to be energised. 'I'm going to walk up to that taverna and see Andreas again, he was such a gentleman, if that isn't too stupid a word.'

'That's exactly what he is and he'd be so happy to see you again. Give him our best, won't you?'

'I'll do that,' David promised.

'And I too have several things to do today. Later on, when they're all awake in California, I'll call my son. But first I'm going to find Vonni – she didn't come home to her shed last night.'

'How on earth do you know?' David was surprised.

'Because normally she pokes around in there with her torch, she didn't do that last night. But when I find her, this time I'm going to *insist* that she stays in her own bedroom, I'm getting tetchy and antsy just having her living in that place in the yard.'

'*Antsy?*' Fiona asked.

'I know, it's a great word, isn't it. Means something irritates you, gives you ants in your pants.'

'Shane will love that,' Fiona said happily.

And neither of the men could think of anything to say.

Elsa was in her apartment. She knew that she would not sleep so she sat on her balcony and watched the dawn come up in Aghia Anna.

She saw the little town come to life. Then, as if she had finally accepted that the night with all its fears and nightmares was over, she went in, had a long shower, washed her hair. She put on a fresh yellow cotton dress and sat down with a cup of coffee to watch the ferry getting ready to leave.

He would leave on the 8 a.m. for Athens. She was utterly certain of this. Dieter knew she wasn't coming with him, so why wait for the 11 a.m.? He wasn't a person to hang about. He had sent Claus and the others ahead of him by the chartered helicopter yesterday. He knew there was no point in searching the town for her. He would never see her on this balcony, but she would be able to see him and know that he had gone.

She couldn't pick him out in the crowd that lined up before the brightly coloured gangplank. Yet she knew he would be there. They knew each other very well despite everything.

And then she saw him, his hair tousled, wearing an open-necked shirt, and gripping that leather grip bag which she had seen so often.

His eyes were raking the crowds around as if he were going to see her in their number. He saw nothing, nobody he recognised, but he knew her well enough to assume that she was watching. He put down his bag and raised both his arms in the air.

'I love you, Elsa,' he called out. 'Wherever you are I will always love you.'

Some of the young men near him clapped him on the back approvingly. Declaring love was good.

Elsa sat like stone as the little ferry sailed across the sea to Piraeus, the harbour of Athens. The tears dropped slowly down her face and splashed into her coffee and on to her lap.

'David, my friend, welcome, welcome.' Andreas was delighted to see him.

David wished that he could have a father like this, a man whose face lit up when he approached, not a man whose features had set in discontent and disappointment over his only son for as long as David could remember. They talked easily about the sad funeral yesterday and how Aghia Anna would never be the same again.

'Did you know Manos well?' David asked.

'Yes, we all know each other here, there are no secrets, we know everyone's history. Manos used to come here to play with Adoni and another boy when he was a child. They made a swing on that tree over there, he used to come up here to escape from his family – there were eight of them. Adoni was an only child so we were so happy to have people come up here and play with him. When my wife, who has now gone to God, was cooking she could look out the window and see the boys playing with the old dog and the swing and she knew he was safe. I wonder if she can see from heaven, David ... see poor Manos buried ... see Adoni over in Chicago cutting himself off from everything here. If hearts can be heavy in heaven her poor heart will be like a lump of lead.'

David wished so much that he had the gentle insights of someone like Thomas. Thomas would have said something thoughtful and helpful, he might even have found a couple of lines of poetry that would be appropriate.

David could think of no quotation that was remotely suitable.

'I only know about Jewish heaven, and I actually don't know all that much about that,' he said apologetically.

'Well, do the people in Jewish heaven see what's going on down here, do you think?' Andreas asked.

'Yes, I think so, but I believe that they have a broader view of things, like they see the whole picture. That's what I heard, anyway.'

Oddly, it seemed to give Andreas some comfort. He nodded several times.

'Come, David, share a lunch with me, we won't see many visitors today.'

David looked at the open cabinets of food the old man had prepared and he felt a lump in his throat. To have got all this ready and then nobody to arrive.

'I never tried that big pasta dish,' he began.

'David, if you don't mind, I can freeze that one. I only made it this morning. Could I persuade you to have the *moussaka* or the *kalamari*? It's not great hospitality asking you to eat only the items that have to go today.' Andreas laughed at himself, embarrassed.

'I'd prefer the *moussaka*, I only said the pasta because it was big. I didn't want to see all your hard work go to waste,' David said.

'What a kind person you are. Sit here in the sunshine and I will get the glasses and plates . . .'

And David sat wondering what that foolish young man was doing in Chicago when he could be here.

Eleni welcomed Fiona back. It was a shock to see all Shane's things gone, his crumpled shirts and jeans, his canvas bag, his tin of tobacco and whatever else it might contain and papers for rolling cigarettes. She had hoped desperately that he might have left a note for her here with this family. But it hadn't happened.

She felt very dizzy suddenly. Perhaps it was the stuffy

room or the realisation that Shane really had gone out of her life.

It would have been so simple for him to scribble her a note and leave it here even if he didn't want to do it at the police station. She felt light-headed and as if she might faint. But she steeled herself in front of the kindly Eleni, whose face was sympathetic and pitying.

Then she felt a hot, wet sensation on her thighs.

It must be sweat.

It was such a hot day.

But as she looked down at her sandals she knew only too well what it was.

And Eleni knew too, as she saw the blood.

The Greek woman helped her to a chair. '*Ela, ela, ela,*' she said and ran for towels.

'Eleni, could you find Vonni for me please, Vonni, you know?' She put her hand to her face to show lines and wrinkles as if to describe Vonni.

'*Xero* Vonni, yes, I know Vonni,' Eleni said, and shouted down to the children.

Fiona closed her eyes.

Vonni would be here soon and would know what to do.

Vonni was sitting opposite Thomas in the apartment over the craft shop.

'I've told you before, I'm telling you again, you are paying me an enormous number of euros so that this is your place. Because of you I am a rich woman, I will *not* take your pity and sleep in your house.'

'Have you no concept of friendship, Vonni?' he asked.

'I think I have, but then we all think that.'

'Then apply it here. I am asking you, not as my landlady but as my friend, sleep in that little room you decorated so beautifully, sleep there, not where chickens are crapping all over you.'

Vonni pealed with laughter. 'Oh, Thomas, you are *so* Californian, so hygienic, there are no chickens crapping on me. A couple of hens in a different part of the building certainly . . .'

'Stay in that room, Vonni, please. I hate my own company. I'm lonely, I need someone in the place.'

'Oh, come on, Thomas, you love peace and time to yourself. You are a sensitive man, don't offer me charity. Please.'

'You are a sensitive woman, don't throw my offer of friendship right back in my face. Please.'

Just at that moment, they heard children shouting something urgently up the staircase.

'I must go,' she said, standing up.

He reached out and grabbed her wrist. 'Vonni, you are not going anywhere unless you agree to what I offer. Do you hear me?'

'I hear, I agree,' she said to his surprise.

'Good, well then, okay you can go.'

'Come with me if you like, you can help, get us a taxi from the square.' To his even greater surprise she snatched some towels from his bathroom and ran down the steps to talk in Greek to two little boys.

'What's happening?' he asked as he ran after her.

'What's happening is . . . that with any luck, Fiona is losing the baby of that little shit who beat her up, but that's not exactly how we are going to phrase it when we get there.'

Thomas ran for a taxi and Vonni bundled Eleni's two

little sons into the back seat, congratulating them for having found her. A taxi ride was a rare treat and they were beaming with pleasure. Thomas had been about to ask if he was really necessary on this particular expedition, but he realised Vonni would not have asked him to come unless she thought so. So he smiled at her and climbed in after her.

'Life is never going to be uneventful with my new room-mate,' he said.

'Good man yourself, Thomas,' she said, with a huge wide smile.

They asked the taxi to wait in case they might need him to go to the doctor's. Thomas stayed downstairs watching the little boys play and make occasional journeys to stroke the car in which they had travelled.

They were not very much younger than his boy Bill who had travelled in a car since he could remember. How different people's lives were.

Vonni had gone upstairs and he could hear the women's voices as they spoke in English and Greek. From what he could make out, Fiona would be all right.

Then Vonni came down and reassured him.

'She's going to be fine, she's lost some blood but she's a nurse after all and she's a sensible little thing about everything except that fool. She thinks he'll be upset when he hears. God protect us! Anyway I'll ask the doctor to have a look at her, give her something to sedate her.'

'Is she all right staying here?'

'I don't think so, they don't speak English in any real sense ... what I was thinking—' Vonni began.

'That she might come and stay with us,' Thomas interrupted.

'No, not that at all. I was going to suggest she spent a couple of days with Elsa, the German girl.'

Thomas shook his head. 'I think Elsa's a bit tied up with her own affairs just now, better if she comes to us,' he said.

'You might find she's not tied up any more,' Vonni said.

'But . . .'

'I hear her German friend left on the eight a.m. ferry,' Vonni said.

'I imagine she must be very upset then.' Thomas was pessimistic.

'No, I think it was her doing, but we needn't necessarily say that we know all this?' Vonni suggested.

'I expect you know where she lives?' Thomas said, smiling.

'I know the apartment building, but perhaps you could take the taxi that's outside and ask her?'

'Would I be the right person?' He was doubtful.

'Nobody better. I'll wait here until you come back.'

A moment later he turned and looked behind. He could see Vonni staggering out with sheets and towels – she was going to wash them there and then. What an extraordinary woman! He wished he knew more about her but he knew she would reveal very little and then only when she wanted to.

'Vonni?'

'You're all right.'

Fiona held out her hand. 'I wanted to say sorry for all the trouble, the blood, the mess and everything.'

'It doesn't matter a bit, you know that. You, of all people, a nurse, know about cleaning up, it's of no importance. What is important is that you are all right, that you recover and get strong again.'

'I don't care if I do or not.'

'Terrific,' Vonni said.

'What?'

'That's terrific. Eleni and I are both worried sick about you, she sent her sons to find me, Thomas brought us all here in a taxi, he's gone to find Elsa to ask if you can stay in her house, we have sent for Dr Leros who is coming to see you here, everyone who has met you and even people who haven't care about you, but you, you don't care. Great.'

'I don't mean that, I meant it's not really important to me what happens now. It's all over, I've lost everything, that's what I meant . . .'

She looked wretched.

Vonni pulled up a chair beside her.

'Very soon Dr Leros will be here, he's a kind man, a real old family doctor person. But you are not meeting him at his best, Fiona, his heart is broken over the accident, and having to pronounce dead, young men whom he delivered into this world. He has been stumbling for hours talking as best he can in English and German to the families of the foreigners who died here, telling them that their loved ones did not suffer much. He doesn't want to hear that a perfectly healthy young girl who has had a miscarriage at a very early stage doesn't care if she lives or dies. Believe me, Fiona, this is not the time to tell him this. Of course it's sad, of course you are upset, but think of other people as you have done all your life as a nurse, as you do about that fellow you claim to love. I will always be here – you can tell me how you may want to die, but don't tell Dr Leros, not today. He has been through just as much as you have.'

Fiona was sobbing. 'I'm sorry, it's just that everyone says Shane was awful, they'll say this was all for the best. It's *not* all for the best, Vonni, truly it isn't. I would have been happy to have his child, I would have loved to have his son or daughter, now it's all gone.'

Vonni held her hand and stroked it. 'I know, I know,' she said meaninglessly, over and over.

'You don't think it was all for the best?'

'Of course I don't! Losing what was on its way to being a person is terrible. I'm so sorry for you. But if the child had lived, you would have had to be strong. All I am saying is that you still have to be strong. And you have friends here, you are not alone. Elsa will be here before too long.'

'Oh, no, why should she take me in, she has her own life, her own fellow, she thinks I was weak to love Shane in spite of everything. She won't want anything to do with me.'

'Mark my words, she will,' said Vonni. 'And I hear Dr Leros arriving.'

'I'll remember what you said,' Fiona said.

'Good girl,' Vonni nodded approvingly.

Eleni's little boys had never known such a day.

A trip in a taxi, people coming and going, sheets and towels being pinned on the line in great numbers to wave in the sunshine. The tall American man with the funny trousers had brought them a big watermelon to share when he came back the second time.

'*Karpouzi!*' he had said proudly, as if delighted that he

knew the name of something so ordinary as a melon. They went behind the house and ate it all, then planted the seeds in the earth.

The American man, who was waiting near the taxi until the women came down, watched them with a pleased expression on his face. Then the woman who had been sick came down with Vonni and their mother and the smart woman in a yellow dress who looked like a film star. Dr Leros was with them, and he kept saying the sick woman was fine but she must rest.

The sick woman's bag had been packed for her, so she must be leaving for good.

She kept talking about money and their mother kept shaking her head. Eventually the man with the mad trousers, who must be a millionaire, travelling all day in a taxi, insisted their mother take some notes and then they were all gone.

Except Vonni, who sat down to have coffee with their mother, but there was something about their faces that made it clear small boys weren't welcome at the kitchen table.

'I'll only stay a couple of days until I get myself together,' Fiona promised when she saw the beautiful apartment that Elsa had.

'I'll be glad of your company,' Elsa assured her as she took out Fiona's clothes from the canvas bag, shook them and hung them up. 'There's an iron here, we can get all domestic later on.'

Fiona looked at Elsa's cream linen dress and navy jacket drying on hangers out on the balcony.

'Aren't you disciplined, Elsa, that's what you were

wearing at the funeral yesterday, and look, you have it all laundered already.'

'I'll never wear either of them again but I wanted to give them away to someone, so I washed them first.' Elsa spoke calmly.

'But, Elsa, that's your best outfit – it must have cost a fortune! You just *can't* give it away!' Fiona was aghast.

'Try it on later, and if it fits you, Fiona, and suits you, then you are more than welcome to it, it's just that I'm *never* putting it on again.'

Fiona lay back against the pillow and closed her eyes. It was all too much to take in.

'I'm going to sit and read. It's too hot outside so I'll be here in the room with you. Try to sleep if you can, but if you want to talk then I'm here.'

'There's not much to talk about now, honestly, is there?' Fiona spoke in a small voice.

'You might feel like it later.' Elsa's smile was warm. She pulled a curtain to darken the room.

'Will you be able to read in the dark?' Fiona asked.

'Sure. There's a nice beam of light coming in here.'

Elsa settled in a chair by the window.

'Did you meet him, Elsa?' Fiona asked.

'Yes. Yes, I did.'

'And are you glad you did?'

'Well, it was just to say goodbye, really. It had to be said, it wasn't easy, but it's finished now. What is it you say ... onwards and upwards?'

'Dead easy to say, but not to do.' Fiona's voice sounded sleepy. The sedative was beginning to work. Soon she was asleep, breathing regularly. Elsa looked at her as she slept. She must be about twenty-three or twenty-four, but she looked even younger. Hadn't it all been a great mercy? But Elsa had heeded well Vonni's whispered advice that whatever she said she must not even hint that it had all been for the best.

Thomas had worked out when best to call his son, Bill. It would be when the boy was having breakfast. He dialled the number, wondering what the chances were that he would get straight through to his son. Three to one probably, or maybe the odds were stacked even more against him since he couldn't expect a child to answer the phone when there were two adults there.

As it happened it was Andy.

'Well, hi, Thomas, good of you to call the other night, one helluva scene that must have been.'

'Yeah, it was very tragic.' Thomas felt his voice becoming clipped and curt. There was a silence between them.

'But apart from that, everything else okay?' Andy asked.

The man was insufferable, to call a catastrophe that ripped the soul out of a small town *one helluva scene*.

'Hunky-dory,' Thomas said scathingly. 'Is Bill around?'

'He's helping his mother do the dishes,' Andy said, as if that's all there was to it.

'Sure, and could you perhaps tell him he might dry his hands and come talk to his father phoning from the other side of the world?'

'I'll see if he's through.' Andy was genial about it all.

'Perhaps his mother might risk letting him leave even if he hasn't *quite* finished.' Thomas realised that his fists were clenched with fury. In the distance he was aware that Vonni was watching him from the kitchen door. It didn't help his mood.

'Hi, Dad.' Bill always sounded delighted to hear from him.

'How are things, son? Good?'

'Yeah, fine. Is your island in the Dodecanese, Dad?'

'No, but if you have your big atlas handy I'll tell you where it is ...'

'No, not beside me, Dad, the books have been put upstairs on the landing,' Bill explained.

'But not the atlas surely, not the dictionary? You *need* these things when you are looking at television, Bill, you can't let him stow away any signs of culture from your life to make room for another rowing machine or whatever.' There was real pain in his voice as he spoke.

At the other end there was a silence as the child tried to think of something to say.

'Get me your mother, Bill, put Shirley on the phone.'

'No, Dad, you and she would only fight, that's what happens. Please, Dad it doesn't *matter* where the atlas is, I can run and get it if you hold on.'

'No, you're right, it's not important where the atlas is. I'll send you an e-mail with a drawing attached and you can look it up. That is if the computer also hasn't been filed away where no one can get at it.'

'No, Dad, of course it hasn't.' He sounded reproachful.

'So what are you going to do today, it's only morning there, isn't it?'

'Yes, well, we'll be going to the shopping mall first, I'm getting new sneakers, and then Andy is going to take me for a run to try them out.'

'Sounds great,' said Thomas in a voice that sounded

sepulchral as it went across the thousands of miles between them.

'I miss you, son,' he said eventually since Bill had said no more.

'Yeah, Dad, and I miss you too, a lot, but it *was* you who went away,' the child answered.

'Who told you that? Was it your mother? Andy? Listen to me, Bill, we discussed this endlessly, better for me to go and give you space together as a family—'

'No, Dad, she doesn't say that,' Bill interrupted. 'And Andy doesn't either, I just said I missed you, and that I was still here and you were the one that was gone.'

'I'm sorry, Bill, we're all upset here. So many people died. Please forgive me. I'll call again soon.' He hung up, as low as he had been in years.

Vonni came towards him with a brandy.

'You made a right dog's dinner out of that,' she said.

'You don't understand what it is to have a son,' he said to her, willing the tears away from his eyes.

'Why the hell do you assume I don't have a son?' she asked him, her eyes blazing.

'You do?' He was astonished.

'Yes, so you don't have a monopoly on being a parent.'

'And where is he? Why isn't he with you?'

'Because like you I made a mess of things.'

He knew she would say no more. And yet critical though she was of him it was somehow comforting to have her there. Much better than four walls to cry to, and rail against what was happening to his beloved Bill.

Yorghis drove up to the taverna. Someone had given him a big leg of lamb. He thought maybe Andreas could cook it for his customers. Andreas explained sadly, nobody but David had come to the taverna today and it didn't look likely that anyone would come tonight. But then Andreas had an idea. Why didn't they cook it at the police station, give all those young boys who had worked so hard at the funeral a real dinner?

They would ask David and his friends to join them, and Vonni. Andreas scraped up all the salads into a big bowl. He was pleased and excited at the thought of cooking for people rather than sitting alone in his empty taverna.

'It's not very comfortable, of course, in the police station,' Yorghis said doubtfully. 'Not very welcoming.'

'We'll get those long red cushions. We can put them on benches.' Andreas would not let the idea die. 'David, run up to Adoni's room and get them, will you?'

David looked at him in surprise. Adoni had been gone for years in Chicago yet he still had his own room in this house.

'At the top of the stairs on the left,' Yorghis advised him and David hastened up the narrow steps.

The room had pictures of Panathinaikos, the Athens football team, and posters of a Greek dance troupe; it had images of the Panayia, the Virgin Mary. He was a man of varied tastes, the missing Adoni.

His bed was made as if he were coming back that night, with a bright red rug folded at the end. On the window seats were long narrow red cushions.

David looked out of the window. The afternoon sun shone down on the hills, over the olive groves to the blue bay of Aghia Anna. What *could* that boy be looking at in Chicago, Illinois, that would be one-tenth as beautiful as this? He grabbed the cushions and went down to help them pack Yorghis's van.

'This will cheer us all up, brother Yorghis,' Andreas said with a happy smile.

David looked at him longingly. Imagine having a father who was so easily satisfied with simple things.

They called first to Thomas and left David there. Thomas sounded very pleased at the thought of the feast. He said he would go out and get some wine. Vonni said she'd check out the situation with Elsa and Fiona. She explained admirably briefly to David what had happened and how Fiona might not feel like joining them.

'That's terrible,' David said. 'But maybe when you think of it, it might be all for the—'

'You know the expression *don't go there* ... David, this is the very occasion that phrase was invented for. You might think it, I might think it, but Fiona most definitely does *not* think it. I thought I'd warn you.'

'Very wise,' David agreed, 'I always say the wrong thing anyway. But what about Elsa? I thought that she had gone off with her German friend?'

'I know I sound like some manifestation of the Sphinx,' Vonni said. 'But to be very honest I wouldn't go there either!'

The young policemen were delighted with the great smells of cooking meat, basted with garlic and oregano. It had been an exhausting and draining time. It was good to relax with their boss, his brother, Vonni and the four tourists. One of the girls looked like a beauty queen, the other very washed out, as if she had been ill.

The two men were very different: one tall and lanky

in ludicrous baggy Bermuda shorts with pockets, the other small and serious with spectacles.

All the visitors made attempts to speak a few words of Greek. They knew wine was *krassi*, so the young police officers taught them *aspro* and *kokkino* for white and red, and how to say *yassu* with exactly the right pronunciation.

In return they were taught how to say *cheers*, *prosit*, *l'chaim* and *slainte*.

Andreas carved proudly and the moonlight made patterns on the sea as the clouds raced across the sky.

'It seems so long since we were in Kalatriada,' Fiona said.

'When the night was full of rain beating against the roof and the walls. It was only two nights ago,' Elsa said. 'And so much has happened since!' She reached out and held the hand of Fiona as a gesture of solidarity.

Fiona's eyes filled with tears, and David flashed a glance at Vonni. How wise she had been to mark his card.

Down near the harbour they saw a group of young men gather in front of the little house that belonged to Maria and Manos. And soon they saw other people leave the cafés and restaurants to come and join them.

'What's happening?' Thomas asked, anxious in case anything was wrong.

Yorghis was peering down. 'I can't see, one of you boys go down and see is everything all right,' and he pointed at one of the policemen. It was possible, unlikely but possible, that someone might have wanted to blame Manos for the whole tragedy. They had better be prepared.

Vonni spoke gently. 'It's no problem. Some of the

young men said they would like to dance tonight in honour of Manos and his friends, outside his house, in memory of how he used to dance *Syrtaki* and other dances.'

'There isn't usually dancing after a funeral here,' Yorghis said.

'This isn't a usual funeral,' Vonni said quietly.

And as they watched, twelve men with black trousers and white shirts lined up, arms on each other's shoulders. The bouzouki players played a few chords and then they began. Bending, swooping, leaping in the night, as Manos and his friends had done until a few short days ago.

Maria and her children sat on chairs outside their little house. When all this was a long-distant memory, perhaps the children would recall the night that Aghia Anna had come out to dance for their father. The crowd grew ever bigger and even from a distance they could see people wiping tears from their eyes.

Then the crowd began to clap in time to the music and dancing, every single person joining in.

From their veranda at the police station, the group watched too. All of them were wordless, watching the scene. It was so different to anything they had ever seen before.

Then Elsa began to clap in time to the music, and Thomas immediately after her. David and Fiona exchanged glances and joined in, as did Vonni, the young policemen and Andreas and Yorghis. They too had tears on their faces as they encouraged the young men in a dance of homage.

Elsa passed a paper table napkin to Fiona who was crying openly.

'What a wonderful thing to do,' Fiona said when she could speak. 'I'll never forget this night as long as I live.'

'Nor I,' Thomas agreed. 'We are privileged to be able to share it.'

The others didn't trust themselves to speak.

And in an unexpectedly clear voice Fiona said, 'Those same stars are shining on Athens and on all our homes. I wonder what everyone is doing and if they have any idea on earth what we are all doing here just now.'

Chapter Nine

In Fiona's home they were talking about her as they did almost every evening. Her mother was looking at the pictures of Aghia Anna in the *Evening Herald*.

'Imagine Fiona being in that very place!' she said in surprise.

'Imagine!' her husband grunted.

'But, Sean, it *was* good of her to ring in case we'd be worried about her. At least she thought that we might be concerned.'

'Why would we be concerned? We didn't know where the hell she was except joined at the hip to that lout.' Fiona's father found very few silver linings in the whole situation, very little cause to see the bright side. He picked up the remote control and turned on the television deliberately to end the conversation.

His wife went over to the set and turned it off.

'Maureen! Why did you do that? I wanted to watch that.'

'No, you didn't want to watch anything, you just didn't want to talk about Fiona.'

'I'm sick to death of Fiona,' Sean said. 'And I couldn't care less if she comes back for the silver wedding.'

'Sean! How can you even say that?'

'I mean it. What's the point of her being here for any celebration, moping, hanging on to the arm of that spaced-out fool, telling us we don't understand him?'

'She's your child as much as mine.'

'She's not a child, according to you . . . she's a woman of twenty-four. She is entitled to make her own decisions, that's what you said when you were standing up for her.'

'Sean, I said that we were only going to alienate her by attacking Shane, that she was old enough to know the choices she was making. I didn't say that any of them were right.'

'Huh,' he said.

'I want you to listen to me. I invited Barbara around tonight to talk to her about everything. They've been friends for fifteen years, since they made their First Communion, and she's as upset as we are.'

'She is not. She's just as bad as Fiona. If a drug-crazed drunken loser like Shane turned up for her, she'd be off too. They're all the same these days.'

'This is *not* the way we must talk, we must try to keep a lifeline open to Fiona, tell her that we are here when she wants us.'

'I'm not sure that I am here if she wants us. She said some very hurtful things to you as well as to me, remember.'

'That's because we said to her things that she thought were hurtful about Shane.' Maureen struggled to be fair.

'She gave up her family, her home, her good job – for what? For a foul-mouthed drug addict!'

'We can't help who we fall in love with, Sean.'

'Yes, we can. We don't all go out looking for lunatics like Fiona did.' He was unbending.

'She never intended to fall in love with a lunatic, wouldn't it be much easier for her if she'd found a nice banker, or a doctor or a fellow who ran his own business? But that didn't happen.'

'You've got very forgiving all of a sudden.' He was confused.

'I'll tell you something, I was touched that she thought to ring us when this terrible thing happened, whether we knew she was there or not doesn't matter.'

The doorbell rang.

'That's Barbara, be nice, be reasonable please, Sean, she may be our only link with Fiona, our only hope.'

'She's heard nothing from Madam either,' he scoffed.

'Sean!'

'All right,' he said.

In David's house in the smart suburbs of Manchester they had been looking at a television documentary on the events in Aghia Anna and were talking about their son.

'It must have been a terrible thing to see,' David's mother said.

'It must indeed have been terrible if he telephoned us,' his father agreed.

'He has been away for six weeks, Harold, we have had ten letters from him. He does keep in touch.'

'Some of them were only picture postcards,' David's father said.

'But he goes and finds a stamp and a postbox,' his mother defended him.

'Miriam, this is the twenty-first century, the boy could find an Internet café, send an e-mail, behave like a normal person.'

'I know, I know.'

They sat in silence for a while.

'Miriam, should I have been different, please tell me?' He looked at her begging for the truth.

She reached for his hand and stroked it. 'You have been a wonderful husband, a wonderful father,' she said.

'So why is our son out in this one-horse town in Greece if I was so wonderful? Tell me that.'

'Perhaps it's my fault, Harold, maybe it was I who drove him away.'

'No, of course not, he adores you, we know that. It's the business he doesn't want. Should I have said something like *be* an artist, *be* a poet, *be* whatever you want to be? Should I? Is this what was needed? Tell me!'

'I don't think so, he always knew you wanted him to run the company, he knew that since his bar mitzvah.'

'So why was that such a crime? I built up this business for my father. He came to England with nothing. I worked day and night to try and show him that his suffering had all been worth while in the end. Where was the problem? I try to hand over to my only son a thriving business, that's bad?'

'I know, Harold, I know all this.' She was trying to soothe him.

'If you understand it, why can't he?'

'Let me tell him, Harold, please let me tell him.'

'No, a thousand times no. I will not have his pity. If I can't have his love and respect, nor even his company, I will not settle for his pity.'

*

Shirley and Bill came back from the shopping mall. Andy had gone up to the university where he and other athletic members of the community gathered to motivate some of the students training for a marathon. They thought it was cool that old guys, who must be well into their thirties, still liked running.

Bill helped his mother to unpack the shopping and stack it away.

'You're a great kid,' she said unexpectedly.

'Am I?'

'Sure you are. I've never loved anyone on earth more than I love you.'

'Aw, come on, Mom . . .' He was embarrassed.

'No, I mean it. Truly I do.'

'But your own mom and dad? What about them?'

'No, they were fine but it wasn't nearly as strong as the love I feel for you.'

'And what about Dad when you loved him? And Andy now?'

'That's different, Bill, believe me. There's something absolutely earth-shaking about the love you have for your child, it's unconditional.'

'What's that?'

'It means that there are no ifs and buts. You are this special kind of person, nothing can get in the way of it. I wish I could explain properly, but when you love a guy or a woman I guess you actually can stop loving them. You don't intend to but it happens, but never with your child . . .'

'And would Dad feel the same about me as you do?'

'Totally the same, Bill, your dad and I didn't see eye to eye about a few things, you know that, but we both thought and do think you were the best thing that ever happened to us. We never argue about you. Never. We just want the best for you.'

'Does Dad still love you, Mom?'

'No, honey, he still respects me and likes me I think, but love, no. We just share our love for you.' She smiled at him encouragingly, hoping he would agree.

Bill thought about it for a while. 'So why doesn't he act like that?' he asked.

'I think he does,' Shirley said, surprised.

'I don't think he does,' Bill said. 'I think he wants me to miss him and be sorry he's not here, and that's very unfair. *He's* the one who went away. I didn't. I stayed right here.'

Birgit saw Claus coming into the newsroom.

'You're back from Greece!' she said, delighted.

'Hi, Birgit.' Claus, the chief cameraman, had no illusions that Birgit was happy to see him. If he were back, then Dieter would be back too. That was what interested her. And interested most of the women in the television network.

Claus sighed.

Dieter didn't even try, and the women just fell over themselves for him.

He waited until Birgit asked about Dieter. He assumed it would be thirty seconds. He was wrong: it was even sooner.

Birgit didn't waste time on preliminaries such as saying it all must have been very sad. 'Dieter back too?' she asked casually.

'No, actually.' Birgit was a hard woman. Claus actually savoured telling her the bad news. 'No, he stayed on a bit. He met an old friend out there. Amazing coincidence, wasn't it?'

'An old friend? Some guy he knew in the press corps?'

'No, it was some woman who used to work here actually. He met Elsa.'

It was a pleasing moment to see her face.

'But it's all over between them,' Birgit said.

'I wouldn't hold your breath, Birgit,' Claus said and moved on.

Adoni looked at the newspaper pictures of the village where he had grown up. He saw the face of his friend Manos whom he had known all his life. There was a picture of Maria too. Adoni had danced at their wedding.

How extraordinary that newspapers all over America would have pictures and stories of his home town. But he wouldn't tell anyone here in Chicago. He had come here all those years ago because Eleni back in Aghia Anna had given him a contact. One of her cousins worked here, he gave a job to a boy who had come with a personal recommendation.

The cousin had moved on but Adoni had stayed. He liked it here, even though he was sometimes lonely. But he would say nothing about the tragedy having taken place in his home town. Why bring grief on himself?

The people here in the greengrocer's where he worked knew little about him and his background. If he told them then they would have to know why he didn't stay in touch, they would learn about his fight with his father, the years of silence. They would never understand. These people that he worked with just lived for family, their fathers were in and out of their houses all the time. What would they think of a father and son who hadn't spoken to each other for nine years?

Of course he could call his father to offer sympathy over what had happened to Aghia Anna. But then his father would take this as some sign of weakness, a giving in, an admission that Adoni had been in the wrong. His father knew where he was. If he wanted to say something then let him say it.

Shane didn't know how to use the Métro in Athens. When they had been here before Fiona had worked it out. The whole thing was called the *Ilektrikos* or something. Had she bought tickets in a kiosk? Or was that for the trolley buses? He couldn't remember.

Shane knew that he wanted to go to the Exarchia area, he had heard on the ferry that it was full of *ouzo* shops and tavernas. He still had plenty of grass in his bag, he could sell it there. Then he would sit down, work out what he would do. He was free now, free as a bird. Nobody would be coming at him with cracked notions that he should be a waiter for the rest of his life in a backwater. Fiona must have been soft in the head to suggest it.

In the end, of course, like everyone else she had let him down. But then Shane had learned to expect that of people. And she wasn't really pregnant. He knew that. If she had been she wouldn't have gone off and left him when he was in the police station. She could well be on her way home to her awful family in Dublin. They would certainly kill a fatted calf for her once they realised that Shane was no longer around.

He worked out that he needed the Métro stop called

Omonia. God, they had really ridiculous names here, and writing that nobody could read as well.

'Come in, Barbara.' Fiona's mother ushered her in.

'You're out late in the evening.' Fiona's father didn't sound very welcoming.

'You know how it is, Mr Ryan, eight a.m. to eight p.m. and we're an hour from the hospital.' Barbara was cheerful and taking no nonsense from anyone. She threw herself into an armchair as she had done for years in this house, her red hair tousled, her face tired after a long day's work.

'Will you have tea, Barbara, or something stronger?'

'Oh, I could murder a gin, Mrs Ryan, specially if we are going to talk about Shane,' Barbara said apologetically.

'Sean?'

'Well, if we're going to have to talk about him then I need an anaesthetic, too,' he said.

'I was wondering if we could write to Fiona and say that we sort of misunderstood the situation.' Fiona's mother served the gin and tonics and sat down looking from one to the other.

Her husband glowered at her. 'I think we understood the situation only too well. Our daughter is infatuated with a bog-ignorant criminal. What else is there to understand?'

'But it hasn't worked, our saying that. She's hundreds of miles away. And I miss her, Sean, every moment of the day. I'd love her to be coming in, like Barbara now, telling us about the kind of day she had. We've only driven her away by our attitude. Don't you think, Barbara?'

'I agree with Mr Ryan, actually, we didn't misunderstand anything. Shane is a real out-and-out bastard because he manipulates her, he makes things seem to be her fault, not his. He plays the victim card, the rest of the world has a down on him, that's the hardest bit to deal with.'

'What I find the hardest is that they say they *love* each other.' Maureen Ryan's face was troubled.

'He's never loved anyone but himself. He'll only stay with her for as long as it suits him and then she'll be alone, miles away with no friends and humiliated. She won't want to come back to us. She'll know that we'll all be thinking, I told you so, even if we manage not to say it.'

'You miss her as much as we do.' Fiona's father sounded surprised.

'Of course I do, I miss her at work every day and I miss going out with her in the evening. I think of a dozen things to tell her and then remember she's gone . . . I was wondering if we could try to build some kind of a bridge?'

'What kind of bridge?' Sean Ryan didn't hold out much hope.

'Well, could you write her a letter sort of implying that we all know now she and Shane will be together in the long run? And I could do the same, like asking would she and Shane be home for your silver wedding or Christmas, something like that?'

'But we can't assume that she's going to be with him for ever, Barbara. What kind of message are we giving the other children if they think we accept Shane as part of their sister's life?'

'Listen, Mrs Ryan, he *is* part of her life, they've gone

off to live together, for God's sake, but deep down I've a feeling it's not going to last that long, and if we pretend that we think it's normal then we stop being part of the Bad Cruel World that's beating up on Poor Misunderstood Shane.' Barbara looked from one to the other.

Fiona's father was shrugging helplessly as if to say it was all beyond him. Her mother's face was working as if to try and stop the tears.

Barbara gave it one more go. 'Believe me, I don't like it either, and I don't like sitting here talking about my friend Fiona behind her back, but I think that we've got to do something or else we've lost her entirely.'

The letter was pushed through the door and fell to the floor. Miriam Fine went to see who could possibly be delivering something by hand at this time of night.

It was a big thick envelope addressed to them both. It contained some kind of heavy card. She brought it in to her husband and they opened it together.

It was the confirmation that Harold Fine had won the coveted Businessman of the Year award and details of the ceremony. It would be presented in November at the Town Hall before an invited audience. They hoped that he would ask a group of family and friends to join them for drinks first with the Mayor and dinner later.

'Oh, Harold, I'm so pleased for you, to see it there in black and white,' she said, tears in her eyes.

'It's amazing.' He looked at the document as if it might fall away or crumble in his hands.

'David will be so proud and pleased, we'll tell him the actual invitation has arrived. It will make it real for him too. I know he will come home for it all,' Miriam said.

'Let's not be too confident, Miriam, from where

David stands, businessmen are bad enough. A Businessman of the Year would be the worst thing he could
encounter.'

'Hi there, Bill.'
   'Hi, Andy.'
Andy sat down beside him on the swinging seat in
front of the house.
   'You down about something, kid? Want a run?'
   'No, running doesn't solve everything.' He didn't
even look up.
   'You're so right there, kid, but it kind of blocks bad
things out for a bit.'
   'You don't have bad things, Andy.'
   'I don't, huh? Then I've been doing a pretty good job
hiding things.' He punched Bill affectionately in the
arm, but this time the boy winced and withdrew from
him.
   'Sorry, kid.' Andy looked at a loss.
   'It's okay, it's not your fault.'
   'So whose fault is it?' Andy asked.
   'I don't know, I think it's mine. I wasn't enough for
them. Mom and Dad. I didn't make them happy
enough.'
   'They're both crazy about you, kid, it's the one thing
that they really see eye to eye about.'
   'So my mom says, but maybe she just wants me to
think that.'
   'Your dad says it too, he told me so before he went
away.'
   'But he went away, Andy.'
   'He did it for you, kid, to give you space, so that you
could get used to me being around and feel part of your

mom's life and mine together. It was good of him to do that.'

'I don't want space,' Bill said.

'What do you want, Bill?'

'I suppose I want him and Mom to love each other still, but I can't have that so I guess I want him to be living nearby. You and Mom don't mind if I see him a lot. That's right, isn't it?' He looked anxiously at Andy.

'Sure it's right, you know it is.'

'And does he know, does Dad know that?'

'Ah, Bill, you know he does.'

'Then if he knows this, why did he have to go so far away?' Bill asked simply.

Hannah, a secretary in the television centre, had over-heard the conversation between Claus and Birgit. She could hardly credit it. Elsa had gone so far away to leave what had been the love of her life and this catastrophe had brought them together.

'Claus, excuse me, can I have a word?'

'Of course!' Everyone liked Hannah, a bright, helpful, confident young woman. She had been Elsa's friend.

'I just wanted to ask is she coming back?' Hannah asked. She too spent no time beating about the bush.

'Would you like her to come back?' Claus asked gently.

'For me, I would. I would like to have my friend back home again. But for her, I think she might be better to stay away.' Hannah spoke from the heart.

'I wish I could tell you what has happened, but truthfully I don't know,' Claus said. 'Dieter told us to go home ahead of him. So of course we did. But she looked different. She wasn't the same Elsa that we know. She was changed somehow, as if she had made up her mind.'

'I see.' Hannah was doubtful.

'I know you probably think that men are hopeless about reading the signs but, believe me, you would have found it difficult to know what was happening.'

'Oh, I know, Claus, it's not easy. Thank you for telling me. We can only wait and hope.'

'And what are you hoping for, Hannah?'

'I'm much more hopeless than you! I actually don't know what I hope. I suppose I hope things turn out for the best,' said Hannah truthfully.

Adoni decided he would telephone his father. He would do it quickly before he changed his mind. It would be evening in Greece, his father would be at the taverna. It would be busy so his father would not be able to talk for long which was just as well. Adoni would say that he was very sorry about the tragedy and that he sent his sympathies. They would not talk about what had passed between them.

He could hear the telephone ringing.

It rang and rang and there was no reply. He must have dialled the wrong number. He dialled again. But in the empty taverna the phone rang and nobody answered.

Before he had left Aghia Anna, he had installed an answering machine for his father. Evidently the old man had never learned to switch it on.

Adoni eventually hung up. In many ways it was probably all for the best.

Shane found exactly the place he was looking for. This was his clientele. It was just the kind of place he would have gone if he had been looking to score. It didn't matter that he didn't know the language. There was an international language over this sort of thing. He spoke to a guy who was some kind of thicko, who understood nothing, then to another who shrugged at him.

The third man looked more promising.

'How much?' the man asked. He was small and round with quick dark eyes.

'How much do you want?' Shane asked.

'Well, how much do you have?' the man wanted to know.

'Enough,' said Shane.

At that moment there was the flash of a Polaroid camera and then another. Right in his face.

'What the hell . . .?' Shane began. Then he felt a hand on his collar, almost choking him. The round face of the man with the quick dark eyes was an inch from Shane's own face.

'Listen to me good. We have two pictures of you, one in this bar, one we will show to the police. If they see you trying to deal again it will be very, very bad for you.'

'You *said* you wanted to buy.' Shane choked the words out somehow.

'This is my father's bar, my family runs this place. I would go very far from here very quickly. That is my uncle holding you. He is expecting you to apologise and leave. In twenty seconds from now.'

'I don't know how to apologise in Greek.'

'*Signomi* will do.'

'*Sigomi*, is it?' Shane stuttered.

'*Signomi* . . . learn to say it, you little shit, and be pleased you got away so easily.'

'I could come back,' Shane threatened.

The man laughed.

'You could, of course. Ten seconds.'

'*Signomi!*' Shane cried over his shoulder to the older man who was holding him. Then the grip was released and Shane staggered out of the door into the warm Athens night.

Chapter Ten

Thomas woke with a slight headache. It didn't take him long to remember why. The red wine they had drunk last night at the police station had not been allowed to age for any respectable time. Yorghis said it could well have been made last month.

Still, a couple of cups of good coffee would cure that. Maybe he would go out and get fresh oranges and hot crusty rolls for breakfast. Possibly Vonni would have a hangover too. There would be solidarity in the cure.

But when he got up, he saw the door to the spare bedroom was open. The bed was neatly made. No sign of any personal possessions around the place. She was truly using it only as a bed for the night. He wondered where she was now. Back in the hen-house? Or like the Pied Piper with a group of children at the harbour?

She was such a self-sufficient little figure, hair braided around her head, suntanned lined face with its broad smile, that made it impossible to know what age she was. Forty? Fifty? Sixty? Hard to know from anyone how long she had been in Aghia Anna. And she told little or nothing about herself, so you would be a long time guessing.

Thomas yawned and went into the kitchen. She had beaten him to it. There were four large oranges on the table and, wrapped in a little check cloth to keep them warm, some fresh bread rolls. Thomas sighed with pleasure and sat down to his breakfast.

Fiona was still asleep.
Elsa left her a note.

Gone down to the harbour. Didn't want to wake you. Why don't you come and meet me at noon. Bring a swimsuit if you feel like it and we can have something in that nice place with the blue and white tablecloths. I can't remember its name. I'd like that.
   Love,
   Elsa

She looked at Fiona as if she were a younger and more foolish sister. To think that, back in the real world, this girl was a competent nurse and yet she was still so foolish as to believe that Shane was somewhere in Athens, worried and concerned about her.

Elsa walked slowly through the narrow streets looking around her at the way life went on. The people washed the pavements in front of their little shops, and laid out their wares. In the cafés and restaurants they were laboriously writing their menus on big blackboards.

There wasn't the same carefree, cheerful way as before the accident. But at least they were getting on with it. Or pretending to. Like Elsa herself.

She felt she was making a fairly good job of hiding the fact that she was numb and empty inside. She thought

143

she was managing quite well, all things considered. She had talked well to the others last night, she had been a rock of strength to Fiona who had cried on her shoulder when they came back.

She was able now to nod and smile at people she passed, saying, '*Kalimera*,' here and there.

But she felt very light-headed and unreal.

She wished that she belonged somewhere, that there were people who cared about her. She had never felt so isolated. No family, no love, no job, and since she had left Germany . . . no home. A father who had abandoned her, a mother who had only been ambitious for her, not loving, a lover who had lied and wanted to go on lying for ever.

Somebody in a shabby, broken-looking van hooted at her. Elsa put up her hand to shield her eyes from the sun and see who it was.

It was Vonni with a load of children.

'We're going for a swim on a really fantastic beach you might not know. Would you like to come?'

'Great, I said I'd meet Fiona at noon in the harbour but I'd be back by then, right?'

Elsa was glad that she had her bathing suit and straw hat in her basket. She was now prepared to go anywhere.

Vonni nodded at her in agreement. 'Oh certainly, we'll be back by then. I can't expose children to the midday sun.' She said something in Greek to the five- and six-year-olds in the back of the van and they all smiled at her and chorused, '*Yassu*, Elsa!'

Elsa felt a sudden lump in her throat as if suddenly her wish had been answered. As if in a small way she did belong somewhere. Just for a while.

*

David had hired a bicycle and travelled five kilometres to where the family he stayed with had told him there was a wonderful beach. He would love to have met the others from last night and talked about the evening, the dancing, the way people had shown respect. But nobody had suggested it and David hated the thought of being a hanger-on.

He puffed up some hills and sailed down the slopes on the other side. The countryside was so beautiful. Why would anyone want to live in a crowded city? Spending hours commuting, breathing in diesel fumes, when they could have this?

He came to where the beach must be and to his disappointment he saw first a parked van. And then he saw Elsa and that strange older woman Vonni, already down on the sand with eight or nine children.

He watched as Vonni lined the children up at the water's edge. She was making great signs with her arms. The children were nodding in agreement. She must be explaining that she would go in first with Elsa, and that nobody must go out any further than the grown-ups.

David lay on a grassy mound and watched them all. Elsa was so beautiful in her elegant turquoise swimsuit, her short blonde hair reflecting the sun; she had a light suntan and moved gracefully in and out of the sea, playing with the children.

Vonni, small and swarthy, her hair in plaits over her head, wore a functional black swimming costume that would not have been in fashion twenty years back. She too ran in and out of the little waves calling and encouraging the youngsters to join her and helping the more timid ones by holding a hand under the chin.

David longed to join them but he felt he would be intruding. Just then Elsa saw him.

'*Ela, ela*, David, come and swim, it is total magic!'

Awkwardly he went to join them. He had his swimming trunks on under his shorts. He took off his glasses and left them on top of his neatly folded clothes.

He greeted the children. '*Yassas, ime Anglos.*'

'As if they ever thought you were anything but English!' Vonni said, teasing him.

'I suppose so,' David said ruefully.

'Come on, David, you're better than ninety per cent of the tourists, you take the trouble to learn a few words of Greek. People are so delighted with that, you wouldn't believe it.'

'Are they?' He was childishly pleased.

One of the children splashed him with a handful of water. 'Very good, *poli kala*,' he said.

'I hope you have six children, David, you'll be a wonderful father,' Vonni said unexpectedly.

Thomas walked down to the harbour. Everything was nearly back to normal. Many of the fishermen had already set out to sea, others were there mending their nets.

They nodded at him. He had been here now for many days, he wasn't a stranger, someone passing through.

One of the men said something which Thomas could not understand. He wished now that he had studied a phrase book like David had, he might have been able to get some hint as to what they were saying.

'I'm sorry, *signomi*,' he apologised.

A man with many tattoos and the appearance of a

sailor said, 'My friend said you and your friends are good people, that you have shared our tragedy.'

Thomas looked at him, puzzled. 'We are all so sad for what has happened here and we were so very touched by the dancing last night. We will never forget it.'

'When you go back to your land you four will talk about it, you and your friends?' The sailor man obviously knew them and was going to translate for the others.

Thomas spoke slowly. 'We are from four different countries – Germany, England, Ireland and the United States – but we will all bring this memory back to our lands when we go,' he said eventually.

'We thought you had been friends for ever,' said the man with the tattoos.

Fiona woke up and read the note. Wasn't life so odd that she should meet by accident such a kind and generous girl? Elsa was almost as good a friend to her as Barbara had been. What an amazing chance! Shane would be so glad when she told him.

He *would* get in contact soon, no matter what they all thought. Fiona washed her hair and used Elsa's hair-dryer. She didn't look too bad. Pale, a bit wishy-washy but nothing that would frighten the birds off the trees, as her father used to say about people who didn't look well.

Fiona thought about her father for a while. He had been such a loving, marvellous father until she had brought Shane home. She wished in many ways that she could be there for her parents' silver wedding party.

But that was her father's mistake.

He had been so definite about Shane. No time must

be spent thinking about it now. She must get on with her life until Shane sent for her. She would dress as well as she could and then walk slowly down to the harbour. She did not want Elsa to think she was some kind of pathetic loser.

She would show her best face.

They left David sitting on the beach learning his ten phrases for the day, then Vonni let the children off in the square and dropped Elsa off from her van at the harbour shortly after 11 a.m.

'Thank you for your company,' Vonni said.

'How do the people in Aghia Anna hand over their children to you, Vonni?' Elsa asked.

'I don't know, they've seen me here for many years now, they believe that I am fairly reliable, I suppose.' Vonni was not at all certain.

'How many years, Vonni?'

'I came here over thirty years ago.'

'What!' Elsa said in shock.

'You asked me. I told you.' Vonni looked impassive.

'Indeed. Forgive me. I am sure you are a person who does not want people to intrude,' Elsa apologised.

'As it happens, I don't at all mind people asking reasonable questions. I came to Aghia Anna when I was seventeen to be with the man I loved.'

'And were you with him?' Elsa asked.

'Yes and no. I'll tell you another time.' Vonni revved up the van and drove away.

'Thomas!'

He looked up at her from where he sat on an old

wooden box looking out of the mouth of the harbour to sea where the wind was lifting the waves.

'Good to see you, Elsa, would you like a nice easy chair?' He pulled over another old box for her.

She sat down as elegantly as if she really were in a drawing room.

He realised suddenly what a good television presenter she must be. Or have been. Never fussed or at a disadvantage, always in control.

'Your hair is damp, were you swimming?'

'Yes, there's a truly beautiful beach in a little lagoon about five kilometres away. Up that coast,' she pointed.

'Don't tell me you've walked ten kilometres today!' He was disconcerted.

'No, shamefully, Vonni drove me both ways. We met David there, he's the fit one, he has actually rented a bicycle. Am I imagining it, Thomas, or is the sea much more attractive here than anywhere else?'

'It sure beats my part of California anyway, very flat where we are. Nice sunsets, but no surf, no changing colours like this.'

'You don't want to think about the sea in Germany, freezing cold up there by Holland and Denmark. Certainly not like this. No wonder people get inspired by the place. I mean, I know it's meant to be a reflection of the sky, but don't tell me that water isn't dark blue.'

'Roll on, thou deep and dark blue Ocean – roll!' Thomas quoted.

To his astonishment Elsa continued:

Ten thousand fleets sweep over thee in vain;
Man marks the earth with ruin – his control
Stops with the shore . . .

He looked at her open-mouthed. 'You can quote English poetry. How dare you be so well educated!'

Elsa laughed, pleased at the praise. 'We had an English teacher at school who loved Byron. I think she was in love with him actually. If you had picked another poet I wouldn't have done so well!'

'But I mean it. I couldn't quote you one verse of German poetry, not a line. What am I talking about German poetry? I can't even speak a word of the German language.'

'Yes, you can, you said *Wunderbar*, and *Prosit* last night,' she consoled him.

'I think I said *Prosit* a little too often last night as it happens . . . oh, I've remembered another German word. *Reisefieber.*'

Elsa pealed with laughter. 'What a marvellous word to know . . . how on earth do you know that?'

'It means "journey fever", doesn't it? Being in a panic at airports and railway stations?'

'That's exactly what it means, Thomas. Imagine you knowing that!' She was impressed.

'There was a guy in the faculty who kept coming up with great words like that, we all took them over.'

They sat companionably together as if they had known each other all their lives.

No wonder the fishermen had thought they had been friends for ever.

Vonni drove the van back to Maria's house.

Maria was sitting at the table in front of an empty coffee cup.

'It's getting harder, not easier,' she said. 'I thought that was Manos coming back in his van.'

'Of course it's getting harder, it's sinking in and that's what hurts so much.' Vonni hung up the keys on a hook on the wall and then produced a pot of hot coffee she had bought at the taverna across the road and some flaky *baklava*.

Maria looked up with her tear-stained face. 'You always know what people want,' she said gratefully.

'I don't indeed. Me? I get it wrong and make more mistakes than the whole of Aghia Anna put together,' Vonni protested.

'I can't remember any,' Maria said.

'That's because you're too young. My more spectacular mistakes were made before you were born.'

Vonni moved around the kitchen, picking up things here and there, rinsing cups, restoring order without seeming to.

Then she sat down.

'The dancing was beautiful last night. He would have loved it,' she said.

'I know.' Maria was weeping again. 'And last night I felt strong and as if his spirit was still here. That feeling has gone today.'

'Well, it might come back when I tell you my plan,' Vonni said, passing her a piece of kitchen paper to dry her tears.

'Plan?'

'Yes, I'm going to teach you to drive.'

Maria actually managed a weak watery smile. 'Drive? Me drive? Vonni, stop joking. Manos wouldn't even let me hold the keys of the van.'

'But he would want you to drive now, I know he would.'

'No, Vonni, he wouldn't, he'd think I'd kill myself and everyone in Aghia Anna.'

'Well, we'll have to prove him wrong then,' Vonni said. 'Because you'll have to drive for your new job.'

'Job?'

'Oh, yes, you're going to help me in the shop, aren't you? And a lot of your work will involve driving to places like Kalatriada and collecting stuff. Save me trekking for miles on buses.'

'But you can drive there in the van, Vonni, it's just standing there . . .'

'No, I can't. Manos would hate that, he saved long and hard for that van, he wouldn't want you just handing it away. No, he'd be so proud of you if you used it for your work.'

And, magically, Maria smiled again. A real smile this time. It was as if she saw his spirit back in the house again and she was squaring up to him as she had done so often when he was alive.

'Right, Manos, this is going to amaze you,' she said.

David came across them during the driving lesson up on a big patch of waste ground at the top of the town.

'*Siga, siga,*' Vonni was screaming as the van jerked and shuddered.

'What does that mean, *siga*? I've often heard it,' David asked, interested.

'Well, you never heard it said with such fervour as this time.' Vonni had got out of the van, mopped her brow and taken some deep breaths. Maria sat gripping the steering wheel as if her hands had been glued to it.

'It means "slow down" but the lady doesn't get the concept.'

'That's the wife of Manos, isn't it?' David peered at the woman still clutching the wheel.

'God knows I never thought of myself as in any way co-ordinated but compared to herself there I could be a Formula One driver,' Vonni said, closing her eyes momentarily.

'Does she need to drive?' David asked.

'I thought so this morning, now I'm not so sure. But of course I had to open my big mouth and suggest it so now we have to keep at it.' Vonni sighed.

'I taught my mother to drive when no one else could. Three driving schools gave up on her,' David said slowly. 'Perhaps I could give it a go?'

'How did you do it?' Vonni said, with hope beginning to show in her eyes.

'I was very patient, I never raised my voice once and I spent hours on the clutch,' he said.

'Would you, David? Oh, dear good kind David, please would you?'

'Sure. If it would help. You'll have to tell me the words for brake and accelerator and gears, though.'

He wrote them down in his notebook and went over to the van. Maria looked at him doubtfully as he sat in beside her.

'*Kalimera*,' he said formally and shook hands.

'How do you say, "Let's go"?' he asked Vonni.

'*Pame*, but don't say it yet or she'll drive you splat into that wall.'

'*Pame*, Maria,' David said gently and with a lurch they moved forward.

Vonni looked on, amazed. She watched as he taught Maria to stop the van. He really did have a gift. The look of terror was leaving Maria's face.

'Drive her home when you've finished, will you?' Vonni said.

'What about my bike?'

'I'll cycle down on it and leave it for you at Maria's house.'

Before he could answer she had swung her leg over the man's bicycle and was heading off down to the town.

David turned back to his pupil. '*Pame* again, Maria,' he said gently, and this time she started the van without stalling it.

Fiona sat at a table outside the little café and was surprised to see Vonni streaking by on a bike. Vonni saw her and did a wheelie turn to come back.

'All on your own?' she asked.

'I'm meeting Elsa here at midday.'

'Oh yes, Elsa did tell me. She helped me take the children for a swim.'

'Did she?' Fiona sounded envious.

'Yes, and David came by on his bicycle, he lent it to me, I'm just leaving it at Maria's house for him. David's taking his life in his hands and teaching her to drive.'

'Lord, everyone's really settling in.' Fiona was wistful.

Vonni leaned David's bike against one of the empty tables.

'I'll sit with you until Elsa arrives,' she said.

Fiona was pleased. 'Will you have an *ouzo*?' she asked.

'No, just a *metrio kafethaki*, little coffee,' Vonni said.

They sat there peacefully watching the life of the harbour around them. That was an interesting thing about Vonni, Fiona observed. She had a great sense of stillness. She knew that you don't need to talk all the time. It was very restful.

'Vonni?'

'Yes, Fiona?'

'I was wondering, could I get some kind of a job here, here in Aghia Anna? I could learn Greek. I could help Dr Leros. What do you think?'

'Why do you want to stay here?' Vonni's voice was gentle.

'It's beautiful here and I want to be sort of settled when Shane comes back for me.'

Vonni said nothing at all.

'You think he might not come back, don't you?' Fiona cried. 'Like everyone else you judge a book by its cover, you don't know him like I do.'

'True.'

'Believe me, Vonni, he has never in his whole life had anyone who understood him until he met me.'

Vonni leaned forward and moved Fiona's hair gently from her face to reveal the bruise. 'And he took a fine way to show you how much he appreciated that you understood him,' she said.

Fiona pulled back angrily. 'That's not the way it is, he is heartbroken that he raised his hand to me, I know that.'

'Sure.'

'Don't be so lofty and patronising, I've had enough of that from everyone at home.'

'Everyone who loves you, I imagine.'

'It's not real love, it's choking claustrophobia, and wanting everyone to settle down and marry a civil servant or a bank clerk and get a mortgage and have two children.'

'I know.' Vonni sounded sympathetic.

'So if you know why don't you believe that Shane will come back for me?'

'You really believe he will?'

'Well, of course I do. We love each other, we went away together for ever. Why wouldn't he come back?'

Vonni swallowed and looked away.

'No, please, tell me. I'm sorry I shouted at you, Vonni, I just get so upset when people come out against Shane, I keep thinking that this is going to go on for ever until we're an old, old couple. Perhaps you know something I don't.'

She looked so anxious, she had her hand on Vonni's weather-beaten arm, her eyes were wide, wanting to know more.

Vonni paused.

After all, she was responsible for Shane going to Athens, she had advised the police chief Yorghis to ship him away from Aghia Anna, she did therefore owe Fiona some kind of explanation. But what could she tell her but bad news?

Yorghis had given Shane a card with the address and phone number of the police station.

Eleni had said she offered Shane a pencil and paper to write a note as he was packing his case, and he had refused it. None of this would bring Fiona any cheer.

'No, I don't think I know anything that you don't,' she said slowly. 'But I was going to suggest that Shane might not expect you to stay on here, you know, without him. If he does contact you . . .'

'He will, of course he will.'

'When he does contact you then, he might contact you back in Dublin. Isn't that a possibility?'

'No, he'd know I'd never go back there, back to them, and admit they were right. Shane knows me too well, he'd never think of ringing me back there. No, one day he'll get off one of those ferries. I want to be here and settled when he does.'

'It's not realistic, Fiona, this is a holiday place. Not a place to settle down in.'

'You did,' Fiona said simply.

'It was different then.'

'Why was it different then?'

'It was, that's all, and I came here not on my own like you are but to live with a man from Aghia Anna.'

'You did?'

'I did indeed, years and years ago, there were hardly any tourists here then, I was considered very unusual, a slut of course. In those days people here, as well as at home, got engaged and married and everything.'

Vonni looked out to sea remembering it all, a different time.

'So then you know it's possible to leave Ireland and come to a beautiful place like this and be happy?' Fiona was trying desperately to find similarities between them.

'In a way,' Vonni said.

'You're not going to tell me you regret it,' Fiona said. 'You're part of the place here, it must have been the right decision.'

'No, heavens, no, what a waste of time regret is, it must be the most useless emotion of all time.' Then she fell silent again.

'And what happened to the . . . er . . . man . . . from Aghia Anna?' Fiona felt daring and asked her a direct question.

Vonni looked her straight in the eye. 'Stavros? I don't know really,' she said and closed down the conversation.

Vonni said she had a hundred things to do and she wanted to thank God above that one of them was not giving Maria a driving lesson.

'Are you all right here on your own?' she asked Fiona.

'I'm fine, and thank you so much for being so kind,' Fiona said politely.

She was glad that the older woman was leaving. She should not have asked Vonni what happened to her man. She saw Elsa coming towards her and waved.

'I'll leave you in good hands then,' Vonni said, and left.

Elsa sat down and told Fiona about the morning on the beach. They ordered a salad and talked easily about life on this island. Just as they were finishing they saw an old van come sputtering past them. It was being driven somewhat erratically by Maria, and David was in the passenger seat. They watched as he opened the van door for her, patted her encouragingly on the back, and finally bent over and kissed her hand.

'God, isn't he going to make someone a wonderful husband!' Elsa said admiringly.

'Yeah, isn't it a tragedy that we can't in a million years fall for people like that,' Fiona said with a heavy sigh. For some reason they both found it funny and were still laughing when David cycled by. He came in to join them.

'Was she dreadful? Vonni said she was a nightmare.'

'Vonni exaggerates. She's okay, just nervous and naturally very upset about everything. Vonni's going to give her a job when she can drive. She's one amazing woman.'

Fiona was going to tell them about the man, Stavros, all those years ago. But then she decided against it. Vonni was very private about things.

The sun was setting and there was a gold-red light over the harbour. Thomas saw that Vonni was still working in her craft shop. He thought about going in to invite her to come up for an evening drink with him. But he remembered how much she liked to be left alone.

She had only agreed to sleep in the spare bedroom after a lot of reassurance that they would not intrude on each other's lives. Yet he did not want to go up to that apartment and be by himself.

He wanted to call Bill. It had been left so awkwardly hanging in the air the last time. He still felt stung by Vonni overhearing him and saying that he had made such a mess of it all. This time he would say the right things.

Thomas sat down in a small street café and made a list of things he would talk about. Like that he had dinner in a police station beside prisoners' cells, like the men coming out to dance after the funeral, like the Germans learning English poetry even though we don't know any of theirs.

He looked at the headings. What dull, odd things he had picked to talk about. A child would not be interested in these things. Maybe he would think it odd that his father was eating dinner beside prisoners' cells. He would be startled to hear that men danced together and particularly at a funeral. What did Bill care about poetry in English or German?

Thomas sat with his head in his hands, thinking how pathetic he was not to be able to find something to say to the boy that he loved with all his heart.

'Vonni?'

'Come in, Yorghis, sit down.'

'You have nice things here.' The policeman looked around.

'Some of it is nice, yes. Thank you again for your hospitality last night, Yorghis, they all loved it.'

'It's not a time to be alone. I hear you've given up on teaching the widow to drive.'

'I turned it over to that nice English boy but it was meant to be a secret!' Vonni laughed.

'In this town?'

'I know, I know.' Vonni stayed still. He would tell her eventually what business brought him here.

'We got a call from Athens, that boy we exported, the Irishman you know ...'

'Oh, yes?'

So he *had* called after all. Fiona had been right. Vonni didn't know whether to be pleased or disappointed.

'What did he say?'

'He said nothing. We got a call from a police station in Athens. He had been taken in for dealing in a bar. They found my card on him and wondered what I knew.'

'And what did you know, Yorghis?' she asked.

'Nothing as yet. I wasn't there to take his call. I wanted to discuss it with you. She's such a nice little girl.'

'I know, so nice she'd probably get on the next ferry and go to Stand by Her Man.'

'That's what I thought,' Yorghis said.

'You know the phrase about locking people up and throwing away the key?' she asked.

'I know the phrase and I'm often tempted. I think I'll just tell them that we had a bit of girlfriend battering and drunkenness here. I don't think I'll say anything specific about Fiona, do you?'

'I think you're right and we might not say anything *to* Fiona either. Do you agree?'

'Is that playing God, do you think?' Yorghis wondered.

'Even if it is, let's do it. God was never around to help when that lout was beating the pulp out of Fiona. Maybe the Almighty needs a hand now and then,' said Vonni with a grim smile of satisfaction.

Much later that night when Vonni went upstairs she found Thomas sitting in his chair in the dark.

'Holy St Joseph, you put the heart across me,' she said.

'Hi, Vonni.' He was very down.

'Did you ring your son and annoy him again?' she asked.

'No, I sat here for hours wondering what to say and I couldn't think of anything so I didn't call him at all,' he confessed.

'Probably wiser in the long run,' Vonni said approvingly.

'What kind of a horse's ass does that make me, not able to find things to say to a nine-year-old?' he asked.

'I'd say it makes you like every father and son in the world, unable to communicate.' She wasn't as unsympathetic as the words might have sounded.

'He's not my son,' Thomas said flatly.

'What do you mean?'

'What I say. Nearly ten years ago when Shirley and I were trying for a baby I went for a medical. Childhood mumps had made me sterile apparently. I walked around all day wondering how to tell Shirley. But when I got home *she* had something to tell me. Wasn't it wonderful – she was pregnant.'

'Did you tell her?'

'No. I needed time to think. I had no idea that she was playing away. Not a clue. And because I didn't speak then I couldn't later.'

'So you never spoke?'

'I love him as much as if he *were* mine.'

'He is yours in every real sense,' Vonni said.

'Yes, that's true. I raised him with her, I got his formulas in the night, I taught him to read, to swim. He's mine as much as anyone's. His natural father must have disappeared from the face of the earth. It wasn't Andy, he only turned up years later. Andy thinks he's mine.'

'Did you raise it during the divorce?'

'What, and lose any chance of access to Bill?'

'Of course,' she nodded.

'He's a wonderful boy, Vonni.'

'I'm sure he is. I'm very sure he is.'

There was a long silence.

'Go back to him, Thomas, it's breaking your heart to be so far away.'

'I can't. We all agreed it was for the best this way.'

'Agreements can be changed, plans can be rewritten,' Vonni said.

'I'd be worse back there than here. Suppose I had to

look at that fool every day, posturing, pretending to be his father.'

'You are his father in every way that counts.' Vonni looked at the floor as she spoke.

'I wish I could believe that,' he said.

'You should believe it, Thomas.' She spoke with quiet certainty as if she knew what she was talking about. His eyes met hers and suddenly it was crystal-clear to Thomas that Vonni really did know what she was talking about.

The night she had told him that he had made a dog's dinner of his conversation with Bill, she had said that she too had a child. A son that she had lost for ever by making the wrong decisions.

Thomas closed his eyes. He had not prayed for a very long time, but tonight he prayed with all his heart. Please may he decide the right thing. Oh, please may he not lose that little boy.

Chapter Eleven

Vonni and David were drinking coffee at the café with the check tablecloths. Maria would be out shortly to have her driving lesson.

'She says you are a very good man and you don't shout at her,' Vonni said approvingly to David.

'Poor Maria, did she expect people to shout at her?' David asked.

'Well, I did for one, and Manos did too, a lot, so I think she did expect it, yes.'

'It doesn't get you anywhere, shouting,' David said.

'I told Maria that you taught your mother to drive. She said your mother was fortunate to have such a son.'

'*She* doesn't think so.'

'Why do you say that?' Vonni asked.

'Because it's a fact. She sides with my father over everything. She parrots him all the time: I have a ready-made business to walk into, I can be my father's right-hand man, his eyes and ears. I am so lucky, most men would love to have a business that they could walk into, a company built up by his hard work.'

'And can you not tell her that you love them but you don't love the work?'

'I've tried and tried, but it ends in recriminations and arguments every single time. I've told them that I feel uneasy and as if I'm having a panic attack or something just as soon as I go in the office doors . . . but you might as well talk to that harbour wall.'

'When you go back you'll find that they have softened,' she began.

'I'm not going back,' he said.

'You can't run away, stay here for ever.'

'You did,' David said simply.

'I'm weary of telling people that those were different times.' Vonni sighed.

'I'm taking Maria up some of those mountainy roads today,' David reported to Vonni.

'God, you're brave as a lion.' Vonni was admiring.

'She's fine on her own where you don't meet too much traffic, she doesn't get fussed.'

'But, David, those awful hairpin bends, those bits where the road sort of crumbles away . . .'

'I know, but aren't these the very roads she'll have to drive to hill villages if she's going to work for you?'

'Yes, but in months or weeks not days.'

'No, she's better away from the town, huge trucks reversing at her out of that big ugly petrol station.'

'Tread softly on that petrol station because you tread on my dreams,' Vonni warned.

'What do you mean?'

'That was my petrol station, I worked there day and night for years.'

'Never!'

'Oh, yes, it was.'

'Did you sell it or what?'

'No, it was sort of taken away from me, too long and

complicated a story to tell you now. What area are you and Maria driving in today? Just so that I'll know to avoid it.'

'I thought we'd go up to see Andreas, that's a windy road.'

'You like him, don't you?' Vonni observed.

'Who wouldn't like him? He's so kind and gentle. He doesn't pressurise people into doing what they don't want to do.'

'He's set in his ways of course,' Vonni said.

'But good ways,' David said. 'His son must be a real fool, not to come back from Chicago and help him.'

'Maybe.' Vonni shrugged doubtfully.

'Why maybe? The boy works in a vegetable shop miles and miles away in the middle of a big noisy neighbourhood, Andreas says, when he could be here in this wonderful place, helping his father.'

Vonni stood looking at David quizzically, her head on one side.

'What is it?' he asked eventually.

'You *know* what it is, David. Couldn't someone say exactly the same about you, you have a father and in your case a mother too who miss you and wonder what *you* are doing miles and miles away.'

'It's different,' David said mutinously.

'Oh yes?'

'It's totally different. My father isn't reasonable, he's just never wrong. No one could live with him.'

'There were ways that Adoni found the very same thing in his father. Andreas wouldn't get lights on the taverna roof, he wouldn't have live bouzouki music to draw the people up the hill in the evening. Adoni could suggest nothing, change nothing. Andreas was always right.'

'I don't see that in him, not a bit,' David said a little coldly.

'No? Well, of course he's polite and respectful to you, people often are not courteous to their own sons.' She looked thoughtful.

'You have a son, Vonni?'

'Yes. Stavros, like his father.'

'And are you courteous and polite to him?' David asked.

'I don't see him, to be courteous or discourteous.'

'You must see him sometimes?' David was startled.

'No. Not at all. But in the days when I did see him I was going through a rather odd period when I was polite to nobody, least of all to him. So he has no way of knowing how much I miss him and how respectful and warm I could be to him these days.'

She straightened herself up and looked purposeful again. 'Right. I'm taking those children with me so that you can take their mother up the Wall of Death or wherever you want to go with her.'

She stood up, calling out something in Greek to the children, who sounded delighted.

'What did you tell them?' David asked.

'I brought up the topic of ice cream, it seemed to appeal,' she said.

'I bet you were always courteous to everyone.' He smiled at her.

'No, David, it would be wrong to think that, but don't go asking about me, they'll tell you nothing. The only person who can explain my troubled life is me.'

At that point Maria came out of her door ready for

her driving lesson. She greeted Vonni and then turned to David.

'*Pame*, David,' she said.

'*Pame*, Maria,' said David.

Vonni watched amazed as she got into the van in the driver's side, looked in the rear-view mirror and slid the van out easily on to the Harbour Road.

If this boy was going to stay in Aghia Anna maybe he had a career ahead of him in teaching everyone to drive.

Andreas and his brother Yorghis were having a game of backgammon in a café near the police station. They saw the familiar van that Manos had hurtled around Aghia Anna drive by.

'That's Maria! Someone's teaching her to drive!' Yorghis explained.

'That will be Vonni, I expect,' Andreas said.

'No, it looks like a man.'

'It's that boy David Fine. Such a good young man,' Andreas said, pleased.

'Yes, isn't he,' Yorghis said. They sat silently for a while.

'Was there any word from . . .' Yorghis began.

'No, no word,' Andreas said quickly.

'Of course they might not have heard over there,' Yorghis said.

'No indeed.' Andreas clicked the pieces on the board.

There would be no more talk about Adoni far away in Chicago. They spoke about their sister Christina, who had had a troubled youth but was happy now living with a kind man on the other side of the island. They didn't talk about her past nowadays. Nor indeed did they talk about Yorghis's former wife who would have known Manos and his friends when they were children. She had not got in touch either.

Thomas found the bookshop.

'*Vivliopolio*,' Vonni had told him earlier.

'Really?' Thomas said. 'It sounds like a vitamin drink.'

'You know the V in Greek looks like a mad B with a sort of leg hanging out of it. When I came here one of the first things I wanted was a bookshop and when I found it I thought that it was *biblionwakyo* or something, like the French word *bibliothèque*.'

'Aren't you funny?' he said to her affectionately.

'I'm a scream,' said Vonni. 'What are you looking for in the bookshop?'

'German poetry as it happens. Do you think they might have any?'

'They might,' Vonni said. 'You never know.'

And she was right. The bookshop had a small section, including a book of Goethe's work, German on one side and English on the page opposite. He bought it and took it outside and sat on a bench near the store.

Thomas studied it carefully until he found something appropriate. Then he took out his notebook and wrote it down.

Kennst du das Land, wo die Zitronen blühn,
Im dunkeln Laub die Gold-Orangen glühn.

He wrote the translation beside it:

Do you know the land where the lemon-trees
blossom,

Where the golden oranges glow in the dark
   foliage.

He would learn it by heart and quote it to Elsa. She must not be allowed to think that he didn't know German writers.

He was just beginning to copy the next bit, which was all about soft winds, myrtles and laurels standing tall, when he felt a shadow fall over the page. It was Elsa looking over his shoulder to see what he was reading. Then she moved back and spoke the lines to him.

Kennst du es wohl? Dahin! Dahin
Möcht ich mit dir, o mein Geliebter, ziehn.

'All right, I give in,' he said. 'I haven't read the translation. What does that bit mean?'

'It means ... let me see ... it means: Do you know it perhaps? It is there, there that I would like to go with you, my beloved.'

And as she said it they looked at each other, slightly embarrassed, as if they had accidentally uncovered something too intimate.

'Did he come to Greece, Goethe? Is this the land where the lemon-trees blossom?' Thomas asked, to move the conversation into safer waters.

'It was the Mediterranean certainly but I think it was mainly Italy he travelled in, he was mad about Italy. But of course he could have come to Greece as well. This is where I am showing my ignorance.' Elsa looked apologetic.

'What about mine? Until now I never read a word he wrote in any language,' Thomas confessed.

'And why are you reading it now?'

'To impress you,' he said simply.

'You don't have to, I'm impressed already,' Elsa said.

Andreas got a phone call from Ireland.

'Is that a taverna in Aghia Anna?' the voice asked.

'Yes it is, can I help you?'

'Fiona Ryan called her family from your taverna on the day of your terrible tragedy.'

'Yes, yes, I remember.'

'I'm Fiona's best friend at home, Barbara. Fiona gave your number in case she got cut off so I rang because . . . well, I was wondering, are they still in Aghia Anna?'

'Yes, is there any problem?'

'No, not a problem really . . . excuse me, who am I speaking to?'

'My name is Andreas, this is my taverna.'

'Oh good, and have you seen her since?'

'This is a very small place, we see almost everyone every day.'

'And Fiona's all right, is she?'

Andreas paused. All right?

The girl looked wretched, she had been beaten by her boyfriend, who had then abandoned her, and gone to Athens where he was now in jail awaiting trial for drug dealing. Fiona had suffered a miscarriage; she still thought that Shane was coming back to find her.

All right? Hardly.

But even though his instinct was to tell this pleasant woman Barbara all that had happened he knew it wasn't his story to tell.

'They all seem to like it here,' he said lamely.

'All? You mean she's been able to make friends with

Shane in tow? Usually people avoid them like the plague.'

'Very nice people. German, American, English,' he said to reassure her.

'Well, that is a surprise. Listen, Andreas, is there anywhere I could send her an e-mail or a fax do you think?'

'Certainly.' He gave her the numbers of the police station.

'And we were all very sorry about what happened there. It must have been a nightmare.'

'Thank you. You are very kind and sympathetic,' he said. And she *was* kind and sympathetic, unlike his cold-hearted son in Chicago.

Andreas wished over and over that he had not written that letter to Adoni.

But he had promised Elsa. And it was too late now, the letter was nearly there.

Fiona had gone to see Dr Leros for an examination and a checkup as she had promised.

'Everything is fine,' he said. 'You are a healthy young woman. Plenty more chances of babies.'

'Oh, I hope so some day,' Fiona said.

'Are you going back to your country?'

'No. I have to wait until Shane comes back here to find me, I was hoping to get a job here. I'm a qualified nurse. Is there anything I could do for you, for example, in your practice here?'

'Well, not really, my dear girl, you see my patients only speak Greek for one thing.'

'Oh, I'm going to learn it,' Fiona promised. 'It would

be such a marvellous thing for Shane to come back and find me settled.'

'And will he be upset that you miscarried?' Dr Leros had heard something of Shane's behaviour before he left Aghia Anna. He knew that the general opinion was that Shane would not return.

Poor soft-hearted mistaken girl.

But there was really no way he could give her a job.

'He will be upset in a way, but maybe it will be better when it's properly planned. He will be so pleased to know your good news that I am healthy.'

'Good. Good girl.'

'And about a job?'

'It's not possible, believe me. Could you try the hotel? The Anna Beach.'

'Yes, but they close in the winter,' Fiona said.

'You're going to live here all year round?' His eyes were wide.

'Vonni did,' Fiona said defensively.

'Ah, that was different.'

'Why was it different?' Fiona cried.

'You didn't know Stavros,' Dr Leros said.

'You knew him?'

'Yes, he was my best friend.'

'And where is he now?'

'I don't know, he left the island.' His face was grim.

Fiona was desperate to know. 'And will he ever come back, do you think?'

'Not now, too much has happened.'

'But no one talks about it?' she asked.

'It was too long ago. Too much has happened since then.' And he stood up to shake her hand and let her know that the consultation was now over.

*

Yorghis was driving around Aghia Anna, he knew he would see Fiona or one of her friends somewhere along the way. He saw her with a straw basket buying vegetables.

'Oh, great, Yorghis, just the man I need. What's the Greek for watermelon?'

'*Karpouzi*,' he said.

'Good! *Karpouzi, karpouzi*,' she said happily.

'I have a letter for you,' Yorghis said.

'Shane! I just *knew* he would get in touch.' Her face was radiant.

'No, it's from your friend Barbara in Ireland.' He handed over the printed-out e-mail.

She barely looked at it, she was so disappointed. She just put it in her basket.

'You can always come up to the station and send an e-mail back,' he offered.

'No, thank you, Yorghis, but is there any way we could find out what's happened to Shane in Athens?'

He bit his lip as he looked at her.

It surely couldn't be right to keep from her the fact that Shane was in detention and would not be coming back for her. But there were pens and paper and telephones in Athens, he could get in touch if he wanted to, and he hadn't wanted to.

Leave things as they were.

'*Karpouzi*,' he said, leaving.

'Is that Greek for goodbye?' she asked glumly.

'No, it's watermelon.' He laughed. 'You'll have to try harder.'

*

She sat down at a café and pulled out the letter.

You must wonder how Sherlock Holmes Barbara tracked you down, but it was easy: your mother had the number you phoned from, and Andreas told me his brother ran the cop shop. He said you and Shane had nice friends from all over the world. That's great news.

Oh, I miss you in the hospital, Fiona, really I do. Carmel is unbearable as Ward Sister. Frightening the patients, terrifying the nurses, upsetting the visitors, stamping round the place like a mad woman on speed. We have two new Filipino nurses, gentle little things, they nearly fled back to Manila until we told them that we were all equally horrified by her.

They were looking for more staff nurses in Orthopaedic, I thought I might apply. It's great working with the new knees and new hips. Any news at all on when you and Shane are coming back? It's just that if it were going to be at the end of the summer there are some really great flats coming on the market, you and Shane could easily get one of them, it would only be a ten-minute walk to the hospital. I'd just love one myself but you'd need two to pay for it.

In fact, I was telling your mam and dad about them, I said that was probably the kind of place the two of you would want to live when you came back. They didn't even flicker an eyelid. Remember when they wouldn't hear his name mentioned? You've certainly laid down the ground rules okay.

They were very pleased you called about that awful tragedy. It must have been terrible.

Anyway, you have my e-mail address now, do tell me how you are and how you both like Greece. I always wanted to go there but never got any further than Spain. Remember that time we went to Marbella and met the two English guys who got burned to a crisp and gave us the keys of their car? Weren't we reckless then? You still are of course!
Love to you both,
Barbara

Fiona sat there stunned.

Barbara sending her love to Shane? Her mother and father accepting the fact that she was going to live with Shane for ever? The world was tilting slightly.

She read the letter again and went back to Elsa's apartment to make soup and a fruit salad.

Elsa stopped by Vonni's craft shop and invited her to join them for an evening meal.

'Fiona is cooking for us, we can have a Ladies' Dinner,' she suggested.

'No, thank you, Elsa, very kind of you both, but I have to work.'

'Work? What on earth do you do?'

'Every week I go to a group of blind people who make rugs. I choose the colours of the wool for them. Then I try to sell the rugs.' She shrugged as if this was everyday work anyone might do.

'Did you always know about rug-making?' Elsa asked.

'Not at all.'

'So why did you take it up, particularly with the blind?'

'Oh, I had to give something back and I realised that the blind could weave with the best – they just needed someone to mark out which was pink and which was orange.'

'What do you mean, you had to give something back?' Elsa asked.

'This place was good to me. I was nothing but a nuisance for years, upsetting them all, howling and frightening their children. They put up with me until I recovered.'

'I can't believe this ... *you* howling and frightening people?' Elsa laughed as if it were a joke.

Vonni looked very serious. 'Oh, I did, believe me. But I had an excuse. My husband betrayed me, you see. He played *tavli* in the restaurants and tavernas – that I didn't mind. It's the way. But then he saw beautiful Magda and he forgot everything we had. He was entranced by her. He would not come home to me. I had a little boy and the people here helped me look after him while I worked up in the petrol station. I'll never forget that ... and it was hard for them to take my side. I was the foreigner – they would have been tempted to side with him rather than me.'

'And what happened?'

'A lot happened,' Vonni said. 'Well, one big thing that happened was that Stavros moved out of our house and into hers.'

'No! In this small place!' Elsa was aghast.

'The size of the place was unimportant, truly it was. It would have been as bad in a big anonymous city. He just would not return. I did a lot of stupid things – that's when the people here were so tolerant and good.'

'What kind of stupid things?' Elsa wanted to know.

'Another time possibly.' The shutters came down in Vonni's face.

'It's just that *I've* done some very stupid things recently. It's comforting to know others did and survived,' Elsa said.

'Is this the man who was staying in the Anna Beach calling out to the stars that he loved you?'

'You know everything!' Elsa exclaimed. 'Yes, it is of course, it is. And I still love him so much, that's the problem.'

'Why is it a problem?'

'Well, it's complicated.'

'It's always complicated,' Vonni said sympathetically.

'I suppose it is, we forget that. His name is Dieter, he runs the television station where I work ... used to work. He taught me everything and I became a sort of star there, presenting the big news programme at night. And anyway we fell in love, got together, whatever you'd call it, and have been together for over two years.'

'You live together?' Vonni asked.

'No, it's not as simple as that.'

'Is he married to someone else?'

'No, it's not that. It's just awkward in the Network if people know.'

Vonni raised her eyes and looked at Elsa levelly. Somehow Elsa felt slightly flustered and defensive.

'You don't know what it's like back there, Vonni, very hot-house. People would think I only got my good job because I was living with him. Easier for him to have his place and me to have mine.'

'Sure.' Vonni was clipped. 'So what are you doing here then?'

'I discovered something very cold and unfeeling about him.'

'More than the fact he just wouldn't commit to you publicly?' Vonni asked.

Elsa was annoyed now. 'You really don't understand, that was a mutual decision.'

'Yes, of course,' Vonni said. 'So what was the cold unfeeling thing?'

'I discovered that he has a child by a woman he knew years back.'

'So?'

'What do you mean – So? He has a child that he has never acknowledged, he's no part of her life. You don't think that's bad?'

'I think it happens all over the world every day of the week. People survive.'

'It happened to me,' Elsa said. 'My father walked away, didn't give a damn.'

'And look at you! Didn't *you* survive, Elsa? So very beautiful, confident, successful at everything. It proves my point.'

'It proves nothing. You don't know what I feel, have always felt. I feel that I must be so utterly worthless that even my own father couldn't be bothered with me.'

'Grow up, Elsa. In the end we all have to rely on ourselves. Ourselves and the friends we make if we are lucky enough to make them. We are not tied to our children, nor they to us. There's no huge law that says *Thou shalt love thy child* and that *Thy child shalt love thee* in return. Happy Families is a game people play with cards, it's not any kind of reality.'

'I don't know what made you so bitter and cynical but I'm glad I don't feel like that,' Elsa said.

'You want him to play Saturday Father to some child he probably never intended should exist.'

'But she *does* exist and that's exactly what he should do.'

'That's not why you are leaving him,' Vonni said.

'I beg your pardon?'

'You're leaving him because you don't trust him. You thought that he would eventually admit that he needed you as part of his life. You are such a beautiful young woman, you are accustomed to getting your own way. If you truly loved him you could put this child out of your mind. But no, you can't be sure that he loves you at all. That's why you are seizing on this episode of his life which took place long before he met you. You are making it the excuse, aren't you?'

Elsa felt her eyes stinging at the injustice of the attack. 'You're so wrong, he *does* love me. You heard him yourself shouting it aloud. And he cried out to me again next morning as he got on the ferry. And I have such a huge, lonely hole in my heart without him. I've decided that I'm going back to Germany as soon as I can to tell him that I love him too.'

Vonni leaned forward. 'You are never in your whole life going to get such good advice as this. Don't go back there, keep going, leave him be. Remain a beautiful golden memory for him. He's never going to love you the way you want to be loved.'

Elsa stood up, not trusting herself to speak. She thought she saw Thomas going up the side stairs in his silly baggy trousers. She didn't want to talk to him. Or anybody. She wanted to get back to her own apartment. Fast.

*

'You're very quiet, Elsa,' Fiona said. 'Don't you like that lovely healthy soup I made you?'

'It's very good. I'm sorry, I just don't feel too cheerful tonight. Don't worry, I'll get over it, I hate moody people.' She smiled a very bright smile.

'Did something happen?' Fiona asked.

'Well, yes, as it happens I had a row with Vonni of all stupid things,' she said.

'*A row with Vonni?*'

'I know it sounds impossible but that's what happened.'

'But what about?' Fiona was astounded.

'She knows about me and Dieter, she wants me to leave him alone, stay away from him.'

Elsa had mentioned nothing to Fiona about her situation up to this point. Fiona was wordless.

'So we saw things a bit differently, if you see what I mean?'

'But you still love him, don't you?'

'Oh yes, most definitely, and he feels the same,' Elsa said.

'Well, there's no question about it then.' Fiona was matter-of-fact and businesslike about it. 'You have to go back to him, Vonni or no Vonni.'

They had all agreed to meet at the harbour café after dinner and the four of them talked about their day.

'Do any of you get the feeling that we are just marking time here – that we should be doing something else?' Thomas asked.

'I'm happy here. I like it,' David said.

'And I do too,' Fiona agreed. 'Anyway, I have to stay here until Shane gets back.'

'I'll probably go back to Germany next week,' Elsa said. 'I'm just thinking it through. What about you, Thomas?'

'Well, Vonni thinks I should go back to California to see my son. I haven't worked it out either,' he said.

'Vonni's busy dispatching us all home! Once Maria can drive that van, Vonni wants me out too, back to make peace with my parents and work with my father.' David sounded gloomy.

'She doesn't think Shane is coming back, she says there are no jobs here, I'd be better to go back to Dublin.'

'She's actually more of a policeman than Yorghis is. She says I should end my relationship with a man who doesn't really love me,' Elsa said, giggling.

'She never put it like that?' David said.

'Almost precisely like that – anyway I'm different to the rest of you, she wants me to keep on the move and *not* to go home.'

They pooled what they knew about her: she came from the west of Ireland over thirty years ago because she loved a man called Stavros. Somehow she managed to buy him a petrol station, where Vonni worked night and day. She had one son, Stavros, whom she didn't see now. Stavros senior had left the island, possibly with Vonni's young son. Vonni had gone through a troubled time but the people of Aghia Anna had looked after her and she felt she owed them in return.

'What kind of a troubled time?' Fiona wondered. 'Maybe she had a breakdown when Stavros left?'

'I think she was an alcoholic,' David said softly.

The others were startled. That quiet, capable, together woman a slave to drink? Impossible.

'Why do you say that?' Elsa asked.

'Well, have you noticed she never drinks any wine or *ouzo* or anything?' David said.

They looked at him with respect. They had all been with Vonni around many a table. Only the gentle, sensitive David had noticed what was now so obvious to everyone.

Chapter Twelve

Vonni had been right when she said that the people of Aghia Anna would close ranks about her. The four of them could get no information at all.

'I believe that Vonni used to run that gas station over there,' Thomas said casually to Yorghis.

Yorghis said something that was neither yes nor no.

'Did she hate giving it up?' Thomas asked.

'I don't really know,' Yorghis said.

'Or it might have been a relief.'

'You live in Vonni's house, I'm sure that you could ask her all about it,' Yorghis said politely.

David got nowhere with Andreas either. 'You must have known Vonni's husband, Stavros?'

'Everyone knows everyone here.'

'And I suppose you knew Magda, too?'

'As I say, it's a very small place.'

'Their son, was he friendly with your son and with Manos?'

'In a village, every child knows every other child.'

'You think I'm asking too many questions, don't you, Andreas?'

'You are interested in this place and the people who live here, that's good,' Andreas said, but told no more.

Elsa tried talking to Yanni in the delicatessen when she went in to get olives and cheese. He was a man of about sixty; he would have been around for all the drama.

'It's wonderful how Vonni is so much a part of this town, isn't it?' Elsa began.

'Vonni is a very good woman, yes,' Yanni said.

'I expect you knew her when she was married to Stavros?' Elsa said.

'Does she talk to you about Stavros?' Yanni asked.

'A little, yes.'

'Then I suppose she tells you all she wants you to know about him,' Yanni said with a huge smile showing many gold teeth, but giving nothing away.

And Elsa, who had been able to interview politicians, business tycoons, authors and actors on German television and make them reveal their stories, had to admit defeat.

Fiona walked out to Eleni's house with sweets for the children. 'I wanted to thank you for being so kind when I was sick,' she said to Eleni.

'Are you good now?' The woman was concerned.

'Yes, I'm fine, but I'm a bit sad because I'm waiting here for Shane,' she said. 'If he comes back for me, you'll be sure to tell him where I am staying.'

'Shane, yes. I tell him, yes. If he comes back.'

'Oh, he will come back, Eleni. He loves me.'

'Yes.' There was an awkward silence between them.

Fiona didn't want to protest any more. She changed the subject. 'Did you know Stavros, the husband of Vonni, long ago?'

'I don't speak English good, I tell this Shane where you stay if he comes back. Thank you for the *karameles* for the children. You are kind, good girl.'

'Vonni, come upstairs for a *portokalatha* when you're through. Okay?'

'So you've finally noticed I only drink soft drinks,' she laughed at Thomas.

'I didn't, David did, he's the one who notices things. Anyway, what you drink isn't important – I want your advice.'

'No, you don't, you want me to tell you that it's all going to turn out fine without you having to lift a finger. Isn't that right?'

'If you could tell me convincingly, I'd sure love it,' he said.

'I'll be up in ten minutes,' she said. He noticed she was wearing a clean, fresh, yellow blouse with little embroidered roses on it. She must keep her clothes in the craft shop.

'That's pretty,' he indicated the stitching. 'Did you do that?'

'No, it was done by someone else. It's thirty years old.'

'Really? Who did it?'

'It doesn't matter now, Thomas, she could sew like an angel.'

Thomas swallowed. He had been too intrusive. 'I guess I ask too many questions, Vonni, forgive me, you don't have to talk about it.'

'Well, I do, really. You four are all anxious to know about me ... you are asking everyone else in Aghia Anna about me.' She smiled at him innocently.

Thomas looked at the floor. 'They told you?' he said ruefully.

'Of course they did!' To her it was obvious.

'I'm sorry, it looks very nosy, but I tell you, Vonni, you're special. We are all fascinated by you.'

'I'm flattered, and astonished. But anyway, I'll tell you whatever you want to know.' She smiled at him encouragingly.

'I don't know. Now that I'm in a position to ask questions, I honestly don't know what to ask. I suppose I want to know if you are happy?'

'Yes, I think I am fairly happy, as it happens. Are you happy, Thomas?'

'No, I'm not, you know that, I've messed up on Bill, you told me yourself. But we're meant to be talking about you.'

'And what will we talk about?' she asked.

'I suppose we wanted to know what your husband was like, and what happened to him,' Thomas said uneasily.

He felt awkward asking probing questions, but Vonni was totally at ease with it all.

'Very hard questions to answer, both of them. His name was Stavros, he was very dark, big brown, almost black eyes, black hair, long always, whether it was fashionable or not. His father was the barber here, he used to say he was ashamed of his wild and woolly son, and that Stavros was no advertisement for his father's barbering skills. He wasn't exactly tall, he was ... I suppose you'd call it stocky. The moment I saw him I knew I never wanted any other man.'

'And where did you see him? Here in Aghia Anna?' Thomas asked.

'No, I met him somewhere very different. The most unlikely place,' Vonni said, almost dreamily.

'Are you going to make me beg or will you tell me?' he asked.

'I met Stavros in Ardeevin, a small village in the west of Ireland in the spring of 1966, before you were born, Thomas.'

'True, but I was born four years later so it was touch and go,' he said.

'He came to work in a garage on the main street. We had never seen anything quite so exotic. A real live Greek man in our main street, well, our only street. Ardeevin didn't run to more than one. He was learning English, he said, and the motor trade, and seeing the world . . .' Vonni sighed at the memory. 'We didn't think Ardeevin was the right place to start seeing the world. What about Paris? London? Even Dublin? But he said he liked it, it reminded him of his home town, Aghia Anna. It felt familiar, comfortable.' She paused to think about it.

Thomas didn't encourage her to say more. Either she would or she would not, it had nothing to do with his promptings.

'I was still at school, in my last year. My family hoped I would get what was described as a Call to Training. It meant a place in a college where you became a primary teacher. A Call to Training was like winning the Irish Sweepstakes, you were educated free into a grand career and a permanent job and a pension.'

'But the call never came?' he said gently.

'I don't know whether it did or not. I never heard because I was so much in love with Stavros nothing else mattered. I had stopped going to school, abandoned studying, examinations had no meaning for me. My only purpose each day was to hide from my sister, to sneak into the back of Ardeevin Motors. I didn't care about anything but being with him.'

Thomas listened enthralled at the calm way she told the story of her first love.

'So Jimmy Keane, who ran the garage, began to think Stavros wasn't concentrating fully on his work and started making sounds that he was going to sack him. I could neither eat nor sleep with the worry of it all. What would I *do* if Stavros had to move on? I went in and sat my school examinations. I could barely understand the questions, let alone answer them.'

'And what kind of results did you get?' Thomas, ever the teacher, wanted to know.

'I have no idea. You see, the most marvellous event occurred in Ireland that summer. There was a bank strike!' Her eyes shone at the memory.

'The banks went on strike? Never!'

'Oh, they did,' she said happily.

'And how did people manage?'

'On trust, mainly, a series of IOUs – they even printed blank cheque-book forms to try and make it seem more normal.'

'And?'

'And what happened then was nothing short of a miracle,' Vonni said. 'Supermarkets would have a lot of cash and no banks to lodge it in, so they cashed these "cheques" for people they knew. The big town ten miles away had a supermarket where I was known, because the manager was a cousin of my mother. So I cashed a cheque for two and a half thousand pounds. And that day Jimmy Keane said he'd have to let Stavros go.'

Vonni began to pace the room at this stage, but she continued the story.

'He told me he would miss me, that I was his true love and that one day we would meet again, that he would go back to Aghia Anna, open up a petrol station and send for me to come and join him. And I asked what was wrong with going right now, that I had the funds to set him up. I told him that it was my savings.'

'Tell me he was pleased.'

'Oh, he was, but my parents weren't. I told them that day that I was seventeen and a half, in six months I could marry without their permission anyway. What were they going to do? Lock me up? They cried and shouted a lot, they talked about the waste, the bad example to my sister, about not being able to raise their heads in Ardeevin. My father was a teacher, a man of considerable importance in the community, my mother was related to big important shopkeepers all over the place. Oh, the shame of it all.'

'But you wore them down.'

'I told them I was leaving that very night, and we did, on the seven-thirty bus.'

'And the money?'

'Ah yes, the money. We were well in Aghia Anna by the time the bank strike ended. A wonderful journey by train and boat, we saved the big money, you see, didn't touch it until we got here. We travelled through Switzerland and Italy, and ate bread and cheese. I was never so happy in my life. *Nobody* was as happy as I was then.'

'And you arrived here?'

'And it wasn't so great. There was this girl, you see, very pregnant with Stavros's child. She thought he had come back to marry her. She was Christina, the sister of Andreas and Yorghis. When she discovered he had *not* come back for her, she tried to kill herself. It turned out that she killed the child she was carrying, not herself. It was a terrible time for everyone.'

'What happened to Christina?'

'She went to the hospital on the hill, you know, on the Kalatriada road.'

'Yes, I know it. And – what happened to you then, Vonni?'

'Me? I learned to speak Greek, I bought the petrol station. I learned how to change wheels, pump up tyres. I went to see Christina every week. She didn't speak to me for forty-five weeks then one day she did. And soon she got better and she married a good man. She has children and grandchildren. They live on the other side of the island. I see her often.'

'You married Stavros?'

'In a civil ceremony in Athens. No one thought it was a real wedding – not my family back in Ardeevin, not his family here in Aghia Anna.'

She had begun to sound tired and weary. Thomas knew he must not push her.

'And in 1970, the very same year that you were born in California, our son Stavros was born. By this time, people were used to me. We had a christening at the church, and even Stavros's father relaxed and sang songs. And Christina came and gave me all the baby clothes she had made when she had thought *she* was going to have Stavros's baby.'

'How amazing,' Thomas said.

'I know. No word from Ireland, of course. I wrote and told them they had a grandson. No reply at all.'

'They must have been very bitter.'

'Well, the money was the final straw that broke the camel's back.'

'Ah, the money,' Thomas smiled.

'Well, I was always going to pay it back.'

'Sure,' he said, with no conviction.

'And I did,' she said, as if it was the most obvious thing in the world.

David opened the letter. It was the first time his parents had written to him. He sat and read unbelievingly of their pride and delight in the actual invitation to this award his father had won. They had sent him a photocopy but described how the wording was embossed on the thick card.

David knew those awards; businessmen patted each other on the back every year. It was a reward for nothing except making money. No achievement, philanthropy, no research, no generosity to charity was being praised. No, it was only the huge god *profit* that was being worshipped here.

His mother wrote on and on – about seating in the Town Hall, what they would all wear, that there would be a table plan. She wondered how soon he would come home for it.

He would calm himself and write a courteous letter explaining why he would not be there. A letter was wiser than a phone call. No danger of anyone losing their temper.

Fiona went to the Anna Beach Hotel and sent an e-mail to her friend Barbara in Dublin.

It was good to hear from you, really it was. Lord,
but it's beautiful here, Barb, I'm so glad we chose
this place. The accident was terrible, but the people
are full of courage, they would do your heart good.
Shane's gone to Athens for a few days on work.
He'll be back any day now. I keep watching the
ferries. Thanks for telling me about the hospital.
Imagine Carmel-the-cow being Ward Sister.
  I'll write again when I know our plans.
  Love,
  Fiona

'There is a fax for your friend the German woman,' the
man at the reception desk said as Fiona was leaving the
Anna Beach.

Fiona marvelled at how everyone knew who they all
were.

'I'll take it back to the villa,' she said.

She was becoming very familiar with Aghia Anna by
now, even knew little short cuts from one side to the
other. She laid the piece of paper on the table in front of
Elsa.

'I'd have read it but it's in German,' Fiona said.

'Yes.'

'Aren't you going to read it? You don't have to
translate it,' Fiona said.

'I know what it says,' Elsa said.

'That's pretty psychic of you,' Fiona said in surprise.

'It's telling me to pull myself together and come back
to where I belong, which is in bed with him two nights a
week, and no more gestures of independence.'

'Maybe it's not that,' Fiona encouraged her.

'All right – I'll translate . . .' She picked up the paper. 'It's fairly short anyway.'

Darling Elsa,
    The decision is yours. Come back to me and we will move together into an apartment openly for all to see. We will even be married. If that's what you want. I will write letters and send gifts to that child if it makes you feel better. We were intended for each other, you know that and I know that. What is the point in playing games? Fax me yes, soonest.
    Love until the world ends,
    Dieter

In Chicago, Adoni took the letter with the Greek stamp. If the kindly Italian family who employed him thought that it was odd he never heard from Greece they didn't say anything. He took the letter to the men's room and sat down to read his father's spidery handwriting.

'*Adoni mou*,' it began and told simply of the boat that had burned in full sight of the town with people unable to get to it in time.

'It makes everything else that has happened seem very unimportant,' his father wrote.

Arguments about the taverna are so small compared to life and death. It would give me great pleasure, my son, if you were to come back to Aghia Anna and see me before my death. I assure you that I would not speak to you in that tone of voice that I did when you were here. Your room is always there if you come for a visit, and of course bring anyone you like. I hope there is somebody to bring.

And Adoni took out a big blue handkerchief to wipe his eyes. And then he cried again because there was nobody to bring.

There was no bail for Shane in Athens so he was brought back to the cells after the initial hearing.

'I'm allowed to make a phone call!' he shouted. 'You're meant to be in the bloody European Union, one of the reasons we let you in was for things like this, so as you'd pay some attention to human rights.'

They passed the phone to him without comment.

He dialled the police station in Aghia Anna. He wished he could remember that old guy's name. But what the hell.

'I'm trying to get in touch with Fiona Ryan,' he said.

'I'm sorry?' Yorghis said.

'I'm phoning from a police station, or jail, or some hell-hole in Athens,' he began.

'We told you before, she is not here,' Yorghis lied smoothly.

'She *must* be there, she's expecting my child, she'll have to get the bail money ...' He sounded frightened.

'As I say, sorry we can't help you,' Yorghis said and hung up.

Shane begged for a second call. He was so anxious, the policemen shrugged.

'Not too long if it's Ireland,' they warned.

'Barbara! They took a hell of a time to find you, it's Shane.'

'I was on the wards, Shane, it's called work,' she said.

'Very droll. Listen, has Fiona gone back to Dublin?'

'What? Have you two split up?' She couldn't keep the pleasure out of her voice.

'No, don't be ridiculous, I had to go to Athens ...'

'For work?' Barbara suggested dryly.

'Sort of – and those half-wits in Aghia Anna say she's left there so it's been a bit of a breakdown in communications, you might say.'

'Oh dear, Shane, I'm so sorry.'

'No, you're not, you're thrilled.'

'How can I help you, Shane, exactly?' Barbara asked.

'You could tell her to contact me at ... no, don't bother, I'll find her.'

'Are you *sure*, Shane? I'd love to help,' Barbara purred. She had never heard better news since the day her friend Fiona had taken up with the dreaded Shane.

Thomas looked at Vonni, who was quietly telling him the story of her life. Now she had told him that she had paid back that huge debt. How many more secrets did she have?

'You paid the supermarket back?' he said.

'It took some time – like nearly thirty years,' she admitted. 'But they got every penny. I started at a hundred pounds a year.'

'Did they thank you? Forgive you?'

'No, not even remotely.'

'But the guy who was your mother's cousin, didn't he say the money was returned?'

'Not in any way that made any difference. No.'

'And do you keep in touch with your family?'

'Cold little note every Christmas. Done out of Christian charity, proving to themselves they are big-hearted, capable of *forgiveness*, that went on for a time. I wrote long letters, sent them pictures of little Stavros.

But it was a bit one-sided. And then of course things changed.'

'Changed? They came round?'

'No, I meant *I* changed. I went mad, you see.'

'No, Vonni, you, mad? This I can't see.'

She looked tired. 'I haven't talked about myself so much for ages, I'm a bit weary.'

'Lie down then, in your own room in there.' He was gentle.

'No, Thomas, I have to feed the chickens.'

'Let me do that for you.'

'Thank you, but no, and Thomas – you can tell the others what I told you. I don't want them bothering people here for my story.'

He looked embarrassed. 'They don't need to know, none of us needs to know anything about your business.'

'I'll tell the rest another time . . . you know, like *New readers start here . . .*' She had a wonderfully infectious smile.

He found himself grinning back.

She did not return to the apartment that night.

When Thomas looked out of the window later on he saw her torch moving around the hen-house.

Thomas told them the story next day down by the harbour. They had got into the habit of turning up at the place with the blue check tablecloths around noon.

David had reported on the latest driving lesson: they had stopped and given some of Maria's neighbours a lift. David couldn't be sure what they had said but it appeared to be great cries of approval.

Elsa and Fiona said nothing about their messages from

home but they told how they had spent the morning helping an old man to paint some wooden chairs. He had wanted them all white until Elsa had suggested painting one blue and another one yellow. He had been delighted with them. Or at least they *thought* he had been delighted.

And Thomas told them Vonni's story.

'She did want you to know, it's as if she were going to take it up with one of the three of you.'

They wondered at the notion of a country where the banks went on strike.

'I remember my father talking about it, he said that the country ran perfectly well without them. There were a few loose cannons like Vonni who went off with small fortunes, but not many,' said Fiona.

'I wonder who she'll tell the next episode to,' Elsa said.

It turned out to be David. Later that afternoon.

Thomas and Elsa had gone for a walk down the coast, Fiona had gone to ask Yorghis had there been any news from Athens. David sat on the harbour wall with his Greek phrase book. Vonni came to join him. She helped him with some pronunciation.

'You'll be speaking like a native soon,' she encouraged him.

'Hardly. But I do like it here, people have proper values, they're not obsessed with making money.'

'Scratch them and you'll find that a fair few of them are,' Vonni said.

He told Vonni about the invitation to his father's award back home, how ludicrous it would all be. He took the invitation from the little music case he always carried with him and she read it carefully. Then he handed her his mother's letter to read as well. To his surprise she had tears in her eyes.

'You'll go back, of course?' she said.

'No, I can't. Six months later it would be something else. I'd never escape, I'd be sucked back in. No, Vonni, you of all people understand how important it is to get away. You never went back to Ireland, did you?'

'No, but I wanted to, a thousand times I wanted to go back and see them. Like for my sister's wedding, like for my father's retirement party, when my mother was in hospital, all those times and many more. But I was never welcome, so I couldn't go.'

'How do you know that you would not have been welcome?' David asked. 'Did you have friends you kept in touch with?'

'No, my friends were all furious with me, I had done all the things they would love to have done – had sex with a grown-up man, abandoned school, cashed a rocky cheque in the bank strike, run off to the isles of Greece. No, they didn't keep in touch – but, oddly, Jimmy Keane did. I think he felt guilty. If he hadn't sacked Stavros, none of this might have happened. So he and he alone replied to my letters. I told him that I was *delighted* he had sacked Stavros, I think that made him feel better. Anyway, he told me all that was going on and I knew something about Ardeevin – not much, but something.'

'And he kept writing, then?'

'Yes, but, you see, I went mad then and that sort of changed everything.' She spoke as casually as if she was saying that she'd gone somewhere on the bus instead of out of her mind.

'It wasn't *really* mad, was it?' David asked.

'Oh, I think so. It was because of Magda, you see. She had a terrible husband, very violent over nothing, always imagining that Magda was flirting with people. But the truth was that she tidied her house, cooked her husband's meals and kept her head down, bent over her embroidery. That's what we thought the truth was anyway. And it might well have been. Possibly she didn't raise her head from her embroidery until Stavros was kind to her. Who will ever know now?'

'And you liked her at first?'

'Oh yes, indeed, she was a lovely gentle woman with a beautiful smile; she had a hard life – no children and a man who was unreliable. Sometimes she had bruises or a cut but she said she was clumsy or tired and had fallen. Stavros played *tavli* in the café with her husband like the other men. He didn't really want to hear stories of what went on in that house. "It's their life, Vonni, their marriage, we should not interfere . . ." And I suppose because I was so busy working long hours and looking after little Stavros . . . Well, I went along with it. Until one day I went to collect a tablecloth, and she was sitting there, the blood dripping down on to the white material. I ran for old Dr Leros, the father of Dr Leros who is here now. He patched her up and he said that this could not go on, we needed a strong man, someone like Stavros, to do something. So I told Stavros what he had said. And for once he listened to me and brought two of his friends with him. I don't know what happened but I gather they held Magda's husband down on the floor for a while and told him what would happen to him if there was another incident.'

'And did he take them seriously?'

'Very seriously, apparently, and Magda stopped being *clumsy*, as she called it, and walked with her head high and looked people in the eye for the first time. That was when people realised that she was very beautiful. Up to then we just thought she had beautiful hair,' Vonni explained in a small sad voice.

'Did you suspect that Stavros was ... well ... interested in her?' David asked gently.

'No, not at all. I was the last to know, the very last person in Aghia Anna. I had heard it's often the way, but I didn't believe it. Or if it happened, I thought the wife must be a spectacular thicko. Anyway it finally dawned on me.'

'How?'

'Well, not the best way really. Little Stavros was at the petrol station – he was four then, going on five. He asked why was Magda always so tired. I said I didn't think she was and little Stavros said she must be, she always had to go to bed when she came to our house, and Papa had to go and sit with her. I remember that moment as if it were this morning. I felt so dizzy and faint. Magda and Stavros? In our house? In my bed? It must be a misunderstanding. It *had* to be a mistake.'

'So what did you do?'

'I closed the petrol pumps and went home early the next day. Little Stavros was playing in the garden. We had a house over there behind Maria's. I took him by the hand across to a neighbour, then I went back. I opened the door very quietly and went in. It was very quiet, then I heard them laughing. He was calling her his little furry rabbit, something he used to call me when we made love. I opened the door and stood and looked at them. She was beautiful with her long dark curls and her olive skin. I caught a reflection of myself in the mirror. Not good. Not the right thing to do.'

There was a silence between them. Then Vonni spoke again.

'And I thought, *why* had I come home and disturbed them? Now it was all out in the open. If I hadn't come back we could have gone on for ever, pretending everything was all right. All of us. But as I looked at her, and how beautiful she was, I knew I had lost. Of course he would want her not me. So I said nothing, just looked from one to the other for what seemed a very long time. Then Stavros said, "Please don't make a scene, Vonni, you'll upset the child." That's what he thought of first, not upsetting little Stavros! To hell with upsetting me! I had left my family and my land to be with him. No worry about upsetting Vonni who had stolen money to buy him a garage and worked in it from dawn to dusk every day to make it a success ... Suddenly things seemed as if they had tilted, like a picture being crooked on a wall. Nothing was right any more ...'

David listened, chilled by her intensity.

'I walked away. Out of the door of our bedroom, out of our house. Past where little Stavros was playing with other children. I walked up to the top of the town and into a little bar. A place where normally only the old men sat and drank. I ordered *raki*, you know, the very rough spirit they have – it's like *poitín* back home. I drank until I could forget the way her round beautiful shoulder had snuggled against his chest. I drank until I fell on the ground.

'They carried me home, I remember nothing of it. I woke up next day in our bed. There was no sign of Stavros. I remembered her there in the bed and I got up to be very sick. There was no sign of little Stavros either. I went to work, but the smell of the petrol and the exhaust of the cars made me very sick again. I went to the bar where I had been the previous day, apologised for my behaviour, asked them how much I owed them. They all shook their heads, they were not going to charge me for becoming incapable on their terrible and probably home-made liquor. Nervously I enquired what had been the reception when they took me home.

'Magda had taken my child, *my* child, to his grand-father the barber. Stavros had just pointed them to the bedroom and left. They couldn't help me further. I had brandy this time, good Metaxa brandy to get me over the shock, and then I sort of crawled back to the petrol station but couldn't talk to anyone so I went home. Home! Huh! There was nobody there. Four days and nights of drinking, then I realised they had taken my child away from me. I heard like in a dream that Magda's husband had gone away on a fishing boat to another island. And then I remember waking up in the hospital on the Kalatriada road. Christina, who had been Stavros's first love, came to see me. "Pretend to be calm, pretend to be better, then they'll let you out," she said. So that's what I did, pretended.'

'It worked?' David said.

'Only for a bit. Stavros would not speak to me, wouldn't tell me what he had done with my son, and I knew I must not raise my voice again or I would be back in that hospital where they locked every door behind them.'

'And Stavros?'

'Had gone across the road, was living with her. I knew they were all watching me, so I couldn't drink in the place at the top of the town. I bought a bottle here, a bottle there, I drank until I passed out. I never slept in that bed again, apart from the night when they carried me home, always on the sofa. I don't know how long it went on.

'Then Christina came and helped me pull myself together. And so a lot cleaner, tidier and relatively sober, I went up to see him. Politely he asked me to go away, to leave him. I could stay in the house. He had changed all the locks on the petrol pumps, the whole place, taken my name off the accounts, cheque books. He said that our son was living in Athens with his aunt and that I would never see him again. He explained as if he were talking to someone with mental problems that soon he would sell the garage, *his* garage, and that he and Magda would go and find little Stavros, settle somewhere new and build some kind of a life for him again.

'And suddenly I realised that this was exactly what would happen. I would be here alone, without my son, without my love, without my garage. Unable to go home, owing two thousand pounds ... I had managed to pay five instalments of one hundred pounds a year, which was hard enough going when I was working nine hours a day. How was I going to find that money now?'

'But in fairness, Stavros knew about the debt, surely he must have said he'd help you?' David was shocked.

'No, he never knew about it. I never told him. He thought it was my money, my inheritance, my savings,' Vonni said.

Then she moved away, and left David sitting on the harbour wall with his Greek phrase book unopened as he thought about the story he had just heard.

*

'Do you know what I don't understand,' Fiona said the same day as they were putting together the jigsaw pieces of Vonni's story.

'Why she didn't get a lawyer?' Thomas suggested.

'She was in no position to do that. Stolen money in her background, he *did* give her the house, and she didn't really know their customs and their ways here in a foreign community,' Elsa said.

'No, wait, I don't understand why Andreas said that little Stavros came up to the taverna on the hill to play with his son Adoni and climb trees, he couldn't have done that at four.'

'Maybe Stavros and Magda stayed for a while longer, even a good time longer,' David suggested. 'That would have been even harder for Vonni to bear if her child just lived across the road.'

'Well, she'll tell one of us, she promised that she would,' Thomas said.

'I didn't want to push her any more,' David apologised.

'You're an easy person to talk to, David, I would not be at all surprised if she came back to you,' Elsa said to him with her wonderful smile.

Vonni came back to David sooner than he had expected.

'Can you do me a favour?'

'I'd love to,' he said.

'I have to deliver some potting clay and moulds to the hospital, for their rehab classes. Will you come with me? You see, I just hate going there on my own. I keep thinking that they'll lock the door behind me as they did before.'

'But you weren't there very long?' David said. 'Didn't Christina get you out by telling you to pretend?'

'Oh yes, that was the first time. But I went back, I was there for years really,' Vonni said casually. 'Will we go and pick up Maria's van now and head off?'

'We will, we will.' David smiled.

'Are you imitating my accent, young fellow?'

'Imitate you, Vonni? I wouldn't dare!' he said.

'There's a very nice part of the garden, I'll show you,' she said when the goods had been handed over. And they sat together looking down from one of the many hills that surrounded Aghia Anna and she picked up her story as if there had been no interruption.

This time she filled in some of the painful gaps.

'Once I knew I had lost everything I didn't see any point in pretending. I sold things out of the house, *his* house I always considered it, and bought drink. So I was back in here and out like a yo-yo. Stavros explained to everyone that I was an unfit mother. We didn't have courts or laws or social workers then . . . or if we did I wasn't sober or sane enough to understand them. I saw little Stavros once a week on a Saturday for three hours. There was always someone else there, not him, not Magda, but Stavros's father sometimes or his sister, or Andreas, they trusted him.'

'Everyone would trust Andreas. You did too?'

'Of course. But the visits were not a success. I used to cry, you see, cry over all I had lost. All that could never be. And I would clutch at little Stavros and tell him how much I loved him and needed him. He was terrified of me.'

'No, no,' David murmured.

'Truly he was, he hated the meetings. Andreas used to

drive him up the hill to his place to the swing on the tree to cheer him up after he had to deal with me, then I would get bladdered with drink to get over it. It went on for years. I mean years. He was twelve when they took him away.'

'They?'

'Stavros and Magda. I was in here then, and oddly it was when they were gone I decided that there was still a life to be lived. A man here killed himself that year and it shocked us all, particularly the drunks. That had been his little problem, too, you see.

'So I got sober. Sounds simple. It was far from simple but I did it. But it was too late.

'My son the teenager was gone. No point in my trying to find out where. The boy's grandfather, the old barber, was even kind to me in the end. But he wouldn't tell me. I wrote to him, young Stavros – letters on his birthday through his grandfather and later through his aunts, every year. Even this year when he was thirty-four.'

'And no answer ever?' David asked.

'No answer, ever.'

'Does Andreas not know? He's such a kind man, he'd tell you or he'd let your son know what you are like now.'

'No, Andreas doesn't know.'

'He'd understand, too, his own selfish son won't come back to him from Chicago, Andreas knows what it feels like.'

'David, listen to me.'

'Yes?'

'There are two sides to everything. I was a pig of a mother when young Stavros was growing up, so how does he know I am mellow and easy-going now? If he were ever to get in contact, it would only be out of pity.'

'Someone might tell him,' David said.

Vonni brushed it away. 'Listen to me, David, Andreas knew everything about running a taverna when Adoni was growing up, how does Adoni know that his father is lonely and sad, and wants him to come home?'

'As I said, Vonni, someone could tell him. Like you, for example?'

'Don't be ridiculous, David, why would Adoni listen to a mad old fart, nearly as old as his father? He has to discover for himself that it might be worth while.'

'Well, they are *so* foolish, these young men, Adoni in Chicago and Stavros wherever he is, why they can't see sense and come back to you both is beyond me,' David said.

'There are probably many people in England who wonder the same about you,' Vonni suggested.

'It's totally different.'

'Do you still have that letter with you?'

'Yes, but that doesn't mean anything,' he said.

'David, you fool, I do like you hugely, but you are such a fool. That letter from your mother, she's *begging* you to come home.'

'Where does she say that?'

'In every line. Your father's ill. He may be dying for all you know.'

'Vonni!'

'I mean it, David,' she said, and looked out to sea as she had so many times from this place when her mind was gone.

Chapter Thirteen

Elsa had written nothing back to Dieter. She still needed time to think about it.

There was no doubt that Dieter meant it. If he said he would marry her then he would be prepared to do that. It would not be easy for him, after years of being on his own. He would get a lot of stick from his friends. He would hate the guilt of admitting that he had abandoned his own child. Which he would have to admit if he opened up a lifeline to little Gerda. He was prepared to do that for Elsa also, he had said as much.

Up to now he had genuinely believed that their lives could run easily together and that there was nothing about the situation that needed to be altered. But when forced to make a choice he had made it. It was up to Elsa to tell him when she would be back home and he would be there, waiting for her.

So what was holding her back?

Elsa walked on her own up one of the windy roads away from town. She had not been this way before, and since she would be leaving soon, she wanted to imprint the whole place on her mind.

No smart restaurants, traditional tavernas or craft

shops on this road. Small poor dwellings, sometimes, with a goat or two outside, children playing amongst the hens and chickens.

Elsa stopped and looked at them.

Would she and Dieter have children? A little blond boy and girl, different from these dark-eyed Greek children in every way except for the smiles.

Would that take away some of the pain? Would her children grow up knowing that they had a half-sister Gerda who didn't live with them?

She was smiling to herself at being so fanciful when, unexpectedly, Vonni came out of a house.

'Heavens, Vonni, you're everywhere!' Elsa exclaimed.

'I could say the same about all of you! I never move but I fall over one of you,' Vonni said with spirit.

'Where does this road lead? I just came up this way to explore.'

'It doesn't really lead anywhere – just more of the same – but I have to deliver something a bit further on, come and walk with me, I could do with the company.'

Vonni looked uncharacteristically downhearted.

'Is something wrong?' Elsa asked.

'That house I was in just now, the woman is pregnant. The father was one of those who drowned on Manos's boat. She doesn't want the child. It's just such a mess. Dr Leros won't hear of doing a termination, so she's going to go to this woman who "manages things", as she puts it, in a village about fifty kilometres away. She could die, she could certainly get septicaemia. Why she can't have this child and love him or her is not clear. I've been there for an hour saying we'll all help her to look after the baby. But will she listen? No.'

'That's an unusual position for you to be in, Vonni. People not listening to you,' Elsa teased her.

'Why do you say that?'

'Well, we all listen to you, and take great notice of everything you say, believe me. We spent hours talking to David about your theory that his father might be ill.'

'Not might be ill, *is* ill,' Vonni said. 'And what did he decide? He wasn't too pleased with me, I can tell you that.'

'Well, he thinks it's all a trap, a way to get him home, and then it will be harder for him to get away again. But you've unsettled him.'

'I didn't want to do that,' Vonni said.

'Yes, you did in a way, you wanted to shake him up, make him think. And you've succeeded – he's going to call his home today.'

'Good,' Vonni nodded her approval. She stopped at a small ill-kept building. 'I'm going into this house – come with me. I have to give Nikolas some magic medicine.' She took a small clay pot from her woollen shoulder bag.

'You make magic medicines too?' Elsa gasped.

'No, it's an antibiotic cream actually, but Nikolas doesn't trust doctors and modern medicine so Dr Leros and I have this little ruse.'

Elsa watched as Vonni moved around the old man's simple house, picking up things here, arranging them there, talking away effortlessly in Greek; and then she produced the magic ointment and applied it solemnly to the sore on his leg.

When they left, the old man smiled at them both.

Elsa and Vonni continued to walk companionably down the windy road. Vonni pointed out landmarks and told Elsa the names of the places they passed and what they meant in English.

'You love it here, don't you?' Elsa said.

'I was lucky to find this place. Maybe I would have found another place, a different place, but Aghia Anna was good to me, I'd never live anywhere else.'

'I'll be sorry to leave, I really will,' Elsa said.

'But you are leaving? Going back to Germany?' Vonni did not sound best pleased.

'Yes, of course, I have to move on,' Elsa said.

'Move back, more like, move back to what you ran away from.'

'You don't know—' Elsa began.

'I know what you told me, how you made up your mind to escape a bad situation, and how he came here, found you and changed your mind.'

'No, *he* didn't change my mind – I changed my mind,' Elsa said, stung.

'Oh yes?'

'Really, Vonni, you of all people should know what it is to love someone and cross a continent to be with him. You did it, for heaven's sake. You should understand.'

'I was a child when I did what I did, a schoolgirl, you are a grown, sophisticated woman, with a career, a life, a confident future. We are not comparing like with like.'

'We are, it's exactly the same, you loved Stavros and gave up everything to be with him because you loved him, I'm doing the same thing for Dieter.'

Vonni paused in her walking and looked at Elsa in astonishment.

'You *can't* believe that it's remotely the same. What are *you* giving up? Nothing. You're getting everything back, your job, your man whom you still don't trust.

You are returning to all that you ran from, and you think that's a victory ...'

Elsa was angry. 'That's not true, Dieter wants to marry me. It will all be out in the open now. We'll live together as man and wife, no more hiding, and then, in time, we will *be* man and wife.' Her eyes flashed.

'And the reason you ran away in the first place ... that was all about forcing him to propose, was it? I thought you said you felt guilty because he had abandoned his daughter and thought it didn't matter. Has all this disgust with him vanished?'

'We only have one life, Vonni. We have to put out our hands and take what we want.'

'No matter who we take it from?'

'You took what you wanted, didn't you?'

'Stavros wasn't promised to anyone else, he was free.'

'What about Christina?'

'I didn't *know* about Christina until I got here, and he had left her, and the baby died, so it was different.'

'What about the money? You took that money. You can't claim to be whiter than white!' Elsa blazed.

'It was only money and I paid it all back, every single penny!'

'You couldn't have, Vonni, that's a fantasy – you earned nothing. You were in and out of that hospital. How could you have raised that money?'

'Well, I'll tell you how. By cleaning floors in the police station, by chopping vegetables up in Andreas's taverna, by cleaning the kitchens in the delicatessen, by teaching English in the school – once I got sober enough for them to trust their children to me.'

'You did all these jobs? Washing floors?'

'I didn't have your qualifications, Elsa ... or your

confidence or your looks. What other way could I raise the money?'

'You got over Stavros in the end, didn't you? Didn't you?'

'Why do you ask?'

'I don't know. I need to know in case I make a different decision.'

'Oh, no, Elsa, you've made your decision: go back and stretch out your hands and take what you want.'

'Why are you so cruel and destructive?' Elsa cried.

'Me cruel and destructive? *Me?* Oh, catch yourself on, Elsa, for God's sake. Just listen to yourself speaking. I told you before that you were too used to getting your own way. And I mean it. There's a careless selfishness about beauty. Magda had it, you have it. It's a lethal thing to have because it gives you too much power for a time. For a time.'

'Did Magda lose her looks? Is this what you're telling me?'

'How would I know?'

'You'd know, someone would have told you,' Elsa said grimly.

'Well, funnily enough, someone did tell me – a few people told me in fact. And she *did* lose her looks, and she has lost quite a lot of Stavros too. Apparently there's a younger woman who works in their business and Stavros sees a lot of this woman.' Vonni smiled at the thought.

'What kind of people tell you these stories? Vindictive people carrying tales?'

'Let me see what kind of people ... Possibly people who think I deserve *some* reward for losing everything and clawing my way back to a position of respectability again.'

'You don't care about respectability,' Elsa scoffed.

'Oh, but I do, we all need respect to be able to live with ourselves and make sense out of the whole thing.'

'You're a free spirit, you don't care what other people think,' Elsa insisted.

'I care what I think of myself, oh, and by the way – I did get over Stavros, though I think of him from time to time. I know his hair is white now, but I would like to see him come up 25th March Street if we could talk as normal people talk. But it's not going to happen.'

'All right, back to my situation.' Elsa was business-like. 'Why should I not go back to Dieter? Just tell me calmly without us arguing about it. Please.'

'It doesn't matter, Elsa.' Vonni sighed. 'You're not going to take any notice of what I say. You are going to do what you want to. Forget I spoke.'

And they walked in awkward silence until they reached the town.

'Shirley?'

'Yes, Thomas?'

'Is Andy there?'

'You don't really want to talk to Andy?'

'No, I was just hoping that I might be able to talk to my son without Andy-the-athlete hopping a ball and getting him away to more training, more workouts.'

'Are you picking a fight, Thomas?'

'No, of course I'm not, I'm telling you straight, I just want to talk to my kid. Okay?'

'Well, hold on, I'll get him for you.'

'And without Muscle Man Andy breathing down his neck, please.'

'You are grossly unfair as usual. Andy always makes himself scarce when you call, then he asks Bill whether he had a good chat with his dad. The only one making any trouble is you.'

'Get him, please Shirley, this is long distance,' Thomas said.

'Well, whose fault is that?'

He could almost hear her shrug.

'Hi, Dad.'

'Bill, tell me about your day,' he said and half listened as the boy went on about a track and field event for families at the university. He and Andy had won a three-legged race.

'Father-son race, was it called?' Thomas asked bitterly.

'No, Dad, they don't call them that now – you know so many families have sort of re-formed themselves.'

'Re-formed themselves?' Thomas gasped.

'Well, that's what our teacher calls it, it's got to do with so many people being divorced and everything.'

It wasn't such a bad word, but it didn't begin to hint at the whole story.

'Sure, so what do they call it?'

'A Senior-Junior race.'

'Great.'

'Are you upset about anything, Dad?'

'Are you on your own now, is it just you and me?'

'Yes, Andy always goes out to the yard when you call and Mom's in the kitchen. Why do you want to know?'

'I wanted to say that I love you.'

'Dad!'

'It's okay, I've said it now. I won't say it any more this call. I got you a wonderful book today, there's a bookshop here in this tiny place. It's stories from Greek myths but written for the modern day. I've been reading it myself all afternoon. Do you know any Greek stories?'

'Is the one about the kids who flew off to find the Golden Fleece a Greek story?'

'Sure it is, tell me a bit about it,' Thomas said, pleased.

'It was about this brother and sister and they rode on the back of a sheep . . .'

'Did you read it at school?'

'Yes, Dad, we have a new history teacher and she keeps making us read stories.'

'That's great, Bill.'

'It'll be great when I have a brother or sister next year.'

His heart felt like a lump of lead. Shirley was pregnant again. And of course she hadn't had the courtesy or courage to tell him. Now she and Andy were starting a family and she had said nothing. Thomas had never felt so alone in his life. But he must keep every door and channel open to Bill.

'That's *great* news, certainly,' he heard himself say through gritted teeth.

'Andy's painting a nursery for it. I told him how you made one for me and put in bookshelves even before I was born.'

And Thomas felt the tears in his eyes as he waded in with his two big feet and broke the whole mood.

'Well, I guess Andy will be busy putting up shelves for trainers and trophies and sports gear for the poor little kid. To hell with books this time round.'

He heard Bill gasp.

'That's not fair, Dad.'

'Life's not fair, Bill,' said Thomas, and hung up.

'Tell me about it,' Vonni said when she saw Thomas's face a couple of hours later.

Thomas didn't move from the chair where he had sat motionless. All day.

'Come on, Thomas, you messed it up again with that kid, didn't you?'

'I got out of his hair, gave him space, did all the things you *should* do, what would you have done?'

'Gone back there, claimed my territory, been a presence for him.'

'Shirley is pregnant,' Thomas said, bleakly.

'He'll need you all the more now if his mother is pregnant. But no, you have to be noble and distant and break that child's heart by giving him space he doesn't want at all.'

'Vonni, you of all people know how hard it is to do the right thing for a child. You've spent a lifetime regretting that. You should understand.'

'Do you know, I *hate* that expression "you of all people" must know this or that. Why should I, of all people, know anything?'

'Because you had a child taken away from you, you know that pain, others only guess at it.'

'I get impatient with people like you, Thomas. Very. I know I am a different generation, my son is your age but I have *never* indulged in self-pity like you do. Especially since the solution is in your own hands. You love this child, nobody but yourself is putting any distance between you and him.'

'You don't understand, I'm on sabbatical leave.'

'They're not going to get out the FBI if you go back to your home town to see your own son.'

'Would that it were so simple,' he sighed.

Vonni went towards the door as if to leave.

'Your bedroom is that way, Vonni.' He nodded his head towards the spare room.

'I'm going to sleep with the hens tonight,' Vonni said. 'They are oddly comforting in a way, just clucking and gurgling. They don't complicate their lives unnecessarily.'

And then she was gone.

Fiona was talking to Mr Leftides, the manager at the Anna Beach Hotel, about a job.

'I could mind the guests' children for you, take them off their parents' hands. I'm a qualified nurse, you see; they would be safe with me.'

'You don't speak any Greek,' the manager objected.

'No, but most of the visitors here are English-speaking, I mean even the Swedes and Germans all speak English.'

She saw Vonni across the foyer, stacking the shelves of the hotel's tiny craft shop.

'Vonni will speak for me,' Fiona said. 'She'll tell you that I can be relied on. Vonni!' she called out. 'Can you tell Mr Leftides that I'd be a good person to work here?'

'As what?' Vonni sounded curt.

'I'm going to need somewhere to live when Elsa goes back, I was asking Mr Leftides if I could work here in exchange for board and lodging and a very little money.' Fiona looked pleadingly at the older woman.

'Why do you need a job – aren't you going home?' Vonni was terse.

'No, you know I can't leave here until Shane comes back.'

'Shane is not coming back.'

'That's not true. Of course he's coming back. Please tell Mr Leftides that I'm reliable.'

'You're not reliable, Fiona, you are deluding yourself that this boy is coming back to you!'

Mr Leftides, who had been looking from one to the other as if he were at a tennis match, decided he had had enough. He shrugged and walked away.

'*Why* did you do that, Vonni?' There were tears of annoyance in Fiona's eyes.

'You are being ridiculous, Fiona. Everyone was sorry for you and kind when you had the miscarriage and all that upset. But surely by now you have come to your senses? You must know there's no future for you here, waiting foolishly for a man who will never return. Go back to Dublin and take up your life.'

'You're so cruel and cold – I thought you were a friend,' Fiona said in a shaky voice.

'I'm the best friend you ever had, if you had the intelligence to see it. Why should a friend try to help set you up in a non-job in this hotel and prolong the agony for yourself? What would you do on your own?'

'I wouldn't be on my own. I have friends, Elsa, Thomas, David.'

'They're all going back. Mark my words you'd be on your own.'

'Would it matter if I were on my own? Shane will come for me, despite what you think. Now I have to find somewhere else to work, to live.' She turned away to hide the fact that she was crying.

'Vonni, you want a Morning Glory?' Andreas often looked into the craft shop and treated her to a little metal dish with three colours of ice cream across the road in Yanni's delicatessen.

'No, I'd prefer a bottle of vodka with a lot of ice,' she said.

Andreas was startled. Vonni never joked about her drinking, and did not refer to her alcoholic past.

'Is there a problem?' he asked.

'Yes, there is. I've fought with every one of those foreign kids, every single one of them.'

'I thought you liked them, they're all very attached to you.' Andreas was very surprised.

'I don't know what it is, Andreas, I'm like a weasel, nothing would please me these days. Everything they say annoys me.'

'That's unlike you, you are always keeping the peace, smoothing things down . . .'

'Not these days, I'm not, Andreas, I feel like stirring everything up. I suppose it was the boat and all the unnecessary waste of life, it makes everything seem pointless. I can't see any sense in anything.' She was pacing around her little shop.

'There's a lot of sense in your life,' he said.

'Is there? Is there really? Today I can't see any. I think I'm a foolish woman perched here in this faraway place until I die.'

'Vonni, we are all perched here until we die.' Andreas was bewildered.

'No, you don't understand, there's a sense of useless-
ness about it all somehow. I used to feel like this years
back, and then I would go up to the top of the town and
hit the *raki* until I was senseless. Don't let me go down
that road again, Andreas, my good friend.'

He laid his hand on hers.

'Of course I won't. You've fought so hard to get out
of that pit you fell into, nobody is going to let you fall in
again.'

'But what a stupid life I've lived – people having to
mind me, look after me, rescue me. I think telling those
young people all about it over the past couple of days
made me realise how stupid I've been, how selfish.
That's why I suddenly want to drink and forget it all.'

'You normally forget problems by helping other
people, that's what gets you by, that's why they all love
you so much here.'

'If that's true then it's stopped working for me, and,
do you know, I don't want to help anyone any more, I
want to blank things out. And people certainly don't
love me any more. I think everyone is running a
hundred kilometres away from me at the moment.'

Andreas made a sudden decision. 'I need your help,
Vonni, my hands are stiff, can you come and help me
make *dolmadhes*? I can't bend the old fingers to stuff the
vine leaves. Please close your shop here and come up to
the taverna with me. As a favour, will you?'

'And of course you'll have plenty of coffee and ice
cream to distract me and keep me away from the demon
drink.' She gave him a weak smile.

'Certainly. That was my very plan,' he said, and they
went out of the door together.

Thomas was running down the whitewashed outdoor

stairs, but he couldn't have seen them as he ran by without saying hallo.

They sat and discussed her at midday by the harbour.

'I can understand her attacking me, because, to be very honest, a lot of people have a problem with Shane,' Fiona said. 'But the rest of you? I don't get it.'

They thought about it for a while.

'It's easy to see where she's coming from with me,' Elsa said. 'I'm a tramp who has somehow blackmailed a poor innocent guy into proposing to her.'

'And did he?' Thomas asked.

'Yes, but it's much more complex than that. Why has Vonni turned on you?' Elsa changed the subject.

Thomas rubbed his chin thoughtfully. 'I truthfully don't know what annoyed her so much about my situation, but she went on about how I had a choice over my son, and she didn't. I felt tempted to say that at least I didn't lose my senses in a vat of alcohol like she did. But I didn't want to offend her, I just wanted her to agree I was trying to be responsible and do the right thing.'

David tried to stand up for Vonni. 'You can see why she envies you though. If she had been allowed any-where near her son she'd have been there. She knows it's her own fault – that's what makes her so enraged.'

'You're very forgiving, David, after all, she lit into you unmercifully as well,' Fiona said.

'Yes, but she got that all wrong, you see, she doesn't know what kind of people my parents are, she doesn't begin to understand. I've read that letter over and over and there's nothing in it to suggest that my father isn't well . . .'

'But David, why did she get angry with you exactly?' Elsa asked.

'Because I was saying what a good man Andreas was and how selfish his son was not to come back and help him. She said I was putting Andreas on some kind of pedestal and that a lot of people might say I was exactly the same as Adoni, staying away instead of helping my father. But, of course, it's a totally different thing.' He looked around the table and thought he saw a look on their faces that suggested it might not be so different after all.

'I have to go and give Maria her lesson,' he said a little stiffly and went over to the house where the black-clad young widow was waving at him from the door.

David could manage a feeble conversation in Greek with Maria by now. It was halting and stumbling, but he managed to understand that she thought he was leaving the island soon. Vonni had told her that his father was ill back in England.

'No!' David cried. 'He is well! Very well!'

'Vonni say you telephone home,' Maria said.

It was hard enough to explain the situation to people who could speak English. With Maria it was impossible.

'No telephone home,' David stammered in Greek.

'*Yiati*?' she asked. It was the Greek word for why. David had no answer.

Vonni rolled up the vine leaves neatly around their little packages of rice and pine nuts. She was very quiet.

Andreas looked at her from under his big bushy eyebrows. She was right to be concerned. She had the same sense of unease and restlessness that had led her to those frightening drinking bouts all those years ago.

He wondered if he should contact his sister Christina. She and Vonni had been good friends and a huge mutual support. But then, he would do nothing without consulting Vonni.

Her face was lined as always, but today she had a deeply worried look. She frowned and gnawed at her lip.

They worked on the open-air terrace looking down over the town. Twice she got up and went into his kitchen for no reason. He watched her without appearing to do so. Once she reached up to where bottles of brandy and olive oil stood on a line on the shelf.

But she took her hand away.

The second time she just went in and looked. She touched nothing. She was breathing fast as if she had run in a race.

'What can I do for you, Vonni? Tell me,' he begged.

'I've done nothing of any use in my life, Andreas. What can anyone do for me? Ever?'

'You've been a good friend to my sister, to me, to all the people in Aghia Anna. That's worth while, isn't it?'

'Not particularly. I'm not looking for pity, I hate that in a person, it's just that I actually can't see any point in the past, the present or the future.' Her voice was flat.

'Well, then, you'd better open the brandy,' Andreas said.

'Brandy?'

'Metaxa brandy. It's on the shelf in there, you've been looking at it all morning. Take it down, drink it, then none of us will have to worry about *when* you're going to do it, it will be done.'

'Why are you saying this?'

'Because it's one way to go. You can throw away the work and discipline and denial of years in an hour or so.

Because it will bring this oblivion you want. It will probably bring it quite quickly since you're not used to it.'

'And you, my friend, would stand by while I did this?'

'If you're going to do it, better it's up here, away from all the eyes of Aghia Anna,' he said philosophically.

'I don't *want* to,' she said piteously.

'No, I know that. But if you see nothing in the past, the present or the future, then I suppose you have to,' he said.

'And do *you* see any point in anything?' she asked.

'Some days it's harder than others,' Andreas said. 'You have good friends everywhere, Vonni.'

'No, I end up driving them away.'

'Who are you thinking about?'

'That foolish little Fiona, I told her her boyfriend won't come back. She was in tears. But then, I know where he is. She doesn't know.'

'Hush, hush, don't you get upset too.'

'I had no right to do it, Andreas. I'm not God.'

'You did it for the best,' he soothed her.

'I must tell her where he is,' Vonni said suddenly.

'I wonder if that's wise?'

'Can I use your telephone, Andreas?'

'Please . . .'

He heard her dial the number and then speak to Fiona. 'I called to say I had no right to shout at you today. To say that I'm sorry. Very sorry.'

Andreas moved away to give her privacy. He knew how very hard it was for Vonni to admit that she was wrong.

In Elsa's villa, Fiona looked at the telephone in her

hand, mystified. Whatever she had expected it wasn't this. She was at a loss to know what to say.

'That's okay, Vonni,' she said awkwardly.

'No, it's not okay as it happens. The reason he didn't get in touch is because he's in jail in Athens.'

'Shane in jail! Oh, my God, what for?'

'Something to do with drugs.'

'No wonder I haven't heard from him. Poor Shane – and would they not let him get in touch and tell me?'

'He did try to get in touch eventually, but only so that you'd get him bail, and we said—'

'But of course I'll get him bail. Why did nobody tell me?'

'Because we thought you'd be better without him,' Vonni said lamely.

Fiona was outraged. '*We* thought, who is *we*?'

'Yorghis and I, but mainly me,' Vonni admitted.

'How dare you, Vonni! How dare you meddle in my life? Now he thinks I haven't bothered to get in touch with him. All because of you.'

'That's why I'm getting in touch now,' Vonni said. 'I'll take you to him.'

'What?'

'I owe it to you. I'll go with you on the ferry to Athens in the morning, take you to the jail, find out what's happening.'

'Why are you doing this?' Fiona was suspicious.

'I suppose I realised that it is your life,' said Vonni. 'I'll see you at the harbour for the eight o'clock ferry tomorrow morning.' Then she came back and sat down with Andreas.

'Did that work?' he asked.

'I don't know, tomorrow will tell. But I feel stronger

somehow. You know the way you said a while ago that some days are better than others? How is it for you today?'

'Not great. I wrote to Adoni in Chicago and he would certainly have got the letter by now. But there's no word from him. It was hard to write, and it's even harder to bear that there's no reply. But I think we have to keep struggling on, Vonni. Manos and those boys on the boat didn't get a chance to, so I'm going to keep going until the end.'

'You wrote to Adoni?' Her eyes were bright and interested.

'Yes, nobody knows but you and Yorghis.'

'I'm so glad; you are great to do that. He'll get in touch. Believe me.'

'Why should I believe you? Seriously, you don't believe in anything yourself. Why should anyone heed what you say?'

'I know he'll ring. Is your answering machine switched on? You're always forgetting. Adoni will come back, I know he will. Suppose he comes back soon? Is his room ready?'

'It's as he left it,' Andreas shrugged.

'But we should paint it, make it smart for him.'

'He may never come back, we are only storing up more heartbreak.'

'We must not be defeatist, that's the worst crime, let's do it today. I've finished the bloody *dolmadhes* – stick them in the refrigerator and get out some paint. Have you got brushes?'

'Yes, in the shed at the back – they may be a bit hard and stiff, I'll see if we have paint remover.'

'Right, but keep a beady eye on me, one whiff of that and I could be on the slippery slope.'

He looked at her in astonishment. She truly had turned a corner. There was life and enthusiasm in her face. It was worth painting the bedroom with her just to keep it going.

Even if that boy never came, it would be worth it.

Chapter Fourteen

'Mother?'

'David!' The delight in her voice was hard to take.

'Mother, I got your letter. About the award.'

'Oh, David, I just knew that you'd call. I knew it. You're such a good boy to phone so quickly.'

'Well, you see, I'm not certain yet what's happening ...' He did not want to be railroaded into dates of return, times of flights, seating plans and what he would wear to the function.

'Your father will be so pleased when he hears you called. It will make his day.'

Already he felt the familiar heavy weight that their pressure always created, it was in his chest and around his shoulders.

His mother was still talking excitedly. 'He'll be back in about an hour and that will really cheer him up.'

'He's not in the office on a Saturday surely?'

'No, no, just ... um ... out ...'

David was surprised.

His father did not go to synagogue every week, only

at the High Holidays. Saturdays were always spent at home.

'What's he doing?' David asked.

'Oh, you know . . . this and that . . .' His mother was evasive.

David felt suddenly cold. 'Is Father ill?' he asked suddenly.

'What makes you think that?' He could hear the fear in her voice.

'I don't know, Mother, I sort of got the idea that he might have an illness and that he wasn't telling me, neither of you were.'

'You got that feeling suddenly, far away in Greece?' She spoke in wonder.

'Sort of.' He shuffled. 'But is it true, Mother?'

He felt that time was standing still as he waited for her to answer. It could only have been seconds but it felt like an age. He watched from the phone box by the harbour as the day's work went on, crates being loaded and unloaded on boats, crowds going about their business normally as he waited.

'Your father has cancer of the colon, David, they can't operate. They've given him six months.'

There was a silence on the line as he caught his breath.

'Does he know, Mother? Has he been told?'

'Yes, that's what they do these days, they tell people. He's very calm.'

'And is he in pain?'

'No, amazingly, he has a lot of medication.'

David gave a gulping sound, as if he were trying to stifle a sob.

'Ah, David don't get upset, he's very resigned, he's not afraid.'

'Why didn't you tell me?'

'You know your father, he is such a proud man, he didn't want you coming back just out of pity, he wouldn't let me tell you.'

'I see,' David said miserably.

'But he didn't bank on your knowing by telepathy, David. Imagine you sensing that from all that distance away. It's uncanny, but then you were always sensitive.'

David had rarely felt so ashamed in his life.

'I'll call again on Monday,' he said.

'With your plans?' his mother said eagerly.

'With my plans,' he said wretchedly.

Thomas called his mother.

'Don't call me from so far away, son, wasting all the money on me.'

'It's okay, Mom, I get my full salary, I told you, plenty to live on like a millionaire out here, and to pay support for Bill.'

'And to send me treats too. You're a good boy, I love those magazines you send me every month. I'd never go out and buy them for myself.'

'I know, Mom, everything for us, nothing for you. That was always your rule.'

'It's what most people do when they have children, not that it always works. I've been blessed with you and your brother, it's not always the way.'

'It's not easy being a parent, is it, Mom?'

'I didn't find it too bad, but then my spouse went and died on me rather than take up with someone else like yours did.'

'It takes two to break up a marriage, Mom, it wasn't all Shirley's fault.'

'No, but when are you finding yourself a partner?'

'One day, I assure you, and you'll be one of the first to know. Mom, I called to ask you about Bill. Do you talk to him at all?'

'You know I do, son, I call him every Sunday. He's doing fine at school, playing lots of games – he loves sport now.'

'Sure he does, now that his boring old father isn't there to annoy him with books and poetry and things.'

'He misses you like hell, Thomas, you know that.'

'Hasn't he got Golden Boy Andy and a new brother or sister on the way? What does he want me for?'

'He told me you didn't feel good about the new baby,' his mother said.

'I was meant to dance with joy about it, I suppose,' Thomas said bitterly.

'He said he thought you would love the new baby, like Andy loves him even though he's nothing to him.'

'He honestly thought I'd love the new baby?' Thomas was astounded.

'He's a child, Thomas. He's just nine years of age, his father has left him, left America. He was clutching at straws. He thought that maybe you would come back if there was a new baby for you to be stepfather to, like Andy is to him.'

'Andy is a horse's ass, Mom.'

'He may well be, son, but he's a kind horse's ass, Thomas,' his mother said.

'*I'm* kind, Mom.'

'I'm sure you are, in fact I know you are, but I'm not entirely sure Bill knows that.'

'Come on, Mom, I've done the right thing, given him

his freedom, not crowded him out. I've let him adjust to his new life.'

'Yeah, and at the age of nine a child will understand all that?'

'What do you think I should do?'

'I don't know, be near him, not thousands of miles away, I guess.'

'You think that would sort it?'

'I don't know, but at least Bill wouldn't think you, who are his flesh and blood, had abandoned him.'

'Sure, Mom, I hear what you say.'

Elsa read the second fax from Dieter.

> *I know you read what I wrote last week. They told me in the hotel that the message had been given to you. Please stop playing games, Elsa; just tell me when you are coming back. You are not the only player on the stage, I have my life to lead too. Why should I tell anyone anything about us until I know that you are coming back and when.*
>
> *Please answer me today.*
> *I love you for ever,*
> *Dieter*

She read it over and over and tried to hear his voice as if he were speaking the words. She could hear it very well. Dieter speaking quickly, decisively and urgently. *Please answer me today.*

It was he who was playing the central figure on the stage. Had he forgotten that this was all about her life, her future? How dare he ask her for such a speedy answer. She went to the little business centre in the Anna Beach where you could send e-mails.

It's a big decision. I need time to think. Don't hassle me. I'll write in a few days.

I love you for ever also, but that's not the only consideration.

Elsa

Fiona woke very early, she saw the dawn come up over Aghia Anna. She could hardly believe the conversation that she had had with Vonni last night.

She was still furious with Vonni and Yorghis for having lied to her. How dare they tell her that Shane had not been in touch? How dare they leave her with this sick feeling that Shane might possibly have abandoned her, left her because she was too stupid, too thick? But he *had* tried to contact her and these old busybodies had interfered.

They said his motive was only to get her to raise the bail money. Well, of course he had to get bail first to get out, to get on with life. What did they expect?

She was so glad that she would see him today.

She was not relishing the thought of the ferry trip with Vonni as a companion. She wished too that she hadn't told it all to Elsa last night. Elsa had been less than supportive.

Fiona wished mightily that she could turn the clock back. Why had she asked Elsa to help her raise the money? To lend her a thousand euros, just for a few days until Barbara could send it to her from Dublin.

'Lend you money to get him out to finish off your face?' Elsa had scoffed.

'That was different,' Fiona began. 'He was in shock, I told him the news all wrong you see.'

Elsa had lifted Fiona's hair. 'The discoloration and the bruises are still there,' she had said softly. 'Nobody on earth, Fiona, is going to lend you money to get that guy out of a place where he should be kept permanently.'

Fiona must have looked desolate because Elsa had become contrite immediately.

'Look, I'm as bad as Vonni lecturing you, I know it's hard, I *know* this. But I'll tell you what I'm trying to do, I'm trying to stand outside myself to look at things, my own situation, I mean, objectively. Look in on it rather than be a part of it. That might help you too.'

Fiona had shaken her head. 'I don't think it would do anything except make me see from the outside poor Shane, who loves me and who tried to contact me, languishing in a Greek prison. That's all I can see, Elsa, Shane thinking I've abandoned him. And it isn't helping me at all.'

Elsa had looked at her with the kind of look you might give to a picture of a starving orphan in an advertisement for famine relief. It was a look of pity, concern and bewilderment that such things were allowed to happen in the world.

When Vonni and Fiona met at the harbour, Vonni had bought the tickets. Two day returns. Fiona opened her mouth to say that she would not be coming back today. But closed it again.

'You've brought a big bag with you?' Vonni said, surprised.

'Well, you never know.' Fiona was vague.

The ferry pulled out of the harbour and Fiona looked

back at Aghia Anna. So much had happened since she came here such a short time ago.

Vonni had gone downstairs to where they were serving coffee and drinks. Suppose she suddenly went back on the drink. Here on this boat. It could happen. Andreas had told David that Vonni was very low and for the first time in years had actually mentioned the possibility of drinking. Please God may it not happen when they were out on the high seas.

To her relief she saw Vonni returning with coffee and two sticky-looking cakes.

'*Loukoumadhes*,' she explained. 'They're honey frit-ters with cinnamon. They'll give you great energy for the day.'

Fiona looked at her gratefully. The woman was making every attempt at an apology. Fiona knew she must be gracious.

'You have been kindness itself,' she said, patting Vonni's hand.

To her surprise she saw tears in Vonni's eyes. And they sat companionably and ate their honey cakes.

'Yorghis?'

'Andreas! I was just thinking of you, come in, come in!' The chief of police pulled up a chair for his brother.

'Yorghis, something has happened . . .'

'A good thing or a bad thing?' Yorghis asked.

'I don't know.'

'Come on, you must know.'

'No, I *don't* know. There was a message on the answering machine in English. It was from the store where Adoni works. They said that as soon as I saw him I was to ask him to telephone about the keys to a storeroom which none of them could find. It was a complicated message but it was as if they thought . . . as if they believed he might be . . .'

Yorghis grasped his brother's hand. 'Do you think that means he might be coming home?' he asked, almost afraid to get the words out.

'It might mean that, Yorghis, it might,' said Andreas, his face alive with hope.

In the newsroom, Elsa's friend Hannah saw Dieter sitting alone and went up to him. Normally people didn't approach the great Dieter unless it was very important indeed. But she judged that this was fairly urgent. Hannah had just got an e-mail. Very short and to the point.

> *I feel very safe and peaceful in this small town. It's a good place to make decisions. But everything moves slowly here including my brain. If Dieter does ask about me, can you please say that I'm not playing games. I am thinking things through and will be in touch. He probably won't ask you, but I wanted you to be prepared.*
> *Love, Elsa*

Hannah laid it on Dieter's desk.

'I know you didn't exactly ask . . .' she said hesitantly.

'But I am very pleased to read this. Thank you, Hannah.' He had remembered her name, which was unusual for Dieter.

Vonni pointed out the places the ferry passed by. This was an island where there had once been a leper colony;

that was a place which had suffered in an earthquake; this was a place where they had a festival in the springtime; here was a headland where a whole village left overnight and went to Canada, no one knew what made them leave.

'Weren't you lucky that you came to this land, Vonni? You love it so much.'

'Lucky?' Vonni said. 'I sometimes wonder about luck.'

'What do you wonder about it?'

'I don't think there's any such thing really. Look at all the people hoping for luck, buying lottery tickets, all the thousands going to Las Vegas, the millions reading their horoscopes, people hunting for four-leafed clovers or not walking under ladders. It's all fairly pointless, isn't it?'

'But people need to have some hope,' Fiona said.

'Sure they do, but we *make* our own luck, we make decisions which turn out well or badly, there isn't anything outside us that works like a black cat crossing our path or being born under the sign of Scorpio.'

'Or a prayer to St Jude?' Fiona suggested with a smile.

'You're surely too young to have heard of St Jude!' Vonni said.

'My gran relied on him entirely to find her spectacles, for her numbers to come up at bingo, for her horrible little yapping Jack Russell terrier to get over his fits. Anything at all, St Jude was called on. And he always obliged.'

'Always?' Vonni was sceptical.

'Well, maybe not in the case of her eldest granddaughter! Gran had St Jude on standby to find me a nice rich doctor to marry. That one didn't take.'

Fiona grinned proudly as if single-handedly she had defeated St Jude, the famed patron saint of hopeless cases, and thwarted his plans by sticking resolutely to Shane.

'Are you looking forward to seeing him?' Vonni asked.

'I can't wait, I hope he won't be angry that it took me so long.' The sense of accusation and outrage was still there.

'I told you, I'll explain, I'll tell him it wasn't your fault.'

'I know you will, Vonni, thank you . . . it's just . . . you know . . .' Fiona was twisting her hands awkwardly, trying to explain something.

'Tell me,' Vonni encouraged her.

'Well, you've met Shane, he can be a bit difficult you know, say things that sound much more aggressive than they are. It's just the way he reacts. I wouldn't want you to think . . .'

'Don't worry, Fiona, I won't think anything,' said Vonni through gritted teeth.

'Elsa! I'm delighted to see you,' Thomas called.

'Well you must be the only person on this island who is,' Elsa said.

'You can't mean that. I was going to rent a rowing boat and go out for a couple of hours, would you trust me enough to come with me?'

'I'd love it. Shall we go now?'

'Sure. David's not coming to the café, his father is ill, Vonni was right about that anyway. He's going to arrange a ticket home.'

'Poor David.' Elsa was sympathetic. 'And Fiona's

gone to Athens with Vonni. She left this morning, very angry with me, because I wouldn't lend her money to bail Shane out of prison.'

'So we're on our own,' Thomas said.

'I'd love a farewell boat journey, I'll help with the rowing if you like.'

'No, lie back and enjoy it. A farewell journey? You *are* going back to Germany then?'

'Oh yes, I don't know exactly what day, but I am going.'

'Is he very pleased, Dieter?'

'He doesn't know yet,' she said simply.

Thomas was surprised. 'Why haven't you told him?' he asked.

'I don't know, there are a few things I haven't sorted out in my mind,' Elsa said.

'I see,' said Thomas, in the voice of one who didn't.

'And you, Thomas, when will *you* go back?'

'It depends a bit,' he said.

'On what?'

'On whether I really believe Bill wants me there.' He spoke candidly.

'Of course he does, that's obvious,' Elsa said.

'How is it so obvious to you?' he wondered.

'Because *my* father left us when I was young. I would have given anything to have had a phone call saying that he was on the way home to live near our street and I could see him every day. That would have been the best thing that could have happened. But it never did.'

Thomas looked at her, astounded. She made it seem so simple, so easy. He put his arm around her shoulder and headed down to where they hired out the brightly coloured boats.

*

In the crowded harbour of Piraeus, Fiona followed, lugging her heavy bag with her, as Vonni led the way to the *Ilektrikos* and bought the tickets.

'It's a fine place on its own apart altogether from being beside Athens,' Vonni explained. 'Full of marvellous little fish restaurants, and there's a great big bronze statue of Apollo – but we've no time for any of that now.'

'Do you know, I'm a bit afraid of seeing him again,' Fiona said, as they got on the Métro for Athens.

'But he loves you, he'll be delighted to see you, won't he?' Vonni asked doubtfully.

'Yes, yes of course. It's just that we don't know how much the bail will be, and really I'm not sure how I'm going to get it when we *do* know. It's not the kind of thing that they're going to help me with from Dublin. I might have to tell them back home that it's for something else.'

Vonni said nothing.

'But of course he'll be very pleased to see a friendly face.'

'You're not really afraid of seeing him, are you?' Vonni asked.

'Well, I think you're always a bit nervous of someone you love,' Fiona said. 'It sort of goes with the territory, doesn't it?'

Yorghis had phoned ahead to let them know that Vonni and Fiona were on their way. He had given a short thumbnail sketch of who they were. The policeman at the Athens station listened to him until he finished.

'Well, if this foolish girl can somehow raise the bail

and get him out of our sight there will be nobody more pleased than us,' he said grimly. 'We'd nearly give her the money ourselves to be rid of him.'

As they went into the police station Fiona paused to take out her compact and comb. Vonni watched stricken as the girl applied makeup to the yellowed bruise on her forehead and arranged her hair so that it disguised it still further. She put on some lipstick and sprayed cologne on her wrists and behind her ears.

She smiled at her own reflection to give herself confidence.

'I'm ready now,' she said to Vonni in a shaky voice.

They only told Shane ten minutes before the visit that Fiona was on her way.

'Has she got the money?' he asked.

'What money?' Dimitri, the young policeman, asked.

'The money you bloodsuckers want, to give me back my human liberties!' Shane shouted, kicking at the side of his cell.

'Do you want a clean shirt to wear for her visit?' Dimitri was impassive.

'You want it all to look good and squeaky clean – no, I don't want a bloody fresh shirt, I want her to see things as they are.'

'They'll be here very shortly.' The policeman was curt.

'They?'

'She has another woman from Aghia Anna with her.'

'Another lame duck, that's just typical of Fiona, she takes her time getting here and then she drags someone else in on the act.'

As he closed and locked the door, Dimitri reflected on

the nature of love. He himself was engaged to be married. He was a solid, reliable person, and sometimes he worried that he might be too dull for his glamorous-looking fiancée. They often said that girls liked a whiff of danger. That old policeman in Aghia Anna had said that the young woman who was coming to see Shane was a nurse, a gentle soul, an attractive girl . . . Heigh-ho as they said. He must not make generalisations.

'How old are you, Andreas?'

'I am sixty-eight years old,' Andreas said.

'My father is sixty-six, and he is dying,' David said.

'Oh, David, I am so very sad to hear that, really so very sad.'

'Thank you, Andreas, my friend, I know that is the truth.'

'You will go home to be with him?'

'Yes, I will, of course I will.'

'And he is going to be so pleased to have you there. Believe me. Can I advise you on something? Be very kind to him. I know you were all upset when Vonni tried to give you advice . . .' Andreas sounded hesitant.

'Yes, I was annoyed, but it turned out that she was right, I tried to find her and tell her, but she's not here . . .'

'No, she went to Athens today, but she will be home tonight.'

'Suppose you were ill, Andreas, what would you like your son to say to you?'

'I think I would like him to tell me that I had been a reasonable father to him,' Andreas said.

'I'll say that when I get home,' David said.

'He will be happy to hear that, David.'

*

They led Vonni and Fiona to the holding cell to see Shane.

Dimitri opened the door. 'Your friends are here,' he said tersely.

'Shane!' Fiona cried.

'You took your time.'

'I didn't know where you were until yesterday,' she said, moving towards him.

'Huh,' Shane said, not responding to her arms held out to him.

'I was responsible for all that, I did not pass on the fact that you had been in touch,' Vonni said.

'Who the hell are you?' Shane asked.

'I'm Vonni, from Ireland originally, but I've lived in Aghia Anna for over thirty years. I'm sort of a local there by now.'

'What are you doing here?' he asked.

'I came with Fiona to help get her here to see you.'

'Okay, thank you. Can you piss off now and leave me with my girlfriend?' he asked with darkened brow.

'Up to you, Fiona,' Vonni said pleasantly.

'Not up to her actually. Up to me,' Shane said.

'Perhaps you could wait for me . . . a bit . . . outside, Vonni?' Fiona begged.

'I'll be there when you need me, Fiona,' Vonni said and left.

Dimitri was waiting outside the door.

'*Dhen pirazi*,' she said to him.

'What?' he said, alarmed.

'I've lived here for years,' she said in his own language. 'I am married to a Greek, I have a Greek son older than you are, I was saying, *Dhen pirazi*, it doesn't

245

matter, nothing matters, that fool of a girl is going to forgive that horrific boy everything.'

'Perhaps women *like* those kind of men.' Dimitri had misery written all over his face.

'Don't believe it. They do not love nor even like people like that. For a time, they might think it's love. But it passes, women can be foolish but they are not idiots. Fiona will soon realise what a horror that boy in your cell is. It's only a question of when.'

Dimitri seemed pleased with her confidence in this matter.

'Who's that old bat you brought with you?' Shane asked.

'She was very kind.'

'Sure,' he scoffed.

Fiona moved towards him to kiss him, to hold him to her, but he didn't seem to be interested.

'Shane, it's so great to see you,' she said.

'Did you bring the money?' he asked.

'Sorry?'

'The money, to get me out!' he said.

'But, Shane, I don't *have* any money. You know that.' Fiona's eyes were enormous. Why was he not reaching out to hold her?

'Tell me you didn't eventually turn up here with nothing to say?' he asked.

'I have plenty to say, Shane . . .'

'Say it then.'

Fiona wondered why were they still not embracing, but she knew she must keep talking. She didn't know whether to tell him the good news or the bad news first.

'Well, the good news is that I heard from Barbara.

There are lovely apartments very near the hospital and we could easily get one and go back there.'

He looked at her uncomprehending.

Fiona spoke quickly. 'But the sad news is that we lost our baby. It was awful but it happened. Dr Leros said that there are no problems – as soon as we want to try again . . .'

'What?'

'I know you're upset, Shane, I was too, desperately, but Dr Leros said—'

'Fiona, shut up talking rubbish about Dr this and Dr that. Do you have the money or do you not?'

'Sorry, Shane, what are you saying?'

'Have you the money to get me out?'

'Of course I don't have the money, Shane, I told you, I came to see you, to talk about it, to tell you that I love you and it will all be all right . . .'

'How will it all be all right?'

'Shane – I'll borrow it and we'll get this flat back in Dublin and we'll pay the money back . . .'

'Oh, Fiona, stop wittering on, for Christ's sake. Where are we going to get the bail?'

He still hadn't touched her, held her or talked about their dead baby.

'Shane, aren't you sad about the baby?'

'Shut up and tell me where on God's earth we're going to find the *money*!' he said.

'I lay in a bed and our baby drained away,' Fiona said.

'That was not a child, it was a period. You *know* that, Fiona, so just tell me where we are going to get the money?'

'We'll ask them, Vonni and I will, how much it is they

want and then I'll try and raise it – but that's not the most important thing, Shane . . .'

'So what's the most important thing?' he asked.

'Well, that I've found you and that I love you for ever.' She looked at him waiting to see a response.

There was nothing.

'I adore you, Shane . . .' she said.

'Sure,' he said.

'So why don't you kiss me?' she asked.

'Oh God, Fiona, will you shut up about love and think who might get us the money,' he said.

'If we are able to borrow it, then we'll have to get a job to pay it back,' she said anxiously.

'*You* get a job if you want to, as soon as I'm out of here I have people to meet, contacts to make. I'll have plenty of money then.'

'You're not coming back to Aghia Anna?'

'That dump? No way.'

'So where will you go, Shane?'

'I'll hang round Athens for a bit and then I might move up to Istanbul. It depends.'

'What does it depend on?'

'On who I meet, on what they say.'

She looked at him levelly. 'And am I to go with you to meet people and go to Istanbul and everywhere?'

He shrugged. 'If you want to, but you're not to nag me about settling down and getting jobs and dragging me back to that one-horse town. We left Ireland to get away from all that kind of shit.'

'No, we left Ireland because we loved each other and nobody understood it, they kept putting difficulties in our way.'

'Whatever,' Shane said.

She knew that tone of voice. It was his switch-off voice. He used it when talking to people who bored him rigid. When they had escaped from such people, Shane would sigh with relief and say that there were so many laws and restrictions in place, why wasn't there a law against bores?

Fiona knew now that she bored Shane. She began to understand that he had never loved her.

Never at all.

It was staggering and almost impossible to take in but she knew she was right. It meant that all this had been for nothing, all her hopes and dreams. All the fears and anxieties of the last few days when she had been sleepless in case he would not get in touch. He would never have got in touch if he hadn't wanted the money for bail.

She knew that her mouth was open and her eyes widening. She knew that from the way he was looking at her.

'What are you gawping at?' Shane asked her.

'You don't love me,' she said in a shaky voice.

'Oh, Lord God above, how often do I have to play the record? I *said* you could come with me if you wanted to. I just begged you not to nag me. Is that a crime? Tell me.'

There was a wooden chair in the corner. Fiona sat down and buried her head in her hands.

'No, Fiona, not now. Not when we have to think what to do. This is not the time to go all weepy and emotional on me. Leave it off, will you . . .'

She looked up at him, her hair was back from her face. Despite the makeup, the bruising was still very visible.

He stared at her.

'What happened to your face?' he asked, as if somehow repelled by it.

'You did it, Shane. In the restaurant out on the point.' She had never before referred to his having beaten her. This was a first.

He began to bluster. 'I did *not*,' he said.

Fiona was calm. 'You've probably forgotten. It's not important any more.'

She stood up as if to leave.

'Where are you going? You've only just got here, we have to work this out.'

'No, Shane, *you* have to work it out.'

'Stop threatening me.'

'I'm not threatening you, nor nagging you. I've seen you and now I'm leaving.'

'But the money? The bail?' His face was distorted. 'Look, I'll say all that stuff about love if it's what you want ... Fiona, don't go!'

She knocked on the door and Dimitri opened it for her. He seemed to have taken in the situation. There was a smile on his face.

This drove Shane into a frenzy. He leaped towards Fiona and caught her by the hair.

'You are *not* coming in here playing games like this with me!' he roared.

But Dimitri was more speedy than anyone would have thought. He had his arm across Shane's throat, forcing his chin upwards. It meant he had to let go of Fiona in order to fight off the policeman.

It was no contest.

Dimitri was big and fit. Shane was no match for him.

Fiona stood at the door for a moment, watching, then

she moved out into the corridor and walked to the front office.

Vonni was sitting there with a senior policeman.

'They're talking about two thousand euros,' she began.

'Let them talk about it, he's not getting it from me,' Fiona said. Her head was high, her eyes were bright.

Vonni looked at her, hardly daring to hope. Could it really be over? Could Fiona be free? It looked very like it indeed ...

Chapter Fifteen

Thomas rowed the little boat back to the harbour. It seemed like coming home.

They looked up towards the hills and pointed to the places they knew. That was the hospital in the Kalatriada road. And that was the road up to Andreas's taverna.

And there, finally, was the harbour and the café with the check tablecloths. It was all so different from California and Germany. They sighed as they came into the arms of the harbour.

It was as if the escapism were over.

Thomas and Elsa had returned the little boat.

'It was good, your voyage?' the old man asked.

'Very good voyage,' Elsa said with a smile.

'*Avrio*? You come again for the boat tomorrow?' Business had been slow and the old man wanted to secure as many bookings as he could.

'Possibly, but not certainly,' Thomas said. He didn't want to promise something that could not be delivered. He knew that Elsa would be spending tomorrow getting ready for her trip back home. They hadn't talked about it but they both knew the leisurely row along the coastline had been a form of goodbye.

They walked up the harbour road towards the town.

'I wonder if we'll forget this place eventually,' Thomas said.

At exactly the same moment, Elsa said, 'Imagine all this busy world going on without us!'

They laughed at thinking almost the same thought, and as they were passing a café, Thomas indicated that they should sit down.

'Why not?' Elsa was pleased. 'By this day next week there'll be very little chance of dropping into a café, let's make the most of it.'

'Ah, you speak for yourself,' Thomas said. 'I'll still be here dropping into cafés, rowing boats, reading in the sunshine.'

'No, you'll be on your way back to California,' she said with a great sense of being right about it.

'Elsa! You're as bad as Vonni. I told you I'm only three months into my sabbatical, I'm not going back until the year is over. And even if I could, it would only make things worse.' He was puzzled at her certainty.

'I'll send you a postcard, you'll be there to get it,' she laughed.

'You are so wrong. Why should I go?'

'Because the great goddess of this island Vonni has said you should go, and when she speaks, things happen. And look, David is leaving tomorrow . . .'

'But he's the only one, and his father *is* dying – he *has* to go, she was right about him. The rest of us aren't taking any heed of her. Fiona's gone to Athens to find her madman, you're leaving, I'm staying. One out of four – that's not a great strike rate.'

'The game isn't over, I'd say she'll have a much higher strike rate in the end.'

Andreas came over to their table.

'May I join you? I have some good news to share.'

'Adoni?' Elsa gasped with excitement.

Andreas shook his head. 'No, not as good as that, alas, but still good. The little Fiona has turned her back on Shane, she has walked out on him, straight out of the police station. She and Vonni are on the last ferry, they will be back by sunset.'

'How do you know?' Thomas asked.

'One of the police telephoned Yorghis with the news. She did not even try to raise his bail – just left.' Andreas spread out his hands at the mystery of it all.

'But why? Why on earth did she go to all that trouble and then walk out on him?' Elsa was mystified.

'Apparently he hit her, or hurt her somehow,' Andreas said hesitantly.

'Well, he sure did that before and it didn't worry her,' Thomas said grimly.

'This must have been different. Something happened there to make her see him as he is.' Elsa was thoughtful.

'Well, it is all very much for the best,' Andreas said. 'And David is coming up to dinner in my taverna tonight to say goodbye, he is leaving Aghia Anna tomorrow afternoon. I wanted to ask you to join us. Yorghis will pick up Fiona at the ferry and take her there. Say yes?'

Thomas asked, 'And will Vonni join the dinner too?'

'I hope so, yes indeed.' Andreas's smile was warm at the thought of cooking for so many friends.

Thomas spoke quickly. 'You are so kind, Andreas, but alas Elsa and I have to meet someone tonight for dinner. What a pity, we would have much preferred to have gone to you.'

Elsa picked it up quickly. 'Yes, that's such bad timing,' she said. 'Can you tell David we'll see him at the harbour at midday?'

Andreas understood.

He understood more than they realised. Of course, it was very last-minute, he reassured them. But he could read signs as well as anyone. These two wanted to be alone.

He didn't say it, however, he left them courteously.

They watched as he saluted the waiters and many of the customers.

'Amazing to be so centred, so rooted in a place like he is,' Thomas said admiringly, watching the old man leave.

'Why did you say that, about us having dinner?' Elsa asked.

Thomas was silent for a moment. 'I don't really know, Elsa, but I knew you didn't want another run-in with Vonni, and as it happens I share your view. Neither do I. I also didn't want to hear one word tonight about Shane. And . . . and . . .'

'And what?'

'And I'll miss you when you go. I wanted some more time together before you left, just the two of us.'

She gave him one of her extraordinary smiles.

'Those were all very good reasons, Thomas, and as it happens – to use your phrase – I share every one of them!'

Fiona and Vonni walked through Piraeus. Such a busy place, a city in its own right. They were jostled by the crowds as they walked together, Fiona dragging her large bag.

But she was very cheerful.

'You were right, Vonni, about all those fish restaurants. Can I treat you to a meal? I don't know what we'd call it, late lunch, afternoon tea?'

'Oh, I'd love some *barbouni*,' Vonni said, clapping her hands like a child being offered an ice cream.

'That's red mullet, I know that much. Here, does this place look all right to you?'

'It looks fine, shall I tell him it's *barbouni* and fries for two?' Vonni asked.

'Great, and I could murder a bottle of retsina.'

'Sure,' Vonni said in a clipped voice.

Fiona bit her lip. What a thoughtless thing to have said to a woman who must never touch alcohol.

'Or fizzy water,' she said lamely.

'Oh, for God's sake, Fiona, drink the retsina, you're entitled to it, and if I'm going to break out, it won't be because my dining companion has her snout in that paint stripper of a wine. Even in my worst days I couldn't swallow it. So you're not putting me in any temptation.'

They talked companionably of the life of a big port like this, sailors coming and going, fishermen unloading their catch. Students with backpacks getting off boats, and the rich yachting set driving to their berths further on.

It was a lively scene.

At no stage did Vonni mention what had happened at the police station. Nor the future for Fiona without Shane. Fiona would bring the matter up when and if she wanted to, and they were both easy with that.

When it was time to leave for the ferry that would take them back to Aghia Anna, Fiona asked for the bill.

'*O logariasmos!*' said the waiter, presenting it to her.

'You know, it's like the word for those logarithms we did at school ...'

'Do they still have those? Here, let me pay half,' Vonni said.

'They may be gone since my time,' Fiona agreed. 'No, put your money away, you bought the ferry tickets.'

'I have a job, which is more than you do,' Vonni protested.

'Look at it this way: I'm actually two thousand euros to the good because of today's events. I call that as good as winning the lottery.' And the two women smiled at each other. In many ways it was better than winning the lottery.

On the boat back to Aghia Anna, Vonni saw Fiona gripping the boat rail and looking out to sea.

Her lips were moving. She might be praying. Or crying. Or just working something out. Whatever it was, Vonni didn't think she needed any assistance, or even conversation.

David helped Andreas in the kitchen.

'I'll miss all this so much,' he said.

'Perhaps you could cook for a while for your father.'

'It's not the same.'

'No, but it won't be for very long and he might like it. Take out your notebook and write this down. I tell you how to make a good *moussaka*. Do you have *melitzanes* in England?'

'Aubergines? Yes, we do.'

'Then I'll show you, it will please him to see you cook for him.'

'Do you think so?' David was doubtful.

'I don't think so, I *know* so,' said Andreas.

Yorghis telephoned from the harbour. He had way-laid Fiona and Vonni, they would be at the taverna in fifteen minutes.

'Yorghis says that Fiona is in great form,' Andreas said.

'She must have got that fool out of jail then,' David said glumly.

'No, on the contrary, I was about to tell you. She turned her back on him. Left him there.'

'For the moment. She'll go back for him.'

'I think not, but I suggest that we let her tell us herself. Do you agree?'

'Oh yes, that's always my policy,' David said. 'And is she speaking to Vonni still?'

'The best of friends apparently, according to Yorghis.'

David laughed. 'Aren't you a wonderful pair of old gossips!'

'If you can't gossip with your own brother, I ask you, then who is there to gossip with? Where is your notebook? Right, a kilo of best minced lamb, next . . .'

'Would you like to go to the Anna Beach?' Thomas suggested to Elsa.

'No, it's too . . . I don't know . . . too full of chrome and opulence. Besides, it doesn't have good memories for me. What about that little place out on the point where the waves break?'

Thomas didn't want to go there. 'It reminds me too much of the day that savage hit Fiona. He came at her with his fist – he could have broken every bone in her face . . .'

'But it didn't happen and now she has left him,' Elsa soothed. 'So where should we go? It can't be too public, we did say we were meeting someone . . .'

'Why don't we get some kebabs and wine and go back to my place?' Thomas suggested.

'Sure, that's great. And if Vonni sees us we can say something . . .'

'She's on hen-house duty at the moment, she won't come in. But just suppose she does, we'll tell her that our friend, an unreliable German, didn't turn up.'

'No! She'd never believe that. A German unreliable? Not in a million years,' Elsa laughed. 'Let's make it an unreliable American . . .'

'How grossly unfair and racist of you. No, I won't have such a slur on my people. An unreliable Irishman maybe?'

'No, Vonni's Irish, she'd know him – reliable or unreliable. It had better be something else. English, I think.'

'That's so unfair on poor David, who is by far the most reliable of the four of us. But these are desperate times needing desperate measures. English he is then, the bad man who let us down.'

'I'll leave a note for Fiona saying I'll be back later and then let's go buy supper.'

There was a definite change in Fiona, they could all sense it. She held her shoulders back, she smiled more readily. She had lost that stooped and slightly defensive tone. Suddenly you could see the kind of girl she had been before.

She ran around helping to get things organised for the evening dinner.

There were three tables of customers, all of them English-speaking. Fiona translated the menu and advised them all to start with *dolmadhes*, which, she explained, were little fat packets of stuffed vine leaves. They were made on the premises, Fiona assured them, and were excellent. She suggested the house wine, which was inexpensive and good. Soon she had them so well organised that little Rina, the girl who helped in the kitchen, could serve them.

That meant that Andreas could sit down with his party and look at the lights going on down in the heart of Aghia Anna.

'A pity Thomas and Elsa couldn't join us,' David said.

'Oh well, you know,' Andreas shrugged.

The others didn't know, but it wasn't something to argue about.

'I'll never forget this place, never,' David said with a catch in his voice.

'You'll come back and visit us again often.' Andreas spoke quickly before David became emotional.

'Oh, I will, it won't be the same, but I will,' he promised.

'And you, Fiona, you are very good with people, you look after them well, would you like to work here?' Andreas said unexpectedly.

'Work? Here?' She was disbelieving.

'I watched you with the customers – you were just what I need. You could even stay here in Adoni's room. You'll need somewhere to stay when Elsa leaves.'

Fiona laid her hand on his. 'If you had asked me this last night or even early this morning I would have cried with gratitude. But now, now I say thank you from my heart, but I will not be able to come and work here.'

'It is too far up from the town?' Andreas asked.

'No, Andreas, not too far. It's just that I'm going home. Back to Dublin.'

She looked around the table at their astonished faces.

'Yes, I thought about it all the way back from Athens on the ferry. I just came back to say goodbye.'

Hannah wrote an e-mail.

Dear Elsa,

I don't quite know what you want to hear. But anyway I showed Dieter your last e-mail. He read it carefully and thanked me. Very politely. That's not his usual form. I thought you should know. Also you should know that Birgit has done everything except strip in front of his desk to attract his attention and he is only greatly irritated by her.

I tell you these things, Elsa, so that you should be in full possession of the facts before you make whatever decision you do.

Naturally I would love you to come home. But wherever you are we will always be friends.

Love,

Hannah

Thomas and Elsa finished their meal and sat on the balcony looking out over the rooftops.

'You have a nicer view from your place,' Thomas said.

'You can still see the stars from here, that's all that matters,' Elsa said.

'What is the stars, Joxer?' Thomas quoted in a heavy Irish accent.

'Will you say that I am showing off if I say I know where that's from?'

'Go on, tell me, shame me, put me down!' he laughed.

'It's by Sean O'Casey,' she said.

'Top of the class, Elsa. Another devoted teacher?'

'No, Dieter and I went to London, on a secret trip, and we saw it there. It was brilliant.'

'Are you looking forward to being back with him again?' Thomas asked.

'There's a problem,' she said.

'Isn't there always?' he sympathised.

'I suppose so. This problem is an unusual one: he has promised that there will be no more deception and hiding and sneaking away from people. It will all be out in the open.' She sounded doubtful.

'That's better, isn't it, in the open?' Thomas asked, surprised.

'Well, I think so, but in a way it might not be.' She chewed her lip.

'You mean you get a kick out of it being secret, clandestine?' he asked.

'No, I don't mean that at all. It's just that he never owned up to something else. Like the fact that he and another woman had a child.'

'Since you and he were together?' Thomas asked.

'No, years before, but the point is that he never acknowledged that little girl.'

'Is that what you ran away from?'

'I did not run away, I left my job and went to see the world. But I did think less well of him. Anyone who has a child, either deliberately or accidentally, must be there for that child.'

'And he didn't agree?'

'No, and somehow I was revolted by it. I felt I could never trust him again. I felt ashamed of loving him. I told him all this.'

'And so what has changed? What makes you think that it's right to go back to him now?'

'Meeting him here, knowing he loves me and will do anything for me.' She looked at him, hoping he understood.

Thomas nodded. 'Yes, I would have believed him, too. If you love someone you'll pretend anything to keep that person. I did, I know.'

'What did you pretend?' she asked gently.

'I pretended that I believed Bill was my son, I loved Shirley then so much I couldn't face her with the absolute proof that he couldn't be.'

'He's not your son?' Elsa was astonished.

Thomas told the story simply and without emotion. The tests that had proved him to be sterile, the joyful announcement of Shirley's pregnancy, and the totally unexpected bonus that when Bill arrived Thomas discovered that he adored the boy, and biological parenthood was not important any longer.

He hadn't bothered to find out who the real father was, it was irrelevant anyway.

And looking back he had been right not to create a drama. If Thomas had disputed the paternity of Bill then he would have been denied access to the child after the divorce.

'Do you still love her? Shirley?'

'No, it sort of passed like influenza does, or a summer

storm. I don't hate her either. She irritates me, and now she and Andy are having a child together and that irritates me too. Greatly. The fact that they *can* for one thing, and for another that Bill is so excited about it . . . his new brother or sister.'

'Did you ever think Shirley was having an affair?'

'No, not remotely. But let's put it this way, the very existence of Bill meant that Shirley was not exactly the faithful type. I guess I thought it was just one fling.'

'It probably was,' Elsa said.

'Yes, I think so, but for whatever reason we found less and less to say to each other. And then we got divorced.' He looked gloomy.

'And did you find anyone else?'

'No, I guess I didn't really look. I cared so much about Bill, you see. And I was really very surprised when she brought Andy to meet me so that they could tell me their plans. Shirley said she wanted things to be "civilised". She said she just hated secrets and pretence. I swear she sounded positively virtuous about it all. Said she wanted us to be up-front about everything.' He was scornful.

'Well, what was wrong with that?' Elsa asked.

'Oh, there had been months of secrets and pretence there! People in love can be so smug, and they expect everyone else to fit in with their plans.'

Elsa was silent. She was thinking hard, working something out.

'Sorry for droning on,' Thomas said.

'No, not at all, you've just clarified something for me.'

'I have?'

'Yes, if Dieter is to be any kind of a worthwhile

human being, he must accept the fact that he has a daughter, and recognise her.'

'Even if it means losing you?' Thomas asked.

'He wouldn't lose me over it, if he could really believe that this girl needs a father. The problem is that he might just put on some kind of an act. He thinks that what I want is a diamond ring, respectability, commitment. All that sort of thing.'

'He doesn't know you very well then, does he?' Thomas said.

'How do you mean?'

'I mean, you have been with him for over two years and he doesn't understand your values.'

'That's completely true, he doesn't understand me at all, but it never mattered. The love part of it pushed all that under the carpet. And what you just said about people in love being smug and uncaring about others – that is *so* true. I never thought of it before.'

'Well, what is a friend for except to come up with an idea now and then?' Thomas laughed.

'But you think I should give him up, don't you?'

'What I think doesn't matter.'

'It matters to me.'

'All right then, I think you should be with someone who does understand you . . . as well as the other thing.'

'What other thing?' she laughed.

'You well know what I mean, sex, love, attraction. All of those are very fine but if you held out for the understanding as well then you'd be very happy.'

'And where would I find all that in one package, Thomas?' Elsa asked.

'Ah, if I knew the answer to that I'd run the world,' he said, raising his wine glass to her.

*

At the table in Andreas's taverna they were still stunned by Fiona's news. Rina cleared away the dishes and they sat with their little cups of coffee.

'Do your parents know yet?' David asked.

'No, I only just know myself, nobody else knows except all of you, my friends here,' Fiona said.

They murmured approval, agreeing on the need to get back to real life and nursing. Nobody mentioned Shane. Andreas said he felt sure that her mother and father would be overjoyed. Yorghis asked would she get her job back in the hospital. David asked would she continue to live at home.

Again, nobody mentioned Shane.

The only person who didn't join in the conversation was Vonni. Very unusually for her, she sat and stared ahead of her.

Eventually Fiona spoke to her.

'You were right all along, Vonni, I'm the first to admit it. Aren't you pleased you were right?'

'It's not a game where you score points or lose points, it's your whole life, it's your future.'

'All the more reason to be pleased then,' Fiona said. 'To say "I told you so." You deserve to say it.'

'I don't want to say it, I've said enough to all of you. And I managed to annoy you all. That was always my trouble, knowing what was right for everyone except myself. Andreas and Yorghis here will confirm this. Stupid, bossy Vonni, who could run the world but couldn't run her own life.'

There was a silence. Then Yorghis spoke.

'You certainly knew how to run our sister Christina's

life for her, she would never have recovered without you,' he said.

'And every day of the year you do something to make someone's life better here, getting Maria to drive, minding the children, visiting the sick. That doesn't seem stupid and bossy to me,' Andreas said.

'I would never have known my father was dying if it hadn't been for you, Vonni,' David said. 'Think of the guilt for the rest of my life if I had not discovered.'

'And you came with me today and never once did you try to influence me. I don't think you were interfering at all. You just happened to be right,' Fiona said. 'And you left me to my thoughts. I'll never forget that.'

Vonni looked from one to another. Her heart was so full she didn't trust herself to speak. Finally she managed two words in the Irish language.

'*Slan abhaile*, Fiona,' she said unsteadily.

'What does that mean?' David asked.

'It means "Safe home",' Fiona said.

Thomas and Elsa talked on the balcony, as old friends talk. It was impossible to believe that they had known each other not for years but only a dozen or so days. They knew the secrets of each other's heart.

'So you will go back long before the year is over, before Shirley's baby is born?' Elsa asked.

'You think I should?' He looked at her.

'Hey, I'm not telling anyone what to do, remember how angry we all were with Vonni when she told us what we should and should not do. You didn't tell *me* what to do.'

'That's different,' Thomas said. 'I'm asking you and I really do want to know what you think.'

'Okay . . . I think that you love Bill, and that he loves you, and in life it's so hard to find a good generous love like that so I believe it's a great waste for you not to be near him. It's not as if you are putting him out of your mind and getting on with your own life. You worry about him all the time. So why not be near him, have a home he feels welcome to visit. He'll be jealous when the new baby arrives, he'll need a place where he is king.'

Thomas listened to her carefully.

'It *was* a good generous love once, but I became mean-spirited about Andy. I diminished that love.' He looked very sad.

'Then maybe you should try to stick it back together, firm it up before it all trickles away,' Elsa suggested.

'In my head I agree with you, but in my heart I fear I'd make such a mess of it that I'd truly be better off out of his way . . . for his sake just as much as for mine.'

'Well, Thomas, you'll come to the right conclusion. I know you well enough. Now come on, before you leave, and you will leave, are you going to tell me what to do with my messy life?'

'I suppose I could tell you that we can and do get over loving people and I hope you might contemplate getting over him.'

'But why, why do you want it to be over? You're my friend, you're out for my good as I am for yours. You know that Dieter is quite simply the love of my life.' She was confused.

'You asked me what I thought, I told you.' Thomas spoke simply.

'But I can't think why you would want me to give him up, get over him . . .'

'I could comfort you.'

She looked at him open-mouthed. 'Thomas, this is not true!' she gasped. 'You and I are mates, friends. You don't fancy me, as you put it, it's only the wine and the stars.'

'You never thought of me in that way at all?' he asked, his head on one side.

'I did think that it would be very easy to love a gentle, thoughtful person like you rather than a restless urgent man like Dieter. But then I've often wished idly for things that didn't happen. Couldn't happen.'

'All right, then I think you should go back to him tomorrow. Why hang around?' he said.

'You give up pretty easily,' she said flirtatiously.

'Come on, Elsa, everything I say is wrong. I did you the courtesy of considering what you said. You are not doing that.'

'I'm only playing with you,' she said.

'Don't,' said Thomas.

She was contrite. 'I know I'm like those feminists who get annoyed if a man stands up to give them a seat and get annoyed if he doesn't. I'm only playing games because I don't know what else to do. I know what you should do. It's so obvious and easy. And what everyone else – Dieter, David, Fiona, Andreas, Vonni – all of you, should do. It's just my own decision that isn't clear.'

'What should Vonni do?' Thomas asked with interest.

'She should get Andreas and Yorghis to find her son and tell him what kind of person she is now. Young Stavros would come home if they told him.'

Thomas smiled at her. 'Elsa the Crusader,' he said affectionately, and patted her hand.

*

In the taverna they talked about Fiona's journey home and when she should leave.

'Perhaps you could come on the last ferry with me tomorrow,' David said. 'We would be company for each other, and you might even fly to London with me.'

'That's not a bad idea, it would make it much less hard to say goodbye.'

'For a while,' Vonni said. 'You'll come back again, you've both got many friends here.'

'Tomorrow I'll go and say goodbye to Eleni and thank her for everything and call on Dr Leros as well.'

'And I'll give Maria a last driving lesson and tell her that Vonni will take over now. Is that right, Vonni?'

'Has she *any* co-ordination these days?' Vonni asked.

'Much improved,' David soothed. 'And she's great if you can manage not to shout at her but to build up her confidence.'

'Aren't we all great when people don't shout at us and build up our confidence,' Vonni grumbled.

'Have you told them, yet, in Ireland that you are going back?' Andreas asked Fiona.

'Not yet, I'll call from the Anna Beach tomorrow.'

'Go in and use my phone,' he said, as he had said all that time ago on the day that Manos had perished with his boat.

'Just a quick call then to my friend Barbara. Thank you so much, Andreas.' And Fiona ran into the kitchen.

'Isn't it unusual that you young people don't have mobile phones?' Yorghis wondered.

'Yes, it is odd. Not one of the four of us has one that works here,' David said.

'It's not unusual at all,' Vonni said. 'You're all

running away from something. Why would you want a phone so that you could be tracked down?'

'Barbara?'
  'God Almighty, it's Fiona!'
  'Barbara, I'm coming home!'
  'Well, that's *great* news, when will the pair of you be back?'
  'Not the pair of us. Just me.'
  There was a silence at the other end.
  'Shane is staying there?' Barbara said eventually.
  'In a manner of speaking, yes.'
  'Well, that's a pity,' Barbara said neutrally.
  'Don't be such a hypocrite, Barbara, you're delighted.'
  'That's not fair – why should I be delighted that my friend is upset?'
  'I'm not upset, Barbara – could you and I share a flat, do you think?'
  'Of course we could, I'll start looking right away.'
  'Great, and Barbara, could you sort of tell my ma and da?'
  'Sure, what exactly will I tell them?'
  'That I'm coming home,' Fiona said, surprised that there should be any question about it.
  'Yes, but you know the way people of that generation always want to ask questions . . .' Barbara began.
  'Oh, head them off at the pass,' said Fiona casually.

Thomas walked Elsa back to her villa and kissed her on the cheek.
  '*Schlaf gut*,' he said.
  'You're learning German just to impress me?' She smiled at him.

'No, I think I'd have to do much more than say, "Sleep well", to impress you, Elsa,' he said ruefully.

'Like what?' she asked.

'I'd have to be restless and urgent. I could try but it might take a long time.'

'You're better the way you are, believe me, Thomas. See you midday tomorrow at the harbour.'

'You won't have gone back to Germany by then?'

'Nor you back to California?'

'Goodnight, beautiful Elsa,' he said and turned away.

Fiona was in Elsa's villa already packing her suitcase.

'Before you say anything, I want to apologise, I was completely out of order with you, trying to borrow money and everything,' Fiona said.

'It doesn't matter a bit, anyway I was very short and harsh with you, I am the one to be sorry.'

'It doesn't matter now. I'm over Shane. I'm going back to Dublin. I suddenly looked at him and saw what the future would be like with him, and that it wasn't worth it. I suppose you'll say or think anyway that it can't have been real love if it vanished so quickly.'

'No, it was real love all right,' Elsa consoled her. 'But as you say it has ended, and that will make life easier for you.'

'I didn't give him up to have an easy life,' Fiona explained. 'I just suddenly saw him in a different light, like you all saw him in, I suppose, and then it was quite easy to walk away. I'm sorry of course that he wasn't the person I thought he was. It's not like your situation.'

'Why do you say that?'

'Well, Shane only tolerated my attaching myself to him. In your case, Dieter writes begging you to come back to him, promising to change for you. That's real love.'

Elsa ignored this. 'What was it that finally made you choose to walk away from Shane?' she asked.

'I think there was a kind of indifference in his tone, he didn't care.'

'I know what you mean,' Elsa nodded slowly.

'You can't know! Your guy is down on his knees beseeching you to come back to him. That's utterly different!'

'Something you said there about a tone of voice seemed fairly relevant to me. I'm going out on the balcony to look at the sea, do you want to join me?'

'No, Elsa, I'm exhausted. I've been to Athens and back in one day, changed the whole direction of my life. I'm going to have to sleep.'

Elsa sat for a long time looking out at the moonlight on the sea then she went back into the sitting room. She took some paper and began to write a letter which she would fax the next day.

My dear Hannah,

You have been such a good unselfish friend. Asking nothing and always ready to listen. It was, as it turned out, a very good decision for me to come here. And it was even better that I met Dieter again as now I can make a decision based on the facts as they are, not on some fantasy world. I'm still not sure what I am going to do. But a few more days on this peaceful island will make it all clear to me. I heard two things tonight, one from an American man who told me that we can get over people. He just said it casually, like you can get over whooping cough. I don't know if he's right. Then an Irish girl said to me that I was lucky because Dieter had promised to change for me. And I have been wondering why we should want to change people. Either love them as they are or move on.

It's late at night and I am writing this by moonlight. I've been thinking in a way I never did before about my life with Dieter. I went into it as an escape. I had a fair amount to escape from. My father left home when I was a child and I always hoped he would get in touch when he saw me on television, but he never did. My mother and I were never close, possibly we were too alike, always striving for perfection.

But in the weeks I have been travelling I have learned that there really is no perfect life, so we must stop seeking it. I have met many people on this voyage whose problems are much greater than mine. Oddly it has calmed me down.

And I thought of you, Hannah, and your happy marriage to Johann. On the day you married five years ago, you said there was nothing about him you would change.

I envy you that, my dear, dear friend.
Love from Elsa

Chapter Sixteen

Miriam Fine had prepared David's room for him, bought a new lilac-coloured duvet cover and matching curtains, laid out dark purple towels.

'They look nice and manly, somehow. I hope he'll like them,' she said.

'Don't fuss over him, Miriam, he hates fuss,' David's father said.

'You tell me not to fuss? What will you do, yes, tell me what will you do the very moment he comes in the door?'

'I'll do nothing to upset him.'

'You'll start talking to him about responsibility. If there is anything guaranteed to fuss him it's that!'

'No, I won't talk about responsibility, at least he's seen sense and decided to give up these mad ideas.'

'He's coming home because you're ill, Harold. He worked that out for himself, you saw the letter I sent. I never mentioned it. Not once.'

'I don't want his sympathy, I will not have his pity.' The man's eyes filled with tears.

'But you might want his love, Harold, after all, that's why he's coming home, because he loves you.'

Fiona's father turned the key in the lock. It had been a long tiring day in the office. It was a week from his fiftieth birthday. He felt eighty-five. His shoulders were stiff and cramped. There were young fellows in the office snapping at his heels. He might well be passed over for the next promotion.

He had been tempted to go and have three pints in his local pub, but realised that Maureen would have his supper ready. It wasn't worth the hassle.

As soon as he opened the door she ran out to meet him.

'Sean, you just won't believe this! Fiona's coming home. This week!' Maureen Ryan was overjoyed.

'How do you know?'

'Barbara rang when you were out.'

'Could that lout not draw his dole money out there? Is that what happened?' Sean grumbled.

'No, wait till you hear, she dropped him – she's coming home on her own!'

Sean put down his briefcase and his evening paper and sat down. He put his head in his hands. 'Someone asked me at lunch today did I think there was a God,' he said. 'I told the lad to grow up, of course there wasn't. What kind of a God would allow all this mess and confusion to go on? But now I may have to rethink my answer. There might well be something out there. She's really coming back?'

'Tomorrow or the day after, she asked Barbara to tell us, she's looking for her old job back.'

'Well, isn't that great – do the girls know yet?'

'No, I waited to tell you first,' Maureen Ryan said.

'And I suppose you've been doing up her room?' He smiled wearily.

'No, and I'll tell you why, she wants to live in a flat with Barbara.'

'Well, that's all right, isn't it?'

'I think it's all for the very best, Sean,' said Fiona's mother with tears in her eyes.

'Big surprise, Bill, I'm going to take you and your mom on a little trip!' Andy said.

'Hey, that's great, where are we going?'

'Your grandma is going with a group to the Grand Canyon, remember she told you?'

'Yeah?' Bill looked very excited. Dad had often told him about the Grand Canyon, showed him pictures of it. Told him that they would go there some day. 'Do you mean we might go there too?' Eagerness shone in his face.

'Well, I said to Shirley we always intended to go there and why not do it when you could meet your gran as well?'

'And what did Mom say?'

'Well, she said I was a kind man, and that pleased me, but I didn't do it to be kind, I suggested it because I thought it would be good for all of us.'

'You are kind, Andy,' Bill said.

'I'm very fond of you, Bill, you know that, and when the new baby comes I'll be as lucky as you are. I'll have two children to love.'

'How does that make you as lucky as me?'

'You have two dads, don't you? And talking about

that, you should call your dad in Greece and tell him you're going on this trip.'

Bill dialled the number in Greece but there was only an answering machine.

He left a message.

'Dad, Andy is driving us to Arizona to see the Grand Canyon, we're going to cross the Sierra Nevada and we're going to meet Gran there, she's going with her book club. Andy says I can call you when we get there so that Gran and I can both say hallo.'

Then Andy took over the phone.

'Thomas, just in case you don't get this message before we leave and you want to call Bill, this is the number of my cellphone. I'll try and show things properly to your boy; we have the atlas out now looking at the journey, but I guess there'll be a lot I miss out. Maybe he could go again with you some time when you get back.'

'That's if he *ever* comes back,' Bill said before Andy had hung up the telephone.

Because Andy had not yet hung up when Bill said this, it was there on the message when Thomas came back from walking Elsa home and turned on his answering machine.

He sat up for a long time wondering about the world. He saw the torchlight moving around in the hen-house. He had been right in assuming that Vonni would not come to sleep in the guest room tonight. He thought of the strange tortured life she had lived amongst these people in Aghia Anna.

He thought of the beautiful, bright Elsa going back to that selfish German who only looked on her as a trophy.

He thought of the simple, decent Andy, the man whom he had always demonised.

Who was only doing his best.

He thought of his Bill who believed he might never come home. He sat there thinking until the stars faded from the sky and the early light came up over the hills.

They met for a last lunch at the restaurant with the blue check tablecloths.

'Imagine, we have been coming here so often and we don't even know its name,' Fiona said meditatively.

'It's called Midnight,' David said. 'Look at the letters.' And he spelled it out slowly: *Mesanihta.*

'How on earth do you work that out?' Elsa asked.

Painstakingly he went over the Greek letters again: the thing that looked like a V is actually an N.

'You would be a great teacher, David,' Elsa said, very sincerely.

'I don't know, I don't have all that many certainties,' he said.

'All the better for a teacher,' Thomas said.

'I'll miss you all, I don't have very many friends back home,' David said.

'Me neither, but I'd be very surprised if you were without friends for long,' Thomas said. 'And don't forget, you'll make a whole new circle through your driving lessons!'

'It's easy here, a bit different with motorways in England,' David said. 'I don't think I'll set up my own school.'

'Do you have a lot of friends back in Germany, Elsa?' Fiona asked.

'No, hardly any, a lot of acquaintances but only one

good friend, Hannah. When you're in the fast track, or think you are, and have to keep yourself ready and available, then there's no real time for friends.' She spoke regretfully.

They all nodded, it was easy to understand.

Fiona announced that she was going on the train to see David's parents with him, help smooth over the homecoming, try to explain something about the life on this magical island and how it had seduced them.

'Like the Lotos-eaters,' Elsa said.

'Elsa is showing off how much English literature she knows.' Thomas looked at her affectionately.

'It's Tennyson,' she smiled, ignoring him. 'When they all arrived where the Lotos-eaters lived and ate nectar, in a land in which it seemed always afternoon, one of them said, "Oh rest ye, brother mariners, we will not wander more." This place has that effect on all of us, I think.'

'Except Fiona and I are leaving,' David said sadly.

'But you'll be back here again one day. It's different now from Tennyson's time, he was back in the nineteenth century with no cheap air tickets, or indeed any air tickets then.' Thomas was cheering them up.

'I'd love my friend Barbara to come out here with me one day, but it won't be the same without you,' Fiona said.

'Vonni will always be here, and Andreas, Yorghis, Eleni – loads of people.' Thomas was still looking on the bright side.

'Will you be here for much longer yourself, Thomas?' Fiona asked.

'No, I don't think so. I think I'll go back to California fairly soon,' Thomas said. His eyes had a faraway look.

They didn't want to ask him any more. It was clearly a decision not fully made.

'And when are you going back to Germany, Elsa?' David asked gently, to change the subject.

'I'm not going back,' she said simply.

'You're staying here?' Fiona gasped.

'I'm not sure, but I'm not going back to Dieter.'

'When did you decide this?' Thomas leaned forward and looked at her very intensely.

'Last night, on my balcony, looking out at the sea.'

'And did you tell anybody, like Dieter for example?'

'I wrote to him. I posted the letter this morning on the way to meet you all. He should get it in four or five days. So now I have all that time to make up my mind where to go.' She smiled at Thomas, one of those slow warm smiles which had made her the darling of television all over Germany.

'You're not going to go down to *Mesanihta* to say goodbye to them, Vonni?' Andreas asked as he called into the craft shop.

'No, I annoyed them all enough while they were here. I'll let them go in peace,' she said, not looking up.

'You are a difficult woman, Vonni, prickly like a thorn bush. Both David and Fiona said last night how grateful they are to you.' Andreas shook his head, mystified.

'Yes, they did, they were very polite, as were you and Yorghis and I thank you. And by the way, the urge to drink seems to have passed over like a summer cloud. But it's the other two, Thomas and Elsa, I really upset them, I don't want to sit there pontificating like some old bat. You and I heard plenty of advice years ago, Andreas, but did we ever take it? The answer is no.'

'And what would you have changed if you could have your life all over again?' he asked.

This was unfamiliar territory for Andreas. Normally he left things as they were, without question or analysis.

'I'd have fought Magda for Stavros. I wouldn't have won then, but I might have won later. He might have come back when he tired of her. And of course I should have fought Stavros for the petrol station. The people here are fair, they would have known I bought it for him. I could have raised my son. But no, I thought the solution was somewhere at the bottom of a *raki* bottle. So it didn't happen.' She looked around her despondently.

'Did anyone give you any advice like that at the time?' he asked gently.

'Yes, Dr Leros's father did, and your sister Christina, but I had my face so far into drink I couldn't listen to them.'

'You haven't asked me what I would change if I were given the chance,' he said.

'I suppose you'd have managed to keep Adoni here. Am I right?'

'Yes, of course I should have done that. But would I listen to people who told me that? No, I would not.' His eyes were sad. 'And also I should have asked you to marry me twenty-five years ago.'

She looked at him, astounded. 'Andreas! You don't mean that. We never even remotely loved each other.'

'I didn't love my wife either, not in any real sense, that is. Not like people read about and sing about, we got on all right and we were company for each other. You and I could have been fine companions.'

'We *are* fine companions, Andreas,' she said in a weak voice.

'Yes, but you know . . .' he muttered.

'No, it would never have worked, not for five minutes. Believe me. You did the right thing there. You see, I loved Stavros exactly the way you read about, sing about and dream about. I could never have settled for any other kind of love.'

She said it in a matter-of-fact way which brought normality back to their conversation.

'So it was all for the best,' Andreas said.

'Definitely. And listen to me, Andreas, I meant it when I said Adoni will come back to see you. I *know* it.'

He shook his big head. 'No, it's only a wish, a fairy tale.'

'The man is thirty-four, you wrote to him, of course he'll come back.'

'Why has he not called or written then?'

He didn't want to tell Vonni about the mysterious phone call which seemed to assume that Adoni was already here. It could have all been a mistake, a misunderstanding, he didn't want to raise her hopes like he had raised his own and his brother's. But even though she knew nothing of the call, Vonni's faith was unshaken.

'He needs a little time, Andreas. Chicago is a long way. He'll need to get his head around it. But he'll be here.'

'Thank you, Vonni, you are indeed a good companion,' Andreas said, and blew his nose very loudly.

*

'Hey, Dimitri?'

'Yes?' Dimitri's voice was cold. He had never seen such a violent attack on a gentle girl who had come to visit this Shane in love and good faith.

'Can I write a letter?'

'I'll get you paper.'

He looked in from time to time and Shane was writing and thinking and writing again. Eventually it was finished and he asked for an envelope.

'We'll put it in an envelope. Just tell me where it's to go.' Dimitri wasted little time with him.

'Like hell you will, I'm not having you read my letter,' Shane said.

Dimitri shrugged. 'Please yourself,' he said and left.

A few hours later Shane called out to him.

Dimitri wrote down the address ... Andreas's taverna, Aghia Anna.

'How strange!' Dimitri said.

'You asked for the bloody address, don't start criticising it,' Shane said.

'No, it's just that I know that man's son, Adoni, he and I are friends.'

'You are, huh? Well, his father doesn't think much of him,' Shane said.

'They had a difference of opinion, it's something that happens to many fathers and sons,' said Dimitri with a great sense of dignity.

They agreed to meet at the ferry half an hour before departure. And they all headed off from the café they now knew was called Midnight, in their different directions.

Fiona and David went to say their goodbyes and collect all the gifts that were being offered to them.

Maria had made a cake for David to take home to his parents. Eleni had made a lace collar for Fiona.

Yorghis had got them worry beads made of amber-coloured glass.

Andreas had a photograph of himself and David framed in a little carved wooden frame.

Dr Leros had given Fiona some coloured tiles she could put on her wall to remind her of Greece.

They couldn't find Vonni. She was not at home.

'She'll come to wave us off,' David said.

'She's very sad these days, she's lost her sparkle somehow,' Fiona said.

'Maybe she's envious with you going back to Ireland ... something she was never able to do,' David speculated.

'Yes, but she says herself it turned out all right, her love affair, for quite a time, and she did have a son to show for it, which is more than a lot of people do.'

'But where is he now?' David asked.

'She claims she doesn't know, but I bet she does,' Fiona said.

'Wouldn't it be wonderful if he came back? If he met Adoni somewhere out in Chicago and they decided to go back and swing again on the old tree up at the taverna,' David said.

'Ah, David, and they say the Irish are the sentimental ones believing in fairy tales.'

Fiona pealed with laughter and patted him on the arm to show she was laughing with him, not at him.

*

'You're a dark horse, Elsa, all these plans and you never told me.' Thomas tut-tutted in disapproval as they walked together up in the little town.

'I did tell you.'

'But when everyone was there?'

'Well, that's where we were, with everyone else, when the subject came up.' Elsa was totally unrepentant.

'But I thought you and I had sort of discussed things fairly intimately . . .' He was hesitant.

'We did, and I enjoyed it,' she said.

'Where are you off to now? I was thinking of having a siesta personally.'

Elsa laughed. 'Where am I going? I'm going to find Vonni.'

Vonni wasn't in her hen-house, nor in her craft shop nor at the police station.

Elsa decided she would go out on the road to the old man who didn't believe in modern medicine. She might find her there.

The sun was high in the sky and she wore her white cotton sun-hat against the heat. The road was dusty. Children came from the tumbledown buildings and saluted her, opening and closing their little fingers.

'*Yassas!*' they called out to her as she passed by.

Elsa wished she had brought some candy, *karameles*, they called it. But she hadn't thought that there would be this reception committee.

She remembered the old man's house and gathered together some sentences in halting Greek to say she was looking for his friend Vonni. But they weren't necessary. Vonni was there, sitting by the old man's bed holding his hand.

She didn't look remotely surprised to see Elsa.

'He's dying,' she said in a matter-of-fact tone.

'Should I go and get the doctor?' Elsa was practical.

'No, he wouldn't let a doctor cross the door, but I'll tell him that you are a herbalist and he'll take what you give him.'

'You can't do that, Vonni.' Elsa was shocked.

'You'd prefer he died in pain?'

'No, but we can't play games with someone's life . . .'

'He has about six or seven hours more of life, if that. If you want to help go to Dr Leros, you remember where he lives from Fiona that time. Tell him the situation here, ask him for morphine.'

'But won't I need . . .'

'No, you won't need anything, call into my shop and get a pottery bowl as well. Go quickly now.'

On her way back down the dusty road an old van came along. Elsa stopped it and said she needed to go to the doctor for medicine. The two men looked at her admiringly and drove her willingly to the doctor's. As Vonni had predicted there was indeed no problem getting the drugs, the men in the van waited while she picked up the bowl and then drove her back.

'That was very speedy,' Vonni said approvingly, and Elsa held the old man's thin hand and repeated to him over and over, '*Dhen ine sovaro, Dhen ine sovaro*. It's not serious, it's not serious.'

Vonni ground up the morphine tablets, mixed them with honey in her pottery bowl and spooned the mixture into the old man's mouth.

'It would be better if we could inject it, more instant relief, but he wouldn't hear of that.' Vonni was grim.

'How long will it take for him to feel it?'

'A matter of minutes. It's really magic this stuff,' Vonni said.

The old man mumbled something.

'What did he say?'

'He actually said that the herbalist is very beautiful,' Vonni said wryly.

'I wish he hadn't said that.' Elsa sounded sad.

'Come on, these are the last things he's going to look at – your face and mine. Isn't it good he has yours to concentrate on?'

'Vonni, *please*.' She had tears in her eyes.

'If you want to help, keep smiling at him, Elsa, he'll start feeling less pain quite soon.'

And indeed, his face began to relax a little, his grip on her hand was less frantic.

'Think of him as if he were your father, put love and warmth in your eyes,' Vonni instructed her.

Elsa felt that this wasn't the time to remind Vonni that she hardly remembered the father who had abandoned her. Instead she looked at this poor old Greek man and thought of him and his strange odd life that ended with an Irishwoman and a German woman at his deathbed, giving him a very large dose of morphine . . .

'Yorghis, it's Dimitri here in Athens, remember, we've talked a few times . . .'

'Of course I remember you! How are you, boy, it's good to hear from you! Are you getting ready for your wedding?'

'Yes, don't women go to a great fuss about one day? I mean it's the life afterwards that matters, isn't it?'

'For us, yes, but for them the day itself is very important.'

'You know that Irish dope pusher?'

'Shane? Indeed I do, but the most important thing was that the girl left him. Walked out on him in front of you, didn't she?'

'That's right, how did you know?'

'Vonni told us, the woman from here who went with her. She said you were quite a hero.'

'Oh, you know the old woman? No, I was nothing like a hero, I'm afraid. But I wanted to tell you he's written a letter to your brother, sent to the taverna. It was in English and I can't read English very well, but I wondered what it was about.'

'He probably thinks Andreas is a soft touch, but it's not going to work. Little Fiona is going back to Ireland, Andreas and I are going down to the ferry tonight to say goodbye to her. So whatever he writes to Andreas it will be too late.'

'Good,' said Dimitri. 'And while I'm talking to you, did Adoni ever come back to Aghia Anna? Remember I knew him here in Athens and I've been thinking about him today.'

'No, he never did.'

'Making too much money over there I suppose?'

'Not that I heard, and we *would* hear if anyone from here did well in the United States. But there you go! Funnily, a day or so ago I thought he might be coming back, but it was a false alarm.'

'How do you mean?'

'Oh, some garbled message came through from Chicago wanting to know where he had put some set of keys. I thought . . . I hoped he might be on his way here but, alas, no.'

'I suppose we all do what we want to do in the end,' Dimitri sighed.

'You are a philosopher, Dimitri my boy. And old men go on hoping that the world will become easy and people will remember that life is short, and no row is worth prolonging.'

A queue was forming to get on the last ferry from Aghia Anna.

Fiona and David stood in the middle of a crowd of well-wishers. Maria and her children were there, Eleni from the house where Fiona and Shane had stayed was there with her children. Vonni and Elsa both looking tired and anxious, but obviously friends again. Thomas was there in his ridiculous trousers. He had bought a little book about the island for each of them, and a copy of a photograph of the four of them at their café.

He had written 'Midday at the Midnight' on the pictures. Andreas and Yorghis were there with promises of more roast lamb when they came back.

Vonni could see that the two who were leaving were becoming quite emotional.

She spoke authoritatively. 'Now you can't leave us all here clinging to this rock in the Mediterranean without knowing what happened when you got home,' she said sternly. 'You can write it to me and I'll come down to the *Mesanihta* and read it to the others.'

They promised her faithfully that they would indeed write.

'Twenty-four hours after you get back, remember,' Vonni said fiercely. 'We want to know what happens.'

'It will be easy to write to you lot, we don't have to tell you any lies,' David said.

'Or put on an act,' Fiona agreed.

And just on cue at that moment the ferry hooted aggressively and they went up the gangplank amongst the people carrying baskets, and some that looked like bags of washing. A few definitely had hens and geese in boxes with holes punched in them for the air to get in.

They waved until the boat had left the harbour and turned along the coast and they were out of sight of their friends.

'I feel desperately lonely,' Fiona said.

'Me too. I could have lived there happily for ever,' David said.

'Could we? Or are we just fooling ourselves, do you think?' Fiona wondered.

'It's different for you, Fiona, truly it is, you love your job, you have friends, your family aren't going to overpower you, suffocate you.'

'I'm not sure quite *how* they're going to react, I'm the eldest of the family, I didn't show much example to my sisters by running off with a certifiable lunatic.'

'But at least you have sisters, I'm the only one. I bear the whole brunt of it. And my father is dying. I have to look at him every day and tell him I'll be proud to work in his company.'

'Maybe it won't be as bad as you think.' Fiona was hopeful.

'It will and worse since I let go of the reins as he calls it. You're very good to come and help me break the ice.'

'Will they think I'm your girlfriend, a frightening Catholic coming to destroy your tradition?'

'They already do,' he said gloomily.

'Well, it'll cheer them up enormously when I hare off

to Ireland next day,' Fiona said cheerfully. 'They'll be so relieved they'll gather you to their bosoms.'

'We were never slow on the bosom gathering – that's part of the problem,' David said.

And for some reason they both found this incredibly funny.

Elsa and Thomas watched until the ferry was out of sight. Then they walked slowly back up to the town.

'Where were you this afternoon?' he asked. 'I was looking for you, I thought we could take off in the boat again.'

'Tomorrow would be lovely,' she said. 'That's if you're free.'

'I'm free.'

'I'm interested that you really are going back to California,' she said.

'And I'm very interested that you're really not going back to Germany,' he said.

'So let's make the most of what time we have here,' Elsa said.

'How do you mean exactly?' Thomas enquired.

'I meant by renting a boat tomorrow, having a picnic, another day taking the bus to Kalatriada, I'd love to see that place again when I'm not so stressed. That's what I meant.'

'There, that's settled,' he said. And they both smiled conspiratorially.

To change the subject he asked, 'You didn't tell me what you were doing all afternoon.'

'I was in a small cluttered house with Vonni, watching an old man die. An old man with no family, no relations, only Vonni and me. I never saw anyone die before.'

'Oh, poor Elsa.' He leaned towards her and stroked her hair. 'Poor Elsa.'

'Not poor Elsa, I am young, I have my life ahead, he was old and lonely and frightened. Poor old Nikolas. Poor old man.'

'You were kind to him, you did what you could.'

Elsa pulled away from him. 'Oh, Thomas, if you could have seen Vonni. She was wonderful – I take back everything I ever said about her. She fed him honey on a spoon and made me hold his hand. She was like a sort of angel.'

They walked together back to her place.

'Tomorrow we'll take out a little blue boat and go to sea,' he said and as she turned to leave, she gave him a big hug.

'Andy, is this an okay time to call?'

'Sure, Thomas, for me it's fine, but I'm afraid Bill and his mother aren't in the car, they've gone exploring.'

'Exploring?'

'I mean shopping really, they call it exploring. Could you call in thirty minutes, or make it forty-five? You know what shopping can turn into, I don't want to waste your nickel just talking to me.'

'I'm happy to talk to you, Andy, because I want to ask you something.'

'Sure, Thomas, ask what you want.' He could hear the slightly wary note in Andy's voice.

'I was wondering, if I came back, like a bit sooner than anyone thought, do you think that would be a good thing?'

'Came back? Sorry, Thomas, I'm not entirely with you. You mean come back here to town?'

'Yes, that's what I meant.' Thomas felt cold. The guy was going to say that it would be a bad idea. He knew it.

'But you leased your apartment for a year, didn't you?'

'Yeah, but I thought I'd get a place, a bigger place, with a yard for Bill to play in.'

'You're going to try and take Bill back?' Andy's voice was choked.

'Not back to live, of course not, just a place he could visit.' Thomas tried not to sound impatient.

'Oh, I see.'

God, Andy was slow. It took for ever for an idea to sink in and another age for him to answer.

'So what do you think? Andy, do you think it would be something Bill would like . . . to have me down the street from him? Or would it confuse him? You're the guy on the spot. Tell me. I just want to do what's best.'

Across thousands of miles, Thomas could almost hear the slow smile crossing Andy's handsome, empty features.

'Thomas, that boy would love it, it would be like Santa Claus and all his birthdays coming together!'

There was no doubting the utter sincerity of the man. Thomas could hardly stumble out the words. 'I won't tell him just yet, if that's okay with you, I'd like to set it up and give him a definite date before I begin talking to him about it. Does that make sense to you, Andy?'

'Sure it does, I'll say nothing until we hear from you.'

'Thanks for understanding,' Thomas mumbled.

'Understanding? That a man should want to be near his own flesh and blood? What's to understand?'

Thomas hung up and sat for a long time in the dark. Everyone believed that Bill was his flesh and blood.

Everyone except Shirley. And indeed for all he knew she might believe it too. After all, he had never told her about the doctor's report. It had been too late to tell her.

She might well not know.

Vonni settled herself down in the shed that Thomas called her hen-house. She had seen him talking on the telephone. And earlier she had seen him holding Elsa's hand. They had so much ahead of them, those two.

She sighed with envy.

It would be wonderful to have years and years ahead. Time to make decisions, to go places, to learn new things. To fall in love again. She wondered what they would do. She wondered about Fiona and David taking a late plane tonight to London from Athens.

Would their homecomings be stormy, awkward or emotional? She hoped they would let her know. She had terrorised them into writing to her when they got back!

She looked back on the long hot day and how she had closed the eyes of Nikolas and wiped the honey from his chin before sending for Dr Leros to pronounce what she knew already. She thought about Yorghis up in the police station. Yorghis whose wife was never mentioned.

She tried to imagine what Magda looked like now and if she cried from those huge dark eyes over Stavros paying attention to another woman. She wondered about Andreas announcing that they should have married long ago. He had been quite wrong of course. But if they had married she might have got Adoni back. It would have been so very easy. The boy was aching to be asked. Unlike her own son, who would never come back.

The boy who had once sent a message to say that she

had stolen his childhood and he never wanted to see her again. In all her confessions and recitals of her story she had never told any of them that. It was too hurtful to say, even to think about. And as she had done every night for over thirty years she said a prayer for her son Stavros. Just in case there might be a God out there and the prayer might do some good.

Chapter Seventeen

Elsa had the picnic ready when Thomas came by to pick her up next morning. It was in a basket with a cloth tucked in to cover the food.

'I was wondering . . .' Thomas began.

'What were you wondering, dear Thomas?'

'Don't mock me, I'm a frail poor creature!' he begged.

'I wasn't mocking you, I swear.'

'I was wondering if we might row up the coast to Kalatriada, and stay there. For the night. That's what I was wondering.'

'I think you should wonder no more, it's a great idea.' She began to go back into the villa.

'Where are you going?' he asked anxiously.

'To get a toothbrush, an extra pair of panties, a clean blouse. Okay?' she asked.

'Very okay.' He had been expecting some kind of resistance. She was out in thirty seconds.

'Will the man with the little boats let us take it away for so long?' she asked.

'I've been down there to check, well, in case you said yes, and he said it would be fine.' Thomas looked slightly embarrassed.

'Go on, Thomas, what did he really say?' She laughed at him affectionately.

'He kept talking about you as … my *sizighos* or something …'

'What on earth is that?'

'I looked it up, it's a partner or a spouse or something in that area, I'm afraid.'

'Well, all right, *sizighos*, let's hit the high seas!' Elsa said cheerfully.

They took the little boat and rowed out of the harbour. The old man who cast them off kept explaining that if the weather was bad anywhere they must just go ashore and tie the boat up. Too many people had come to harm.

The sea was calm outside the arms of the harbour and they went up the coast identifying places as they passed. That was the hospital where Vonni had stayed for so long, that was the bathing place where Elsa had been with the children. That must be the wayside shrine where the bus had stopped the morning they had all come back for the funeral. It seemed so long ago now, so very long ago.

About halfway there they found a big wooden platform about a hundred yards from shore. The kind of place that people might swim out to. Thomas could tie their little boat to one of the posts. It was ideal for their picnic. Elsa climbed out of the boat and spread the cloth out between them.

She spread the taramasalata and hummus on the pitta bread, arranged the figs and watermelon on a plate. Then she poured a glass of wine and held it out to him.

'You know you really are quite dazzlingly beautiful,' he said.

'Thank you, that's very kind of you, but it's not important,' she said in a matter-of-fact voice. She wasn't putting him down. She was just stating a fact.

'All right, it's *not* that important, but it's true,' he said and spoke of it no more.

Kalatriada didn't have a real harbour so they tied up to a jetty and walked up the steep road to the little village.

Irini remembered them from the last visit. She took their hands in hers and greeted them warmly. She seemed to think it in no way unusual that this happy, handsome couple asked for two rooms.

'We only have one room free, but it has two beds – one for each person,' she said.

'I think we could survive that, don't you, Elsa?'

'Certainly,' she agreed.

Irini might not have travelled far from her home village but she was wise in the ways of the world. She knew that you must never be surprised by anything.

'Did he say anything at all about this girl he's bringing with him?' Harold Fine asked for the third time.

'Only what I told you, that she and he and two others were friends on the island and they are travelling back together.'

'Hmm,' said David's father.

'I don't think it's a romance,' David's mother said.

'He's never brought a girl home before, Miriam.'

'I know but I still don't think so. She's Irish for one thing.'

'Why would that stop him? Hasn't he been living out in the furthest wildernesses of Greece for the summer?'

'She's only staying one night, Harold.'

'That's what they say now,' David's father said darkly.

'And what in the name of God is she stopping off in Manchester for?' Sean Ryan asked Barbara.

'There wasn't much time to explain but apparently it's someone she met whose father is dying and so Fiona is going to spend a night with the family to ease the situation,' Barbara said.

'Another lame duck,' Fiona's father grumbled.

'Just Fiona being kind,' Barbara said.

'Look where being kind got her before,' he muttered.

'But that's all over now, Mr Ryan.' Barbara sometimes felt that life was all about being relentlessly cheerful both on and off the wards. 'She'll be home tomorrow at six o'clock and without Shane. Isn't that all we ever wanted?'

'And she really doesn't want any of us to come to the airport?' Maureen Ryan was puzzled.

'Yes, she says she hates emotional scenes in front of strangers. Her plane lands at four, she'll be here before six.'

'I wonder, Barbara, if you were free could you ever . . .' Fiona's mother began.

'Like, be here when she arrives . . .' Fiona's father finished for her.

'To ease the situation?' Barbara asked.

'To stop me saying the wrong thing,' Sean Ryan said bluntly.

'Sure, I'll get them to let me change my shift,' Barbara said.

'It's just that words were said when she was leaving,' Maureen explained.

'Oh, words are always being said, believe me.' Barbara wondered if she should hand in her notice and apply to run the world officially. It seemed to be what she was doing in her spare time.

'And do you think she should stay here or spend the night with you?'

'Do you know, Mrs Ryan, I think it would be great if we could all have a lovely welcome home supper here and then she came off with me ... that way, Rosemary wouldn't have to leave Fiona's old room where she's settled now, and there would be no danger of more words being said.'

As Barbara ran for the bus she wondered whether she should take over the United Nations this month or wait for a little bit longer.

'Dimitri?'

'Yes?'

'Did you post that letter?' Shane asked.

'It was posted. Yes.'

'Well, why hasn't that stupid old man replied?'

'I have no idea,' Dimitri shrugged.

'Maybe he can't read anyway, mad old fellow wearing laced-up boots in the middle of summer.'

Dimitri turned to leave. Shane put his hand on Dimitri's sleeve.

'Please don't go ... I'm ... Well ... I'm a bit frightened and lonely here to be frank.'

Dimitri looked at him. He remembered the way Shane's face had contorted when he had held that girl's hair and was about to beat her against the walls of the cell.

'We're all frightened and lonely from time to time,

Shane. We have arranged for a lawyer to represent you
in court,' he said, shaking off the hand and locking the
cell behind him.

Dimitri's telephone rang.

It was Andreas, he had got the number from his
brother Yorghis in the police station.

'It's about the young Irishman.'

'Oh, yes?' Dimitri sighed.

'He wrote to me for news of Fiona, he said he was
very sorry and could I explain that he didn't mean to
hurt her.'

'He meant to hurt her,' Dimitri said.

'Yes, you know this and I know this but he wanted
me to tell her. I wanted to send him a message that I
can't tell her, she has gone. Back to her country.'

'Good,' said Dimitri.

'So will you pass him that message?'

'Could you send a letter, a fax, an e-mail? Something?
He's not going to believe me.'

'I'm not good at writing in English.'

'Is there someone there who could do it for you?'

'Yes, yes there is, thank you, I know who to ask.'

'Before you go I wanted to ask you how is your son
Adoni? I knew him when we did military service
together.'

'He is well, I think, he lives in Chicago now.'

'And does he come back?'

'Not really, why do you ask?'

'Because I would like to see him again. And I am
getting married. I wanted to ask him to our wedding.'

'Well, if I hear from him I'll ask him to contact you,'
Andreas said with a heavy heart.

Dimitri sat looking at the phone for a long time.

People did extraordinary things. Adoni had been a great fellow when they had been together at military camp, spoken lovingly about his father and the taverna on the hill. Dimitri sighed. Nothing got easier to understand.

It was their second night in Kalatriada and, unlike the time that they had been here with David and Fiona, it was a clear starry night.

Irini set a little table for Thomas and Elsa out in the open air where they could see the square and the people walking up and down. She had put two little sprays of bougainvillaea in a white china vase as a decoration on their table.

Thomas took Elsa's hand and stroked it.

'I feel very happy here, calm somehow, as if the storms had died down.'

'I feel the same,' Elsa said.

'Which is, of course, ridiculous,' Thomas said. 'The storms haven't really gone away at all. They're round the corner for both of us, to be dealt with sooner or later.'

'But maybe we feel calm because we think we can deal with them now,' Elsa suggested.

'How do you mean?'

'Well, you are going back to Bill – the only question is when? And I'm not going back to Germany, so the only question is where?'

'You've a quick, bright mind, Elsa. You can sum things up very well.'

'Not all that quick, this is something I should have seen a long time ago.'

'We'll waste no time on regrets though, will we?' he enquired.

'No, I agree, regrets are useless. Destructive even.'

'Would you like coffee?' he asked.

'Maybe – I'm a little nervous actually, Thomas,' she admitted.

'So am I, but I don't think coffee ever calmed anyone down. Shall we go, do you think?' She held his hand as they walked up the wooden stairs.

Irini smiled at them and seemed to understand that this was an important night.

In the bedroom they both felt awkward. Elsa pointed out the mountain peaks, naming this one and that.

'It's a beautiful place to be,' she said softly.

He went towards her, held her to him and kissed her neck gently. She gave a little shiver.

Thomas drew away.

'Was that gross or something?' he asked, irresolute.

'No, it was exciting and lovely. Come here,' she said.

And first she stroked his face and then she kissed him, holding him close. Her hands went up and down his back and gently he opened her blouse.

'Elsa, I don't know ... I hope ...' he began.

'I don't know either, and also I hope,' she murmured. 'But remember, no looking back, no regrets, no comparisons.'

'You're beautiful, Elsa.'

'Hold me,' she asked him. 'Please love me, Thomas. Love me in this beautiful island and let's not think about anything beyond tonight ...'

Vonni sat down with Andreas and wrote to Shane.

I am replying to your letter about Fiona Ryan. She left this island two days ago on her way back to

Ireland where she hopes to resume her nursing career. I could not therefore give her your message of apology but I presume you know how to contact her in Dublin.

I hope that you will co-operate with the authorities in Athens in the matter of your detention. They view all drug infringements very seriously.

Yours faithfully,
Andreas

She translated it for Andreas.

'Is it a little cold, do you think?' he wondered.

'It's very cold,' Vonni agreed. 'Would you prefer to have paid his bail and invited him to stay here for six months?'

'No, I know all that. It's just he is in jail and he did apologise.'

'Andreas, you have a soft heart over everything ... everything except your son.'

'I have a soft heart for him too now, Vonni, but alas it's too late. No, don't tell me you have a feeling, I don't believe in feelings any more.'

'Right. No more on the subject, I swear. Will we mail this letter or ask Yorghis to fax it, do you think?'

'You want it sent as it is, even though you agree it's cold?' he asked.

'My opinion, and of course I could be wrong, is that there's a time in life for coldness and this is one of those times.'

'You, wrong, Vonni? Never!' He smiled. 'Let's fax it and put the poor fool out of his misery.'

'I'll drop it in to the police station on my way home,' she said.

'Where's home tonight? Is it your apartment or your hen-house?' Andreas asked.

'Now you are worse than Thomas! Making fun of my domestic arrangements no less! But since you are so curious, tonight I will sleep in the little guest room. Thomas and Elsa have gone to Kalatriada together, I will have the place to myself.'

'They have gone back there together.' He stroked his cheek. 'I see . . .'

'I know. Imagine,' she said.

'And when will they come back?' Andreas asked.

'Thomas left a note; he said if it all went well it might be a few days.'

'Let's hope it goes well for them,' Andreas said.

'You are a dear man,' Vonni said.

'You never said that before.'

'No, but over the years I said a lot of rubbish. You always had the wisdom to know what I meant and what I didn't mean. I *do* mean that you are a dear and good person. I hope you know that.'

'I do, Vonni, and I'm happy you think of me like that,' he said.

David sat and talked to his father along the lines that he and Fiona had rehearsed. Nothing about the illness that was ending his life but a lot about the office and the upcoming award.

'I didn't think you'd care about that kind of thing,' Harold Fine said.

'But they are honouring you, Father, why should I not care and be very proud?'

His father nodded and smiled. 'Well, I'll tell you frankly, son, it wouldn't have been the same if you

NIGHTS OF RAIN AND STARS

weren't here to take part in it. What's the point of these things if your own flesh and blood isn't there to share it?'

In the next room, Fiona talked with David's mother.

'Mrs Fine, you are very kind to put me up for the night. I so appreciate it.'

'Well, of course, any friend of David's is most welcome.'

'He told me all about your lovely home but he didn't do it justice, it's gorgeous.'

Miriam Fine was pleased and confused in equal measure.

'And you live in Dublin, David tells me?'

'Yes, I've been away for many weeks now, I'm so looking forward to seeing them all again.' Fiona's smile never faltered.

'And it was a nice place, this island you were all visiting?'

'Oh, it was lovely, Mrs Fine, they were very simple, very kind people. I'd love to go back there again, and I will, I know I will.'

'And what exactly were you doing there?'

'Having a career break,' Fiona said blithely. She and David had agreed there was no need to mention Shane, miscarriages, drugs arrests. Anything that would disturb the even lives of the Fine family.

'And you're a nurse in Dublin?' Miriam Fine was beginning to breathe more easily. This was not a girl with designs on her only son.

'I spent six months on an oncology ward before I went away, and let me assure you that these are the days to be living in, Mrs Fine.'

'I'm sorry?'

'They can do so much to help people nowadays, you'd be amazed. Let me tell you ...'

And to her amazement Miriam Fine found herself sitting down and talking to this girl with an Irish accent who was extraordinarily helpful on many different levels. She could not have asked for a better visitor to her home.

At the desk of the Anna Beach Hotel they held several faxes for Elsa. They were increasingly urgent, asking her to pick up her e-mail. But Elsa was nowhere to be found.

The desk clerk spotted Vonni in the foyer craft shop.

'I wonder could you advise me about these messages? The German woman hasn't come in for a while ...'

Vonni looked at them with interest. 'I can't read German – what do they say?'

'Some man in Germany saying she can't play games like this, can't leave him. That sort of thing.'

'I see.' Vonni was pleased.

'Do you think we should fax him back saying she isn't around?' the clerk asked, anxious that the Anna Beach should not be blamed for inefficiency.

'No, I'd leave it really. Better not get involved. If he calls, of course, you could say that you heard she has gone away.'

'And has she?'

'For a few days, yes, she won't want to be disturbed.'

Dublin

My dear Vonni,

I swore to you that I'd write when I was home for twenty-four hours. So here goes.

The journey was fine, a plane full of tourists, holidaymakers. David and I felt very superior because we knew the real Greece, not just beaches and discos. We took the train up to David's place. He is seriously rich, by the way, his family have this huge house full of lovely antiques and valuable ornaments. His mother is very innocent and fussy and obviously gave in to her husband all her life. Mr Fine looks very badly, he only has a few months to live. Very few. He was quite frightened but actually he was able to talk to me about palliative care. He didn't really know what they did and didn't want to ask. David and I cried at Manchester Airport – people thought we were lovers saying goodbye.

Barbara was at home when I got there, to take the edge off things. Dad was walking on eggshells trying not to say anything that would offend; Mam was like some kind of TV commercial about gravy and home cooking, you'd think I'd been in some gulag or other rather than on an island full of wonderful smells and tastes. I still yearn for the smell of charcoal at the Midnight Café or the roast lamb and pine nuts up in Andreas's.

Do give him my love, I'll write when I start my job and when Barbara and I get our new flat. At the moment I'm sleeping on her sofa and I'll go round to see Mam and Dad every second day. They're fine, actually, and hardly ever mention the bloody silver wedding at all. My two sisters have turned into horrors. I thought it best not to dwell on things like the miscarriage and Shane being in jail. Well, more than not dwelling on them, I didn't really mention them at all.

I can never thank you enough, Vonni, particularly for that day in Athens. I have a hope, a dream that you find your husband and son again. You deserve to.

Love,
Fiona

Manchester

Dear Vonni,

Oh, I miss you and Aghia Anna every hour of every day. How good it would be to wake up to that bright sky and spend a day without care until the stars came out. I suppose there are stars here, it's been overcast so I don't seem to see them.

My father looks awful. Fiona was wonderful with him, by the way. Talking to him as if she had known him all her life and telling him how great the drugs were to take the edges off pain. Even my mother loved her and, having bristled at the thought that I was bringing a gentile girl into the house, she was quite sorry to realise that we actually were just friends. They made her promise to come back nearer the end and I know she will. We cried at the airport. It symbolised the end of everything – the summer, Greece, friendship, hope.

Am I glad I came back? Well, put simply, I had to come back. I feel weak at the thought that I might not have done so if it hadn't been for you. You were so clear-sighted, and strong in making me see what was happening. The awful thing is that I keep getting praised by uncles and aunts and friends for my great 'intuition' in knowing that something was wrong. Some intuition, Vonni! It was you! But as we agreed, I don't tell them that.

The days are dreary, and I will soon be starting to work in the office. I have to concentrate because my father wants to talk about it each evening. The man who was running the show naturally hates me, and is very resentful. He keeps wanting to know when I start. I so want to tell him how I feel about it all. But of course I can't. The award is next week. More fuss and preparation than for a moon landing. I'll write and tell you about it. Can you write to me? I long to know about Maria's driving, about the people in the Midnight, about whether Thomas and Elsa stayed or went, or even got together, which is what I thought might happen.

I dreamed the other night that your son came back. Right into the harbour in a boat with an outboard engine. It could happen, couldn't it?

Love,
David

'When should we go back to the real world?' Elsa asked after days spent wandering around the hills and coves of Kalatriada.

'Do you mean back to Aghia Anna or points further west?' Thomas had picked wild flowers for her and was busy making them into a posy with a length of string.

'I suppose Aghia Anna as a base camp,' Elsa said. They had been living a strange life here, totally disconnected from the real world. They had gone shopping in the markets and bought cheese for their lunch on the hills. There was a bookshop where they had found some

English books. Thomas had asked a potter to make a plate with his mother's name on it.

Because they hadn't really packed for such an extended visit, they bought a couple of extra garments at stalls on market day. Thomas looked splendid in his colourful Greek shirt; Elsa had bought him a pair of elegant cream-coloured trousers in a desperate attempt to get him to abandon the three-quarter-length shorts with all the pockets which he seemed to love.

'*Orea*,' Irini said when she saw him dressed up.

'Yes, indeed, he is beautiful,' Elsa agreed.

'I miss my other trousers,' Thomas grumbled.

'You're the only one that does – they're quite terrible!'

'Oh, Elsa, indulge me, let me wear them, they're familiar like a comfort blanket. Please,' he begged.

'A blanket would be more elegant,' Elsa said. 'Hey, I'm talking like a wife. This will never do. Wear what you like,' she laughed at him.

'Shall we row back to Aghia Anna tomorrow?' he suggested.

'Yes, it's not as if it were goodbye, we can still be together there,' Elsa consoled herself.

'Of course we can, we're in no hurry to go anywhere,' Thomas agreed.

Maria and Vonni knew that they were back from Kalatriada, as they had just seen them returning the rowing boat at the harbour.

'The American looks very well, he doesn't wear those foolish trousers any more,' Maria said approvingly.

'Well, thanks be to the Divine Lord for that,' Vonni said devoutly. 'The Divine Lord helped and ably assisted, I'd say, by a very bright young German woman.' Vonni watched as she saw them kiss each other goodbye, Elsa heading for the Anna Beach, Thomas for the town. They looked relaxed and at ease with each other. The trip had obviously been a success.

'Heigh-ho, Maria, *pame*, let's go. Lots of three-point turns today, and where better than up in the square? I got a message that I have to go to see Takis, the lawyer, he has a message for me apparently.'

'What about?'

'I have no idea. It's hardly a court summons, I've been well behaved now for a couple of decades. But we'll hear.' Vonni was giving nothing away. Maria had no idea that Vonni had been up half the night wondering if the message had anything to do with Stavros. Either Stavros – her husband or her son.

Elsa sat in the Anna Beach with her big organiser diary beside her. For the first time in months she looked up contacts back in Germany, people who worked in the media.

The desk clerk brought her a sheaf of faxes plus four telephone message dockets. The last one said that Dieter would come out in two weeks' time to find her.

Elsa calmly ripped all the faxes in half without reading them and threw them into the wastepaper basket with the telephone messages. Then she went to the business centre where she could log on to her e-mail; and there she began to work.

Her first e-mail was to Dieter.

I have written a long letter explaining why I am not

coming back. Come out to Greece if you like, Dieter,
but I will be gone. It will be a wasted journey.
  Elsa

'Andy, am I disturbing you, it's Thomas.'

'No way. We're down in Sedona today, another canyon, it's real pretty here, Thomas.'

Thomas could hear Bill calling out excitedly.

'Is that Dad? Can I talk to him?'

'Sure, Bill, he called to talk to you. Take the phone and go off to have a real good chat with him.'

'Dad? Is it really you?'

'Nobody else, Bill, just me.'

'Dad, if you could just *see* this place. We've had a great time here, the colours keep changing all the time. And Gran's got all these friends, old, old people, she calls them the girls. And I said they were girls with wrinkly faces and they all laughed.'

'I bet they did.'

'What have you been doing, Dad?'

'I went to a little village, a tiny little place, real old-fashioned. One day I'll take you there.'

'Will you, Dad?'

'I don't ever say things I don't mean. One day I'll have a holiday with you on this island.'

'Was it lonely for you in this little village all by yourself?' Bill asked.

'Um, no, not lonely no . . .'

'So you don't miss us or anything?' the boy asked, sounding disappointed.

'Oh, I do, Bill, I miss you every single day, and do you know what I'm going to do about it?'

'No.'

NIGHTS OF RAIN AND STARS

'I'm going to come back there in ten days' time and we'll have a great time.'

'Dad, that's *fantastic*! How long are you coming back for?'

'For good,' he said.

And as he heard the boy who would always be his son shouting out, 'Mom, Andy, Dad's coming home. In ten days' time and he's going to stay for ever', Thomas felt the tears falling down his face.

'Takis! How are you?'

'I'm fine, Vonni, and you?'

'I'm keeping a slightly beady eye on Maria in case she ploughs through us and knocks down your office.'

'Let's watch her from inside the office, we won't be directly in the line of fire,' he said, leading her in. 'Do you know what I want to talk to you about?' Takis asked.

'No, not a clue.'

'Can you guess?'

'Is it something about Stavros?' she asked hesitantly.

'No, not at all,' he said, taken aback.

'Well then, you'll have to tell me, Takis,' she said. The light had gone out of her face.

Takis spoke quickly. 'It's about Nikolas Yannilakis. As you know, Nikolas died last week.'

'Poor Nikolas.' Vonni looked slightly worried. There surely couldn't be any trouble, any inquiry about giving him the morphine – Dr Leros had been aware of everything and co-operated all the way.

'He left you everything.'

'But he didn't have anything to leave!' Vonni said, wide-eyed.

'He had enough. He came in here six months ago and made a proper will. Left it all to you. His little house, his furniture, his savings . . .'

'Well, imagine him thinking of doing that!' Vonni was stunned. 'I suppose we should give the house to his neighbours, they have a lot of children, they could do with more space. I could sort of clear it out for them.'

'You haven't asked about his savings,' Takis said gravely.

'Sure, poor Nikolas didn't have any savings to speak of,' Vonni said.

'He left you over a hundred thousand euros,' Takis said.

Vonni looked at him in amazement. 'That can't be, Takis, the man had nothing, he lived in a hovel . . .'

'He had it all in the bank, some of it in shares, some in cash, I had to wait until it was totalled before I told you.'

'But where on earth did he get that amount of money?'

'Family apparently.'

'But why in the name of God didn't he use it to give himself some comfort?' She was angry with the dead man for denying himself what he could have had.

'Oh, Vonni, don't talk to me about families, the most extraordinary institution ever invented. Somebody insulted somebody somewhere along the line. Don't ask me because I don't know. But it meant that Nikolas didn't touch the money. So now it's all yours.'

She said nothing.

'And rightly so, Vonni. No one deserves it more than you, you looked after him in a way no one else could have.'

She sat very still, looking ahead of her.

'What will you do, will you travel, go back and visit them in Ireland?'

She still sat in shocked silence.

Takis wasn't used to Vonni being like this.

'Of course, you don't have to make any decisions yet. I'll arrange all the transfers when you've had time to think about things and feel like giving me instructions.'

'I feel like doing it now, Takis, if that's all right.'

'Certainly.' He sat down opposite her, his face to the window looking on to the square.

'Tell me first, is that madwoman Maria obstructing traffic or anything?'

'No, she's fine, she's doing rather big loopy turns but she's fine, everything is steering well clear of her,' Takis said, pulling a pad of paper towards him to write down the instructions.

'I don't intend to touch any of that money. Just leave it where it is. I will as I said give the little house to the family next door, but I would like them to think it came directly from Nikolas. And I want to make a will ...'

'Very sensible, Vonni,' Takis said in a low voice. He didn't think it was sensible at all, but it wasn't his business.

'And I would like to leave everything, my craft shop, my apartment and this legacy from Nikolas to my son Stavros.'

'I beg your pardon?'

'You heard me.'

'But you haven't seen him in years. He never came back to you despite all your pleas.'

'Are you going to make this will for me, Takis, or do I have to go and find another lawyer?'

'I'll have it drawn up by tomorrow at this time. And I'll have two people here to witness your signature.'

'Thank you – and I presume this is all just between us?'

'It is, Vonni. Just between the two of us.'

'Right, I'll go save Aghia Anna from Maria,' she said.

She walked out shakily, Takis noticed, as he stood at the door and watched her as Maria came running over.

'I understand it now, you turn the wheel exactly the wrong way to what you think! In the opposite direction!' she cried triumphantly.

'Whatever you think, Maria . . .'

'And what did Takis want?' she asked.

'To help me make my will,' said Vonni.

'I missed you,' Thomas said to Elsa when she came up the whitewashed steps to his apartment.

'And I you. The lazy days of Kalatriada are no more.' She kissed him lightly and walked into the sitting room. 'That's beautiful,' she added, pointing to a little vase of wild flowers.

'I'd love to say that I went out and gathered them for you on the hills, but actually Vonni left them there. She left a note to welcome us both back.' He passed her the little card.

'So she knows then?' Elsa said.

'I expect she knew before we did,' Thomas said ruefully.

'I wonder what she thinks?'

'Well, look at the flowers! That's a seal of approval, isn't it?' Thomas said.

'That's true, and of course it does also mean we've

signed up for her own kind of messy, complicated lifestyle,' Elsa agreed.

'Messy?'

'Well, look at us! They say the secret of the universe is timing. We timed things spectacularly badly, didn't we? You going in one direction and me going in the other!'

Thomas reached for her hand. 'We'll work it out,' he promised.

'I know,' she said doubtfully.

'Honestly, we'll work it out together,' Thomas said.

'We will,' said Elsa with greater conviction.

Dublin

My dear Vonni,

Thank you so much for the letter. I got so homesick for Aghia Anna when I read it. I was right to come back here, but that doesn't mean I can't ache for the sunshine and the lemon trees and all the marvellous people I met out there.

The Ward Sister here, Carmel, is horrific; she used to be a mate of ours, but all power corrupts ... She thinks I should be punished for having left the hospital and is dreaming up ways. Barbara and I have a terrific flat, we are having a housewarming party on Saturday, so wish us luck.

Mam and Dad have been great, Shane's name is never mentioned, it's as if he has become a family secret never to be spoken of. Which is probably for the best. They've decided to have a much simpler silver wedding, no place names and all that bullshit. Which is a great relief. I telephoned David and he was a bit grim. It was the day of his father's award. He just hates being back. But he'll stay there until his father dies.

Fancy Thomas and Elsa being a number! I never saw that coming. But it's perfect!

Loads of love to all pals,

Fiona

Manchester

Dear Vonni,

You are wonderful, telling me all the things I want to hear. I'm so pleased about Maria's progress. Imagine her driving alone all the way to Kalatriada!

That's wonderful news about Thomas going home, but what about Thomas and Elsa? How will they manage to sort it out?

I am too close to it to write and tell you in any balanced way about my father's award. It was a truly awful day. Worse than I had feared, because my father looked so frail and my mother so ludicrously proud, and everyone there, businessmen of every type, just worshipped the God of money and profit.

I'll write when it's less raw, but it was awful. My father made a speech where he announced that I was to be head of his company from next January. Everyone clapped and I had to look so pleased. But I did hate it, Vonni, and I know it's just self-pity of a high order but I feel my life is over at twenty-eight. I know you'll say something positive to keep me going. I think of you so often, and in a dream life I wish that you were my mother and Andreas my

father. I'd never let either of you down. It's just so hard in my own family.
Love from a disgustingly morose,
David

The days went by. Elsa spent a lot of time at the Anna Beach on e-mail.

'Who on earth are you writing to?' Thomas asked her.

'I'm examining the job situation,' she said crisply.

'But I thought you weren't going back to Germany?'

'It's hard to accept but there *are* other countries,' she laughed.

Thomas spent those hours beside her at another computer. He was in touch with the university. If he did come back early could he have access to his rooms on campus? All these things had to be worked out.

It was two days before Thomas would leave for Athens.

'I want you to come up to Andreas's tonight for dinner,' Elsa said. 'We have a lot to talk about.'

'Is that the right place to talk about it?' Thomas wondered. 'We always seem to be part of a huge crowd up there.'

'No, I'll see that we have a quiet table,' she promised.

She wore a simple white cotton dress that night and had a flower clipped in her hair.

'You look lovely and so dressed up. I'm so pleased I wore my smart new Kalatriada pants,' he said when he saw her.

'I got this dress today to impress you and I have a taxi to take us to the restaurant. How about that for style?'

They went up the windy road to Andreas's taverna,

pointing out places to each other, and watching the usual starry sky unfold out over the sea.

They had indeed been given a little table for two right at the edge of the terrace with an uninterrupted view.

Little Rina served them. Andreas was indoors. Yorghis, Vonni and Dr Leros were in there with him too. They all waved. They would talk to them later. When it was time for the second coffee.

'I need to talk to you about my looking for a job,' Elsa said.

'Yes, I didn't ask too much.'

'Why didn't you ask?'

'Because even though you said there are other countries I was afraid you would be offered a big position back there in Germany. And I suppose, to be honest, I was afraid you might meet Dieter again and . . . and . . .' He rushed on before she could say anything. 'I've been working out just how soon you can come out to see me, and then I'll come and see you. I can't bear to let you go now that I've found you. Maybe I'm mad to risk losing you by going back to Bill.'

'I got a job, Thomas.'

'Where?' he asked in a very shaky voice.

'I'm almost afraid to tell you.'

'Then it *is* Germany,' he said with a defeated face.

'No.'

'Where, Elsa? No games, I beg you.'

'Based in Los Angeles, but roaming up and down the west coast. A weekly column for a big magazine, interviews, politics, features. Whatever I can come up with really.' She looked at him anxiously for a reaction.

'Where?' he asked, dumbfounded.

'California,' she said nervously. 'Is it too soon, too

much of an assumption? I mean I just couldn't bear to lose you . . . but if you think . . .'

A slow smile began to broaden across his face.

'Oh, Elsa darling, isn't that wonderful . . .' he began.

'I don't have to live with you or anything, I don't want to crowd you out, but I thought we could be together a lot . . . you see, I know that we haven't been together long but now I couldn't exist without you . . .'

Thomas stood up and went to her side of the table, he pulled her to her feet and kissed her. He didn't care about the other guests. Someone took a photograph of them but they didn't care, they stood locked in each other's arms as if they were never going to be able to draw apart. Then of course the group in the kitchen came out to join them, and many toasts were drunk. To the couple.

'That man who took your picture, he was German, he recognised you, Elsa, from the television.'

She couldn't have worried less.

'He asked who Thomas was,' said Vonni. 'I explained you were a high-powered American academic and you were Elsa's fiancé.'

'*What!*' Thomas and Elsa spoke at the same time.

'Well, I wouldn't have told them anything, Thomas, if you had been wearing those terrible shorts with all the pockets. Once I saw you in a decent pair of trousers, then I thought it doesn't matter for Elsa if some fan sells the picture to a German newspaper!'

They talked on easily as always, looking down on the harbour way below. The last ferry had come in an hour ago but Andreas's taverna hadn't expected any guests coming from that sailing. It was too late and too far a walk. So they were surprised when they saw someone toiling up the windy path.

It was a man of about thirty. He must be fit because he had a pack on his back and carried a suitcase in each hand.

'There's a dedicated diner,' said Elsa admiringly.

'Maybe he's heard of Vonni's stuffed vine leaves,' said Thomas with a smile. He loved Vonni for calling him Elsa's fiancé even though he was bewildered that everyone had hated his lovely shorts with the pockets.

'It's late for anyone to come up here,' Dr Leros said, mystified.

'Unless they really intended to,' said Yorghis in an odd sort of voice, peering at the gateway.

Vonni had stood up to look at the man hesitating at the entrance.

'Andreas!' she said in a choked voice. 'Andreas, my friend, it *is*, it really is!'

Elsa and Thomas looked from one to the other without any idea what was happening. Andreas had stood up and was staggering towards the gate with his arms out. Everyone watched as his laced boots faltered across the terrace.

'*Adoni* ...' he cried. '*Adoni mou!* You came back. *Adoni ghie mou*. My son, you came back to see me.'

'I came back to stay, Father, if you'll have me?'

The men embraced in a grasp that looked as if it would never end. Then they drew away from each other and stroked each other's faces in wonder. The two men kept saying the same words.

'*Adoni mou!*' Andreas said over and over.

'*Patera!*' Adoni said to his father.

Then Yorghis moved forward, and Vonni and Dr

Leros. And they were a little group talking excitedly in Greek and embracing.

Thomas and Elsa held hands very tight.

'We'll never forget this night,' Thomas said.

Elsa said, 'Was I too forward, too pushy? Tell me, Thomas?'

Before he could answer, Andreas and his son came over.

'Adoni, this is the wonderful young woman who told me that I should write to you, when I wondered if you would care. She said everybody loves a letter . . .'

Adoni was tall and handsome. He had a great shock of black hair which would one day go grey-white like his father's, but not for a long time and then possibly here in Aghia Anna. Elsa, who could summon words at will on television in front of millions of viewers, was without words now. Instead she stood up and hugged Adoni tight as if they were old friends.

'Aren't you just beautiful,' Adoni said admiringly to the blonde girl in the white dress and the flower in her hair.

'Elsa and Thomas are together,' Andreas said hastily, lest there should be any misunderstanding.

Adoni shook Thomas by the hand. 'You are a very lucky man,' he said with great sincerity.

Thomas agreed. 'I am a very lucky man.' And then he stood up to address the group of friends. He looked straight at Elsa as if to answer her question about whether she was too pushy, too forward.

'I want to tell you all that Elsa will be leaving with me. We will be going to California together.'

'Yet another reason to celebrate tonight,' Andreas cried out, tears in his eyes.

Thomas and Elsa kissed again, and then they sat with his arm around her shoulders as they watched the homecoming unfold.

Andreas, Yorghis and little Rina ran to get food and wine for the prodigal son. The feeling was that he had never eaten properly in all those years in Chicago.

Vonni sat beside Adoni, her eyes sparkling.

'And your son Stavros?' Adoni asked.

'Has his own life somewhere ...' she said hastily.

'But why can he not find it in his heart to ...'

'Let's not talk about that now, the important thing is that *you* are back, Adoni! And by the way, your father has changed; he won't be like he was ...'

'Neither will I be as I was, Vonni.'

Then Adoni was borne away by more well-wishers.

Vonni sat flanked on either side by her friends Andreas and Yorghis as she had been for so long.

'One night Stavros will come into that harbour,' Andreas said.

'And it will be a night like this,' Yorghis encouraged.

'Yes, yes, I'm sure,' Vonni said, eyes bright, face hopeful.

They knew she was putting on a cheerful manner. At the same time they each stretched out a hand to hold hers. Now her smile was genuine.

'Of course he will come back one day,' she said as she gripped their hands. 'We only have to look at tonight to know that miracles happen. And there is no point in going on if you don't believe that.'

Dr Leros came out of the kitchen excitedly.

'There are two bouzouki players out there, they want to play to welcome you home, Adoni,' he begged.

'I'd love that,' he laughed.

And as the music rang out into the night and the people in the restaurant began to clap to the beat, Adoni stood up and went into the centre of the terrace. And in front of everyone he began to dance. Adoni danced in front of forty people, some of them customers who knew nothing of what was happening, some like Thomas and Elsa who knew part of the story, and some like his father, his uncle, the doctor and Vonni who knew everything.

His arms high in the air, he swooped and bent and danced, overjoyed to be back where he belonged.

And a little light rain came down but nobody cared.

It didn't get in the way of the stars.